Praise for
the Mr. Terupt novels

Because of Mr. Terupt

An NPR Backseat Book Club Selection
An Indie Next List Selection
An E. B. White Read Aloud Honor Book
An Arizona Grand Canyon Reader Award Winner
An Indiana Young Hoosier Book Award Winner
A Minnesota Maud Hart Lovelace Award Winner
A Connecticut Nutmeg Book Award Winner
A Nebraska Golden Sower Book Award Winner
An Iowa Children's Choice Book Award Winner
A Massachusetts Children's Book Award Winner
Nominated for 17 State Book Awards

"Even the accident toward which this novel is inevitably headed is no accident; it is as masterfully set up and skillfully concealed as the rest of this riveting story." —JOHN IRVING

★ "The characters are authentic and the short chapters are skillfully arranged to keep readers moving headlong toward the satisfying conclusion." —*School Library Journal*, Starred

"This powerful and emotional story is likely to spur discussion."
—*Publishers Weekly*

"No one is perfect in this feel-good story, but everyone benefits, including sentimentally inclined readers." —*Kirkus Reviews*

"Compelling. . . . Readers will find much to ponder on the power of forgiveness." —*Booklist*

Mr. Terupt Falls Again

"A surprising and totally satisfying sequel. The voices ring true."
—JOHN IRVING

"This sequel can be read on its own. Moving and real."
—*Kirkus Reviews*

"A skillful meshing of characters and story lines makes for another great read." —*School Library Journal*

saving mr. terupt

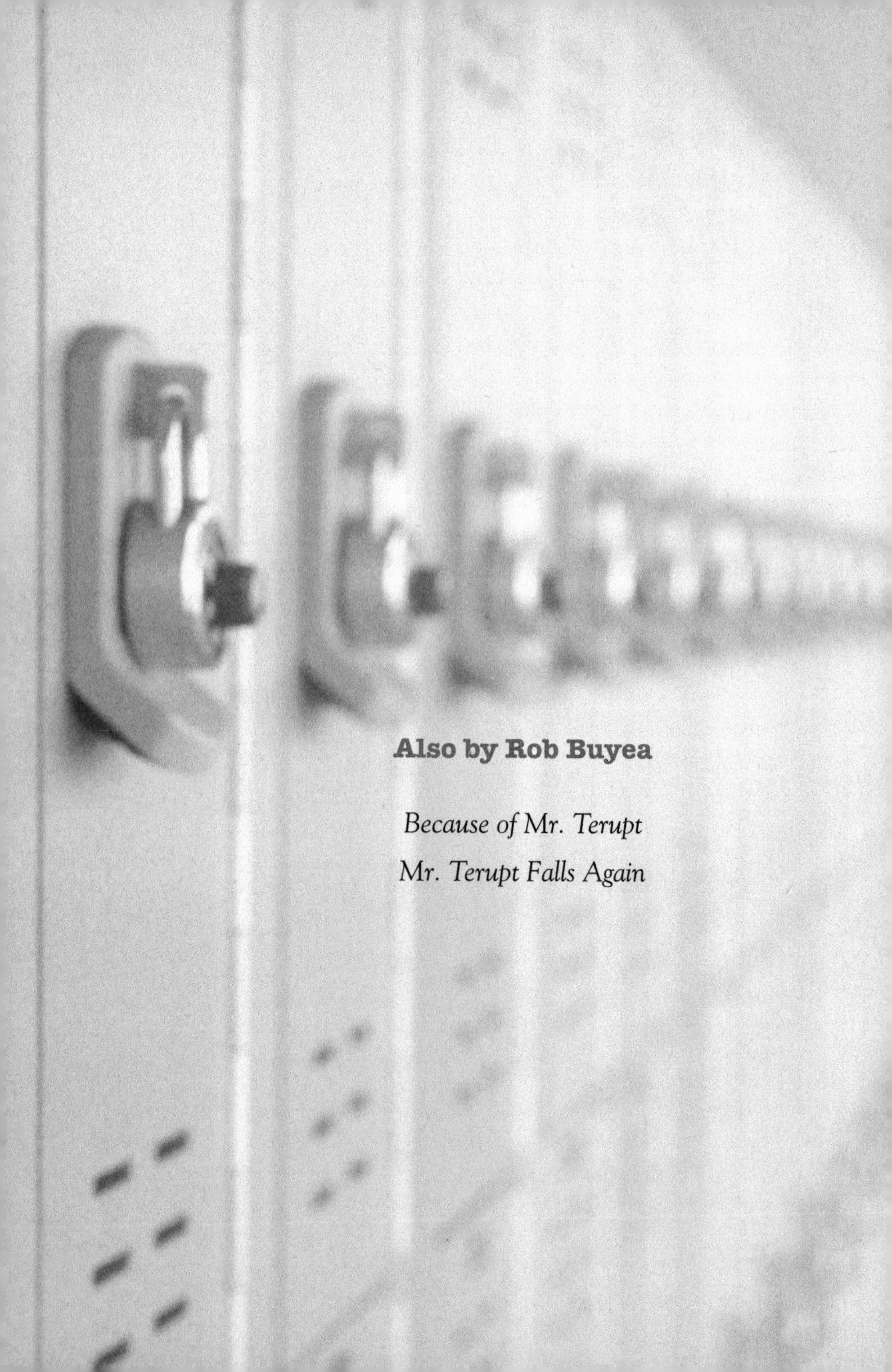

Also by Rob Buyea

Because of Mr. Terupt

Mr. Terupt Falls Again

saving mr. terupt

Rob Buyea

Delacorte Press

Text copyright © 2015 by Rob Buyea
Jacket art copyright © 2015 by Harry Bliss
Interior photographs copyright © 2015 Shutterstock. Pencils: Preto Perola;
lockers: Monkey Business Images; buttons: somartin; signs: albund.

All rights reserved. Published in the United States by Delacorte Press,
an imprint of Random House Children's Books,
a division of Penguin Random House LLC, New York.

Delacorte Press is a registered trademark and the colophon
is a trademark of Penguin Random House LLC.

Visit us on the Web! randomhousekids.com

Educators and librarians, for a variety of teaching tools, visit us at RHTeachersLibrarians.com

Library of Congress Cataloging-in-Publication Data is available upon request.

ISBN 978-0-385-74355-6 (hc) — ISBN 978-0-375-99120-2 (lib. bdg.) —
ISBN 978-0-449-81829-9 (ebook)

The text of this book is set in 12-point Goudy Old Style.
Jacket design by Sarah Hokanson
Interior design by Trish Parcell

Printed in the United States of America
10 9 8 7 6 5 4 3 2 1
First Edition

To my beautiful daughters, Emma, Lily, and Anya,
who tell me stories, give me ideas and sentences—
sometimes without even knowing it—
squeeze me in the best hugs,
and give me a reason to smile every day

PART ONE

SUMMER

Peter

All good things must come to an end, and when you're on the receiving side of a really good wedgie, you want the end to show up in a hurry, even if it means having your underwear ripped clean out of your shorts. To say it was just a *good* wedgie would be a serious understatement, though. My tighty-whities were so far up my back I could feel the Fruit of the Loom tag scratching my neck. My underwear stretched so much that you could've put Jeffrey in there with me. No, it wasn't just a *good* wedgie. I was the victim of one of the greatest wedgies of all time, one that deserved a place in the *Guinness Book of World Records*. Not the sort of thing you want to be known for, but, if I'm being honest, I'd asked for it.

My claim to fame happened at the two-week summer wrestling camp that Jeffrey and I attended together. The camp was definitely the highlight of my vacation. Mr. T had told us that he'd gone to his first camp as a rising seventh grader, and since we were planning to join the school team in the winter, he encouraged us to do the same, and told our parents that it would be a good idea. Mr. T helped us pick the camp and even drove Jeffrey and me there on the day it started. It took place on a college campus I'd never heard of but featured some of the best coaches in the country.

After we were all checked in and settled in our room, Mr. T brought us back to his car and opened the trunk. "I've got something for each of you, now that you're officially wrestlers," he said. He pulled out a pair of his old wrestling shoes and handed them to me. "These babies aren't used to losing matches, so you'd best take care of them," he told me.

I couldn't even get a thank-you out of my mouth. I held those shoes like Jessica cradles her books.

He passed his old headgear on to Jeffrey, who couldn't manage to say anything, either.

"If you pay attention, I know you'll learn plenty," Mr. T promised us. "I discovered some of my best moves at camp. Have fun, work hard, and stick together. And stay out of trouble," he added, looking at me. He closed the trunk and climbed into his car. "I'll see you in ten days." Then he drove away.

I did a pretty good job of following his advice. I paid attention, worked hard, and stuck with Jeffrey. But I did manage to get myself in a little bit of trouble—I couldn't help it.

One of my favorite parts of camp was the dorm. I'd never been away from home like this before. It was great. There was no one harping on us to clean our room. Jeffrey and I kept the place as messy as we wanted. It was also really cool having other kids in the dorm with us. There were ten rooms in our hall, twenty boys total, and Jeffrey and I were the youngest. I used to think the bathroom at school was the best place for messing around, but the dorm was heaven. You could get away with murder.

We were at our morning session, sitting along the mats and changing into our wrestling shoes, when Max, one of the kids a few doors down from Jeffrey and me, started freaking out.

"Eww!" he yelled. "What the heck!" He yanked his shoe off and tipped it over. Shampoo dripped from inside it. Max tossed his sneaker aside, ripped his sock off, and chucked it at Matt, who was cracking up. Matt and his roommate, Josh, were the oldest kids on our floor, which made them the alpha males—or so they thought. I wouldn't say they were mean, but they definitely liked pulling pranks and picking on the younger kids in the pack. They slapped high five and kept laughing their heads off. Poor Max had no choice but to wrestle that session in his bare feet. By the end of practice, they were covered in so many mat burns he could hardly walk.

Let the wars begin, I thought. Jeffrey must've seen my wheels spinning. "Don't even think about it, Peter," he warned me. "Remember what Terupt told you." I might've taken his advice, but later that night, Matt left me with no choice but to get involved.

I had just finished in the shower and went to grab my towel, but it was gone. Someone had swiped it when I wasn't looking and had left me a tiny little washcloth in its place. I was soaking wet, but what could I do? I held the washcloth in front of my waist like a matador and booked it down the hall. My front was covered, but my naked butt shone like a full moon. I thought I was going to make it, but when I reached my room I found the door locked. I pounded on it.

"Jeffrey!" I yelled.

No answer. Then I heard a door at the end of the hall open and close. I didn't even have to look. I knew it was them.

"Hey, nice butt!" Josh yelled. "And cute towel. Perfect for a little guy like you."

I pulled the washcloth tight to my front. "Some jerk took mine and left me with this," I said.

"You don't say. And now you're locked out. Boy, that stinks," he teased.

"Shut up!" I said.

"Tough words from a naked boy."

"Out of my way, little man," Matt said, shoving me as the two of them passed by. "The ladies await. It's time for Matt's Gun Show." He flexed his biceps and strutted toward the exit.

There happened to be a field hockey camp also taking place at the college, so there were girls everywhere. One thing I know about girls is that they always go for the bigger, older-looking guys, and, for once, that was a relief. Thanks to the girls, Matt and Josh didn't have time to torture me at the moment.

Jeffrey showed up a few minutes later, carrying a bag of chips from the vending machine. "Whoa! Where's your towel?" he said.

"Just let me in." I'd gone from relieved to annoyed.

While Mr. Biceps was outside schmoozing with the ladies, I rounded up Max and a few of the other guys on our floor. Even after I told him what they'd done to me, Jeffrey vowed that he was staying out of it. That was fine, but I wasn't going to sit back and do nothing. It was time to get even. Those two had messed with the wrong kid.

At eleven o'clock, every camper had to be in his room for attendance check and lights-out, including the two big shots. At eleven-fifteen, a group of us snuck out and met in the bathroom. Max and I found the biggest trash barrel in the dorm and stuck it in the shower. It took us more than five minutes to fill that sucker with water. The thing must've weighed a gazillion pounds, but we lugged it down the hall and leaned it against Matt and Josh's door. Then we knocked.

Matt must've been just on the other side because he opened it immediately. I was still standing there when the barrel fell and the wave of water rushed into his room like a tsunami, soaking him and drenching everything they had on the floor.

"You're dead meat, little man!"

I took off down the hall. Matt came flying after me.

"Jeffrey!" I yelled.

He opened up just in time. I dove into our room, and Jeffrey slammed and locked the door behind me.

The next morning at session, all the guys kept asking Matt and Josh why their stuff was wet. "Did you get caught in a rainstorm?" Max teased. Jeffrey and I stayed on the far side of the mat, keeping as much distance between ourselves and Matt and Josh as we could. Still, it was only a matter of time.

It was just after lunch, in the middle of the quad, when Matt grabbed me. He lifted me high above his head by the waistband of my underwear as if he were doing shoulder presses. The field hockey girls were watching.

"Look!" one yelled.

"Oh my gosh!" cried another.

Every girl in the quad started laughing and pointing at me.

"Put me down," I said, kicking and squirming.

"Yeah, and who's gonna make me?" Matt challenged.

That was what I wanted to know. My underwear was already in my armpits. I could hear it ripping. And believe me, I felt it. My underwear wasn't the only thing ripping.

"I'm warning you," I said.

"I'd like to see you do something about it," he said.

You really should be careful what you wish for. Turns out Jeffrey is even crazier than I am. Mr. T didn't have any reason to worry. There was no doubt about us sticking together. That's just how it was when it came to the old gang.

Jeffrey

I swore I wasn't going to get involved in Peter's pranks at wrestling camp. I was there to learn, and I was determined to stay out of trouble. But trouble and Peter are drawn to each other like magnets. And sometimes you're guilty by association, which is what happened to me.

Things were fine in the beginning. Coach Terupt dropped us off at camp, and before he left he gave us these incredible gifts. Peter got a pair of his old shoes, and I got his headgear. I spent all of the first day fiddling with the straps, adjusting them so that it fit me perfectly. Just putting it on made me feel like a serious wrestler, which I'd become. I remembered Terupt telling us about wanting to be the best when he was a kid, and that fire had been lit in my belly. I couldn't wait to wrestle for the school team. My goal was to win every single match this season. I understood camp was important preparation if I truly wanted to make that happen, so I was focused at the sessions and learning a lot, as Terupt had promised we would.

One day, we spent two hours going over a position called "out the back door." Imagine being on your hands and knees with your opponent draped across you, facing in the opposite direction and reaching for your ankles. You can easily find yourself like this in a match, especially if you take a shot and your opponent sprawls his legs back and falls on you. From there, if you scoot forward and pick your head up off the mat, you will come out between your opponent's legs, and this is called coming out the back door. Believe it or not, there are about a million different ways to finish your move, and things that can happen from there, and we studied a bunch of them.

Later that night I was sitting in our dorm room, writing down everything we had learned.

"If you write it down, then you'll have a better chance of remembering it when wrestling season rolls around, which is when you want to be able to execute all of those new moves," Coach Terupt had said.

I was midsentence when all of a sudden there was this big ruckus out in the hall. I wasn't going to get involved. But then I heard Matt yelling and Peter calling my name.

I hurried over to our door and yanked it open. Peter dove inside our room. I saw Matt hot on his tail, charging after him like an angry bull. You could hear the water squishing and sloshing about in his sneakers with every step he took. I slammed our door and locked it just in time. A barrage of fists rattled on the other side.

"You twerps can run, but you can't hide," Matt warned.

I turned to Peter. "What'd you do?"

"Dumped a little water in his room."

"It must've been a lot of water," I said. "Matt's soaking wet."

Peter grinned from ear to ear. "Really?"

"Yeah, and now you've got me involved. I didn't sign up to be your bodyguard."

"I didn't want you missing out on all the fun, that's all."

Thanks to Peter's shenanigans, the back-door move we'd learned in practice wasn't the only one we had to perfect. Matt and Josh were determined to get us, so the next day, we snuck out the back door of the dorm, in and out of the gym, and into the dining hall. Those two dummies hadn't caught on, and I was beginning to think we would survive the rest of camp without facing them, but then Peter had a brain fart and forgot to use our secret exit after lunch. Matt was there to grab him as soon as he walked out of the building.

I wanted to kill Peter for involving me, but I couldn't leave my friend hanging in that position. And he was *hanging*—by his underwear! There was a crowd of onlookers pointing and snickering at the sight. I wondered which was hurting Peter more, his pride or his crack. I give him credit, though—he might have been grimacing, but he wasn't squealing. The squeals came from all the field hockey girls after I hit my best move of the week: I ran over and yanked Matt's shorts all the way down to his ankles! For such a tough guy, he sure sported girlie boxers—there were hearts all over them. Peter fell to the ground, and we took off. Matt tried chasing after us, but he tripped on his shorts and face-planted. The place erupted in laughter.

The rest of camp went without incident. Even though Peter and I were the youngest kids there, Matt and Josh knew not to mess with us. We packed a solid one-two punch.

Camp was definitely the best part of my summer, full of

crazy memories (thanks to Peter) and tons of new techniques that I couldn't wait to try. I was going to score a lot of takedowns with my new back-door finishes. I was ready for seventh grade and a new phase of my life as I entered junior high. Of course, I also wanted to catch up with everyone else. Peter was the only one I'd seen since the end of sixth grade. I wondered how Luke's summer had gone and how Jessica and Lexie and Danielle were doing—and Anna, especially. I was excited to tell her everything that my baby brother could do now.

Asher was nearing his first birthday. My family decided we'd celebrate it on the day I found him abandoned by the side of the road. Not only was he now pulling himself to his feet more and more, and getting better and better at his wrestling stance, but he was also beginning to say a few words. He could say *Dada* and *Mama*, and *Jeffrey* came out as "Ree."

He liked to stand at our sliding door and bang his hands on it. His fingerprints were all over the glass. But there was one afternoon when I was with him that he stopped in the middle of his drumming and pointed outside. "My-my." I looked to see what he was pointing at. There was nothing out there, but he kept gesturing toward the old oak tree with its tire swing gently swaying in the breeze. "My-my."

I had no idea what he was trying to say. Maybe Anna would be able to help me figure it out.

Jessica

Dear Journal,

    Mr. Terupt gave you to me at the end of the year. I've never had a better journal. Your cover is made of fine Moroccan leather. Not soft leather—rather, you feel like a hardback book. However, you don't open and close like a novel. Instead, your cover wraps all the way around, and where you meet, you fall together, one end on top of the other, and click shut. There's a hidden magnetic element inside your Moroccan leather, and it keeps you closed until I decide to pull you open again. Luke would be able to explain the science behind it, but I'm content thinking of you as simply holding hands when you fall shut.

    While your outside is wonderful, it's your inside that is important. You're filled with off-white, delicately lined pages.

    "Instead of giving you another book to read, I thought it was time you were given something to fill with your own words," Mr. Terupt said when he handed you to me. "You'll figure out how to use it."

    I take you with me everywhere. I want to keep you close by always, since I never know when I'm going to be inspired to write. I'm not certain I've figured out how to use you yet, so in the meantime, I've decided just to keep you in the loop.

Presently, I'm at theater camp. I'm actually here with Lexie. After seeing how much she liked dressing up and putting on a show last year, I decided to ask her to come with me. I thought she'd really like it. I was right. We're having a blast, and it's fun being here with a friend. Tomorrow we're going to be given a setting and characters and some sort of conflict, and then we'll have the rest of the week to create a play and costumes and props based on that information. We get to share our production on the last day. I'm quite excited, as is Lexie. I'm sure she's having visions of herself all done up as the lead actress, stealing the show.

That's about it for now. I'll let you know how camp turns out, and I'll certainly have plenty to tell you about seventh grade—our year without Mr. Terupt. That sounds incredibly sad, and I like happy endings, so I'll have to figure something out.

Love,
Jessica

P.S. I forgot to mention, the students at theater camp who demonstrate the best talent in writing, acting, set design, and costume design will receive a special invitation to attend a weekend retreat in New York City at a time yet to be announced. The retreat is a once-in-a-lifetime opportunity to work with professionals to create and perform a short production, opening for an off-Broadway show—in an actual theater! I have no doubt Lexie will get in—she's a natural onstage. I'm desperately hoping for an invitation. I haven't wanted anything this badly since Mr. Terupt lay in his coma.

Fingers crossed,
Jessica

Alexia

School isn't the sort of thing you get excited about, unless you're in Teach's class, but like, school shopping—that's a whole different story. And like, oh my God, this year was even better because I got the girls to go with me—to the mall! Our moms came too, but we convinced them to let us do our thing. We agreed to meet them at the food court after two hours. The other girls were each given some money, and then we were off.

I'd spent all summer working with Mom at the restaurant, so I had my own money to burn. I'd been saving up just for this occasion. I had some things I needed. The only week of work I'd missed was when I went with Jessica to theater camp, which turned out to be totally awesome, by the way. Like, I rocked the party games, and we killed on our final production, so there was no way we weren't getting invited to that special weekend retreat-thingy that Jessica was dying to attend. But this shopping trip was the retreat I'd been most looking forward to.

Being the expert in this arena that I am, I took charge from the start. Our first stop was at a small boutique specializing in accessories. Teach had given me the most charming ankle bracelet as a parting gift at the end of sixth grade. Teach knows how to dress and all, but like, I was still shocked that he could pick out such a stylish piece of jewelry. I had to ask him, "Teach, did your better half help you pick this out?"

"Maybe. Why? Would it surprise you if I said no?"

"Maybe," I said.

We laughed, and then I told him, "Thank you. I love it."

I planned to wear it a lot, which was why we had to hit the boutique. I was able to find a set of dazzling charms to put on it. Jessica found a necklace, Danielle got a ring, and Anna a pair of earrings. I also bought some sweet nail polish. Pink, of course—my favorite. I always dazzle in pink. We were off to a good start.

After the boutique, we went looking for pants and shirts, and let me just say, it's a good thing I was with the girls. They were picking tops that were so last year. I took over and found us several cute outfits. Then it was time for our most important stop.

"Lexie, what do we need to go in there for?" Anna asked. Her face was already as red as some of the apparel, and we weren't even inside the store yet.

"We'll just look," I said. "C'mon. It'll be fun."

"I'm not sure my mother would want me in there, Lexie," Danielle said.

"She won't find out if you don't tell her. And you can pray for forgiveness later."

"I don't know," she said.

"Victoria's Secret girls are called angels, Danielle. Not devils. Now, c'mon."

"Maybe you should go without us," Anna said.

"Oh my God! Seriously?! Can you guys stop being such babies?"

"Calm down," Jessica said, stepping forward. "We'll go with you, Lex, but we're going to make it quick."

Danielle and Anna looked alarmed, but Jessica only shrugged. I wasn't waiting for any more objections. I led the way, and my nervous Nellies followed. Seconds later, we were inside Victoria's Secret and surrounded by the most beautiful lacy nightgowns and lingerie I'd ever seen. I didn't have enough money for any of it, but it didn't hurt to look. Tell that to the girls, though. They huddled together, acting as if looking or touching could kill you—Jessica included. In the back of the store, we found the area I was searching for—bras and underwear. I couldn't believe I'd gone through such trouble to make myself look endowed last year when Victoria's Secret had done all the work for me. There must've been five different mannequins, each wearing a different style push-up bra. They had one that made you look two cups bigger just by putting it on.

"Can I help you?" a young store worker asked, startling us. She was talking to Danielle. "We have a special one-day sale today," she said. "Buy one get one free."

That was all I needed to hear. Jessica and Anna slunk away as fast as they could and went and stood over by the lotions and perfumes, but I started shopping. These bras were pricey, but with the sale we could pool our money and it wouldn't be that bad. While Danielle was getting fitted, I browsed through the selection and picked out two different styles. I held one against my body and spun around to look in the mirror. I found Jessica and Anna right behind me, staring at my reflection.

"What do you think?" I asked them.

"It's perfect," Jessica said. "Listen, Lex." She was talking in a hushed voice now. "Do you think you could help us find one, too?"

"Yeah!" I squealed. I couldn't contain my excitement. We were going to be bra buddies. All eyes in the store turned to us. I still had the one in my hand pressed against my body.

"That's a nice pick," the girl who'd been helping Danielle said to me, "but you should try one size smaller. Let the bra do the work for you."

Jessica and Anna started giggling. "Shut up," I said, and swatted them with the too-big bra.

When all was said and done, the four of us walked out of Victoria's Secret with brand-new bras. I thought Danielle was going to die. It was such a wonderful moment. I was reminded of that day in Teach's hospital room when the four of us left together. We'd been that way ever since. I had the best friends in the whole wide world.

Little did I know how much I was going to need them this year.

Danielle

I felt like I was passing through the gates of hell when I stepped into that store of red and pink, but in Lexie's mind, it was clear we'd found heaven. She loved everything in that place.

"Oh, look at that. It's so pretty." She must've said that ten times in the first two minutes. She floated from one side of the store to the other while the rest of us stood frozen in the middle. I stared at the floor, afraid that if I looked up my eyes would catch on fire or God would send his eleventh plague my way. I was surrounded by sinful clothing, and I was standing in plain sight. Anyone walking by the storefront and glancing in could've spotted me. If my mother saw me in there, she'd never allow me to shop on my own for the rest of my life.

Lexie pulled us deeper into the store, where we were hidden from the outside, and I was finally able to breathe. The initial shock was wearing off. Most of the items in that store were things I could and would never wear. And the tinier the whatever, the higher the price.

"Can I help you?" The voice belonged to a young store worker, and she was talking to me! She said something about a sale and then asked, "Do you know what size you are?"

I shook my head. That was all I could do. The rest of my body was paralyzed with fear.

"No problem. I can measure you." She took the tape measure from around her neck and wrapped it around me. "Okay," she said. "Let me show you a few different options." She picked up three different bras and led me to the dressing room. "Try them on. You want to make sure you like how it fits and feels. Let me know if you need any help."

I nodded and went into the dressing room. I still hadn't said anything. I stood there not moving, staring at the bras I was supposed to try on. I liked two of them. The other one was meant more for Lexie than me.

"Psst. Danielle. Where are you?"

It was Jessica. She and Anna had come to rescue me. I opened my door a sliver, and they rushed in.

"Did you try them on yet?" Anna asked.

"No. I can't."

"You should," Jessica said. "They're not bad. And you need one, Danielle. That's why the girl approached you and not us." She picked the top one off the pile and handed it to me. "Try them on. We'll be out here waiting."

It felt different when Jessica and Anna encouraged me to do this than when Lexie did. I tried the bras on—and I wasn't struck by lightning.

"Well?" Anna said when I came out of the dressing room.

"I like the first one," I said.

"So get it," said Jessica.

"I can't."

"Why not?"

"I can't go to the register to buy it."

"Then we'll get one, too," Jessica said. "You heard the girl, it's buy one get one. C'mon, Anna. Friends stick together."

I couldn't help but smile. Anna looked a bit shocked, but Jessica grabbed her hand and took her away.

I found the girl who'd helped me and gave her the two bras I didn't want. "That's a lovely pick," she said about the one I had in my hand.

"Thank you," I said. My mouth was working now.

The four of us made our purchases and then went back out into the mall.

"I can't believe I just did that," I said.

"If any of us need one, it's you," Lexie said.

"I can't let my mother know."

"Will you stop being such a worrywart? Gimme your pink bag and bury your bra underneath your other stuff."

Lexie was so good when it came to these things. Sometimes it scared me, and sometimes it made me feel lucky to have her as a friend. I should've known she wouldn't stay quiet about this, though. She was too excited.

"How did things go?" Jessica's mother asked back at the food court.

"Great!" Jessica said.

"What's with all the pink?" my mother asked, noticing Lexie's bag.

"It's from where the angels shop, Mrs. Roberts," Lexie said.

"Oh," my mother said, sounding surprised. "Sounds like my kind of store."

I almost choked. My mother looked at me, and I just smiled and shrugged.

"Did you find a bra, Lex?" Lexie's mother asked her. She just came right out and asked. No wonder Lexie was so open about these things. I wished I could talk to my mother that easily, but I wasn't very comfortable talking about myself, never had been.

"Yeah, we all did!" Lexie cheered. The news came spilling out of her the same way she had blurted to Mr. Terupt last year that I got my period.

That was it. I was dead.

"That's good," my mother whispered to me. "I was thinking it was time for you to get one."

I stared at her. My mom thought it was good that I got a bra? I couldn't believe it.

"You'll have to show your grandmother and me later," Mom said.

Gulp. I had a lot of praying to do.

Before dinner that night, I sat down with the sketchbook Mr. Terupt had given me at the end of last year. I drew a picture of the four of us from behind, walking by storefronts in the mall, bags in our hands and our heads tilted at all different angles so that you knew we were laughing and talking and having a wonderful time. That's what I remembered most from our shopping trip—how happy I felt to have such close friends.

I didn't get to finish my sketch because I ended up feeling exhausted, so I set it aside and took a nap before heading downstairs to eat. It was a long day, but a good one. And soon, we'd all be together again.

ANNA

Now that Mom and Charlie were together all the time, most of my summer was spent on the farm with Danielle. The two of us were as close as sisters, though I wasn't sure we could be called that. If you thought about it too much, it could get confusing. Someday Danielle would actually be my aunt, and I would be her niece. That just sounded too weird and complicated, so we decided not to worry about it. We settled on being called half sisters. But if her brother was my dad, and she was my sister, then was my dad also my brother? That wasn't just confusing, it was creepy.

No matter. Danielle and I decided Charlie would move into my house so he and Mom could have a place of their own, even though he had to drive to the farm each morning for his chores. Then I could make Charlie's old room my room at the farm. If we were half sisters, then I'd need to spend half my time there. Danielle and I had it all figured out. I planned to record every bit of this special new chapter in our lives in the scrapbook Mr. Terupt had given me at the end of the year, using the camera Mom had passed down to me. Together, the scrapbook and camera were the perfect gift. I'd discovered a passion for photography. It was perfect for me because I liked being out of the frame, and I loved doing cool things with my pictures. The only problem remaining was that Charlie still hadn't officially asked Mom to marry him. What was he waiting for?

As the summer passed by, my patience with Charlie started to wear thin. Being a farmer, Danielle seemed to have more of that than me, but I still convinced her to help out. Like those twins in the movie *The Parent Trap*, Danielle and I started scheming to help Charlie and Mom make it happen since they weren't getting it done on their own. Danielle worked on Mom while I spent time with Charlie, which usually meant hanging out with the cows. Last summer I was more of an observer around the farm, but this year Charlie put me to work. He actually taught me how to milk a cow.

"You want to be careful you don't get kicked when putting the machine on," he told me, "so you should talk to the cow, gently touch her, let her know it's okay. And then everything else between the two of you ought to be smooth as clockwork." Charlie was good at talking to the animals, just not to Mom.

My favorite cow was Bessie. I named her. I felt like she understood me and even smiled at me when I came around. She was small—like me—but feisty when she wanted to be.

The farm was a big place, so if I ever felt like I wanted to be alone, I could do it. But after all those days with it being just Mom and me, it was nice to have so many other people around, especially at dinner. We often gathered as one big happy and complicated family. The food was always delicious, and the conversation was never slow. There was only one instant all summer when it got quiet around the table.

It was after we went school shopping. I was scooping some mashed potatoes when Danielle's mother burst right out and told everybody at the table, "The girls went shopping today and bought everything from pants and shirts to their own bras."

Silence. I felt my face growing redder than the beets we were eating. I couldn't believe Mrs. Roberts felt the need to make an announcement like that. This was one of those times when I was thankful for my younger mother, who still knew enough to understand how awkward that was for Danielle and me.

"I was figurin' *I'd* take the girls shopping," Grandma Evelyn said.

Danielle and I shot each other mortified looks. Imagine Grandma Evelyn in Victoria's Secret! I didn't think so. Shopping with her would've been more embarrassing than going with Lexie. If Lexie thought we were picking out things that were so last year, then I bet Grandma Evelyn would've had us outfitted in clothes that were so last *century*.

"Maybe next time, Grandma," Danielle said.

"Oh, stop being so nice, Danielle," Grandpa Alfred said before turning to face his wife. "She doesn't want to go old-lady shopping, Evelyn."

"You hush up," Grandma said.

"Maybe the girls can take *you* shopping," Grandpa said. "I bet they could teach you a thing or two."

"Now, that's enough, Alfred!" Grandma snapped.

We burst out laughing at the two of them going back and forth, and that awkward moment was quickly forgotten. Grandpa Alfred certainly knew how to test Grandma's patience, same as Charlie was testing mine. Were all men the same? When school started, I planned on asking Luke if he had the statistic on how many women who caught the bridal bouquet, like Mom did at Mr. Terupt's wedding last summer, actually got married within the next year.

LUKE

I had a good summer again this year. It was a busy one, but I wanted it that way. I needed to keep myself from going nuts thinking about my schedule for seventh grade. I was dying to find out when I'd have each subject, which teachers I'd have, and who'd be in my classes. Unfortunately, that information wasn't expected to be delivered until four or five days before the start of school. That meant I had a lot of time for thinking.

My summer started with a two-week Boy Scout camp that was situated in the middle of the woods. I earned several more badges and sharpened my survival skills. I also saw firsthand how annoying and stubborn pine sap can be. I don't know how he managed it, but one of the other scouts got that stuff all over his hands and clothes and in his hair during a game of capture the flag. The kid was still sticky four days later when it was time for us to go home—the poor sap!

Camp was fun, but the best part was when I figured out how to use the pocket compass Mr. Terupt gave me as a graduation present. It wasn't one of those cheesy plastic compasses, but a good one with a silver cover on the top that latched closed. My favorite thing about the compass was what was on the inside of that cover. Mr. Terupt had a message engraved for me. It said: *Luke, may you always find your way.*

After the Boy Scout camp, I attended a science camp at the same place I went to last year. It was another great experience. This time instead of leaving with a bog and two lizards, I came home with my very own snake! This was something I'd always wanted. For some reason, Mom wasn't thrilled, but in the end she allowed it. Stanley was a very handsome ball python. I placed his tank right on top of my dresser.

After science camp, we took a family vacation, a week-long trip to our nation's capital. This came as a surprise. It was my parents' idea. They considered it a reward for my great job all through grade school, and also a perfect opportunity for me to expand my knowledge of America's rich history before studying it in school.

The trip was absolutely amazing! Usually it's math and science that captivate me, but I couldn't soak up enough information about our country's past and its great leaders. I felt inspired by their many accomplishments and famous words, even though I didn't see myself ever joining their ranks.

Above all else, I'll always remember our stop at Arlington National Cemetery. The immaculate state of the place, coupled with the precision and organization, was like nothing I'd ever seen. The ceremonial Changing of the Guard that occurs every half hour at the Tomb of the Unknown Soldier was an unforgettable lesson on honor, loyalty, and respect. I felt all of that without anyone speaking a word. Silence can be powerful. Silence can say a lot. And the Changing of the Guard is a schedule that never falters.

Speaking of schedules, mine finally arrived three days before the start of seventh grade. This is what it looked like:

> 1st Period: Advanced Math
> 2nd Period: English Language Arts (ELA)
> 3rd Period: English Language Arts (ELA)
> 4th Period: Specials (PE or Art)
> 5th Period: Lunch
> 6th Period: Social Studies
> 7th Period: Study Hall
> 8th Period: Music/Home Ec/Computers
> 9th Period: Advanced Science

I was in all the advanced courses that were offered. (ELA was a double-period class, but there wasn't an advanced section for it, or for social studies.) I studied that piece of paper for the next three days. It's important to know what classes you have when, if you want to succeed in junior high school. I decided I had a good schedule. The only thing missing from it was Mr. Terupt.

LUKE'S SEVENTH-GRADE SURVIVAL GUIDE
TIP #1: Know your schedule.

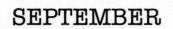

SEPTEMBER

Alexia

Some things never change. Like the first day of school. You always need to look your best. I'd been trying on different outfits all week long. I can have a hard time making decisions when it comes to what to wear. Like, I look good in everything. Mom says I have too many clothes, but I don't see that as the problem. How can a girl have too many clothes? Not possible. Anyways, it was the night before our first day of junior high, and I still didn't know what to wear, so I called Jessica for help.

"Hey, girl. Listen, like, what do you plan on wearing tomorrow?"

"I don't know. I'll figure it out in the morning," she said.

"In the morning! Are you crazy?! Decisions like this need time. Like, this is a big deal. We're not going to *Teach's* class tomorrow, you know."

"Yes, I know," she said. "Don't remind me."

"Oh, don't go getting all sappy on me. What I mean is, we're going to be the newbies in a much bigger school. With the junior high and high school in the same building, there'll be eighth graders *and* high schoolers walking the same halls as us! I've got to look good."

"You always look good, Lex. You know that. But please, nothing crazy like your toilet-paper-stuffed shirt last year."

"I know, I know. Chillax. I'll let the bra do the work for me."

"Well, you've got to put on more than that," she said. "Why don't you tell me what you're thinking about wearing."

I ran through all my choices, carefully describing every outfit. When I finished, Jessica made the decision for me. I don't know how she did it so easily, but she told me exactly what to wear: my new white jean shorts, which gave me plenty of leg to show off, my new pink top, and pink sandals. I chose the accessories, which included silver hoop earrings, a silver ring, and my anklet from Teach. I was all set. Or so I thought. . . .

Jessica

Dear Journal,

I have you concealed inside my first-period textbook. I know I should be paying attention, but it's math, not English. This stuff is boring, especially without Luke or Mr. Terupt getting all superexcited about it. I don't normally do these things. In fact, I've never done something like this; I'm not a rule breaker or a sneaky kid. Perhaps I'm entering a rebellious stage? No, I don't think so. I'll get back to paying attention in a minute—I promise. But first, I need to tell you what happened. There's already been more drama on our first day of junior high school than there was at theater camp.

Lexie kept me on the phone for over an hour last night. She had to describe—in detail—every single one of her potential first-day-of-seventh-grade outfits. Finally, I picked something for her randomly. Near tragedy avoided. Until this morning . . . Tell you more later. Math teacher is getting suspicious.

Love,
Jessica

P.S. Already missing Mr. Terupt.

Alexia

"A*hhhh!*" This couldn't be. Not today. I didn't *believe* it. Staring back at me in the mirror was the hugest pimple I had ever seen. Right on my nose! On the first day of junior high school! Could it get any worse than that?!

It wasn't one with a white head that I could easily pop and take care of, but a hard red lump with pressure underneath it and no way for it to escape. It hurt, and I wanted it gone. I *needed* it gone. So I leaned closer to the mirror and pinched it as hard as I could, until I couldn't stand it anymore. My eyes watered and blurred to the point where I couldn't even see myself in the glass, but after I wiped my tears away, I saw that I had only made things worse. The mass of ugliness on the tip of my nose was still there, and it looked angry. I didn't know whether to blame my week of stressing over clothes, all that stupid restaurant grease, or puberty. I called Jessica in a panic.

"I'm sure it's not that bad," she said once I'd caught her up on my crisis.

"Yes, it is! It's the ugliest thing ever!" I cried. "I can't go to school."

"Okay, calm down," Jessica said. "Stop freaking out. We've got all sorts of makeup left over from camp. Bring what you have, and I'll bring my stuff. We'll get you fixed up in the bathroom before school starts. No one will ever know."

"Are you sure?" I asked, sniffling.

"Yes," Jessica promised. "My mom's driving me to school. I'll have her swing by your place on the way. We'll pick you up in twenty minutes."

There was no lollygagging. We found the girls' room before anyone else saw us. Jessica was armed with several bags of makeup. We had learned some nifty tricks at theater camp, and Jessica was good. She had called in reinforcements, as well—Anna and Danielle. The three of them spent the next ten minutes fussing over me. When they had finally finished, they took a step back.

"Well?" I asked them.

"You look like a ninth grader," Jessica said.

I liked the sound of that. I smiled and posed like a model, sticking out my chest and jutting my hip forward. I was relieved and excited . . . until I looked in the mirror. Then I was devastated. I had myself fooled, thinking they could mask my monster pimple, but the makeup on top just called out more attention to it. The first day of school ranked among the most important events of the year, and mine was ruined before it even started. I wiped off the stupid makeup and left the bathroom. I moped down the hall with terrible posture, which I knew did nothing to help me look attractive, but what did it matter?

"Whoa! Lexie," Peter said. "What is that on your nose, Mount Everest?"

"Be quiet, Peter," Jessica said. "Now's not the time."

Just then, a group of cute older guys came walking by. I

was used to Peter being an idiot. He didn't bother me. But like, when these other boys said something, that was different. I should've kept my head down, but I wanted to see them.

"Look at that girl," one said, and pointed. "Hey, Rudolph!" They thought that was hilarious. They started cracking up. "She's got a tumor on her nose!" yelled their obvious leader.

Peter stepped forward. "Hey, big mouth," he said, his voice cracking. "Shut up."

"Oooh. Better watch out, Zack, her scrawny, squeaky boyfriend's mad," a member of the pack said to his leader.

"You better go back over there with your dweeby friends and fat and ugly girls," Zack said.

"*You* better keep walking," Jeffrey warned, taking a place next to Peter and joining the standoff.

The group of older boys stared at Peter and Jeffrey, who stared back, but nothing more happened. It was typical guy stuff. Macho men full of tough talk and no action. Having boys fight over me on the first day of school might've made my day better, but that didn't happen, so I turned and walked off in the other direction. I was grateful that Peter and Jeffrey had stuck up for me—for all of us—but I didn't know how to show that, not at the time.

"Lexie, where're you going?" Jessica called. The first bell rang. "We've got to get to homeroom."

I shrugged and kept walking. I knew where I was going. I hadn't faked being sick since third grade, but I spent the day in the nurse's office after giving her a made-up story about cramps.

Seventh grade was off to a terrible start.

Peter

After our showdown with Zack and his bunch of losers, I wanted to check on Lexie and tell her I was sorry, but when I turned back around, she was already halfway down the hall. I didn't see her for the rest of the day. I *did* get to meet Principal Lee, though.

After third period, I needed to hit the bathroom. Then I hurried to my locker to dump off my math book. I didn't want to carry that brick around any longer than I had to. (There should be a rule that textbooks can't exceed a certain weight. That ancient piece of junk must've weighed ten pounds—and that was with its back cover missing!) I opened my locker, and papers and folders spilled out all over the floor. I hadn't even been in school for a day yet, and already I had a mess. I scrambled to stuff everything back inside, then I slammed the door and took off down the hall.

Being late to class on day one is not the best way to make a first impression. I was in a full sprint. The bell was going to ring any second, but I was determined to make it. I went flying around the corner . . . and came to an abrupt and painful stop. What is it with principals and terrible timing? Or is it just my rotten luck? The good news is, I didn't plow this guy to the ground like I had Mrs. Williams, our old principal. The bad news is, what happened was way worse. I only had a second to react, and in that instant I managed to spring up on my toes and turn sideways in a desperate maneuver to avert catastrophe. I avoided every part of Principal Lee except his elbow. I bumped that with my hip and sent the hot cup of coffee he was holding splashing all over the front of him—his face, his shirt, and even the crotch of his pants.

"Oh—!" The next word slipped out of my mouth same as my feet did coming around the corner. I wasn't doing myself any favors.

Fortunately, Principal Lee didn't hear what I'd said because he let a few choice words of his own fly at the same time. Then he started dancing a jig, hopping up and down and tugging at his clothes where the coffee was burning him. Like a superhero, he ripped his dress shirt open to get it off his skin. I stood there frozen in fear and disbelief while Principal Lee stood with his hairy belly hanging out, staring daggers at me. It's safe to say he was a little hot after our run-in. I spent the next fifteen minutes in his office, cowering in my chair as he read me the riot act.

"I'm going to be watching you, Mr. Jacobs. And if you slip up even a little bit, I'm going to be all over you like white on rice."

Despite my best efforts, I made it to English Language Arts more than a little late on that first day. I arrived just in time to hear Mrs. Reeder talking about words. *Detention* was *my* word. I had just received three of them.

Jessica

Dear Journal,

I've been dying to get back to you all day. I haven't had a chance until now, fourth- and fifth-period English Language Arts—ELA, as the teacher calls it—with Mrs. Reeder. Isn't that a lovely name for an English teacher? Mrs. Reeder is crazy about books, and words.

"Words," she said. "We will read words, write words, and talk about words. You will find an appreciation for words in this class. Words can be the most powerful thing we know."

"What kind of words?" Peter asked, having just arrived, and quite late, I might add. He handed Mrs. Reeder his pink slip.

She studied it and then said, "Better late than never, Mr. Jacobs."

"I tried my best to make it on time," Peter said.

"Well, let's hope not all of your attempts end with fruitless results."

What sort of trouble had Peter managed to get himself in already? I wondered.

"You may take a seat," Mrs. Reeder said, pointing to an

empty desk. She continued, "'What kind of words?' Mr. Jacobs has asked. That's something each of you will need to figure out for yourself. I challenge you to do something important with your words this year. I will ask you to write in your journals regularly, responding to this very topic, explaining to me how you feel you've accomplished this, or perhaps missed the opportunity. And then, as we near the end of the school year, you will be asked to write a paper of reflection to conclude your study. If taken seriously, this assignment is one that you will find enlightening and rewarding."

I already know this is going to be my favorite class—and how lucky it's a double period. Mrs. Reeder's passion for words reminds me of Mr. Terupt, which only makes me miss him all the more. I miss Luke, too. I haven't seen him all day. I wonder, would he have stepped forward on my behalf like Peter and Jeffrey did for Lexie and Anna and the rest of us this morning?

There's the bell.

Love,
Jessica

P.S. I hope my words at theater camp were powerful enough to earn me an invitation.

P.P.S. We need to visit Mr. Terupt. I'm going to get the gang on this pronto.

LUKE

As seventh graders entering junior high, we were no different from the kindergartners back at Snow Hill School. Once again, we were at the bottom of the food chain in this new and dangerous ecosystem. There was so much to learn. Just walking down the hall was a study in survival.

I was in search of my first-period classroom, reading the numbers on each door I passed, when this group of kids going by in the other direction purposely knocked all the books out of my hands. "Ha-ha! What a dork." They laughed and cheered and carried on like a pack of hyenas.

Traveling in numbers is a strategy exercised by many species in the animal kingdom. There's safety in numbers. But none of my friends had the same schedule as I did. Even my locker was located in a different area. I was on my own. Already, I felt like a lost gazelle, separated from my herd, in danger of being eaten alive in this vast savannah called junior high school.

The second bell rang. I was late. I crawled around, gathering my folder and notebook and papers that had scattered everywhere. I'd always loved school, but the unfamiliar had me scared to death. Where were my friends? Where was Mr. Terupt? My recently honed wilderness-survival skills weren't going to be of much help in this new environment.

LUKE'S SEVENTH-GRADE SURVIVAL GUIDE
TIP #2: Hold your books tightly. Do not hold your books in a stacked pile in front of your body. Do not hold them lying flat. Failure to adhere to this advice will result in your being laughed at, called names, and late for class.

ANNA

We had lockers back at Snow Hill School, but they were no big deal. You dumped your bag and jacket in there at the beginning of the day and then didn't go back to it until it was time to go home. All your books and supplies were kept inside your one and only classroom desk. There was a whole different system in seventh grade. Seventh graders went to their lockers after every period to switch books and folders.

We were issued our locker numbers and combinations in homeroom after the teacher took attendance. "Conveniently, you will find your lockers just outside this classroom," Mrs. Reeder, my homeroom teacher, said. "I suggest you go and find yours and practice the combination. Should any of you be the forgetful type, I will always have your information on file. Please let me know if you need any help."

I didn't have much trouble finding my locker, but getting the combination to work was another story. My locker was old, like most everything at the junior high, and desperately needed a paint job, but I liked it. I decided it was a lot like me. It didn't like opening up any more than I did. I let it be. I knew I'd have to get it to open eventually, but I decided I'd worry about that later.

In many ways, seventh grade was like starting all over again. I made myself as small as possible and did my best to hide. I wasn't interested in being noticed. That was Lexie's thing, though I knew she was hoping to accomplish that in a different way than she had that morning. In class, I raised my hand zero times and had zero teachers call on me.

It wasn't until fourth- and fifth-period English Language Arts that I finally felt somewhat comfortable in a classroom. My homeroom teacher, Mrs. Reeder, was also my ELA teacher, but that wasn't what helped put me at ease. It was that the rest of our group was in there with me, except for Luke. We hadn't seen him all day, but we weren't worried. If anybody had school under control, it was Luke.

Mrs. Reeder jumped right into class and got all excited talking about words. She sounded like a philosopher and challenged us to do something of importance with our words this year. She had me worried. It was going to be hard to do something of significance with my words when all I wanted to do was stay quiet. I was more concerned with getting Charlie's vocal cords to work so he could finally do something special with *his* words—like ask my mom to marry him!

Following ELA, all the old gang minus Luke had lunch. At this point, I needed to get my locker open because I had too many books and folders to lug around after all my morning classes.

"Let me help you," Jeffrey said, startling me. I didn't realize he was behind me. He must've seen me struggling. "What's your combination?"

"Two-zero-two," I said.

"Two-zero-two, huh," Jeffrey echoed, and smiled. "That was our room number with Terupt back in fifth grade."

Once he said that, I knew I wouldn't need Mrs. Reeder to ever remind me of my combination. Jeffrey opened my locker on his first try. I wondered, if he ever tried to get me to open up to him, would he have the same effect on me, and me on him? He didn't exactly reveal himself to the world, either. We were a good match. Did he think so too?

"Thanks," I said in a small voice. "I couldn't get it open earlier."

"Guess I've got the magic touch," he said.

I felt the heat rise in my cheeks. I hoped I wasn't the color of Grandma's beets again.

Jeffrey

Other than our stupid standoff with Zack—thanks to Peter—the rest of that first morning was uneventful, not something you could ever say about Terupt's classroom. I moved from one class to the next, each time hoping I'd find someone I knew. That finally happened in ELA.

This lady had vocabulary on the brain like I had wrestling on the brain. She wanted me to write about important words, and the only ones I could come up with were the ones I had taped on the back of my bedroom door: *I will win every match this season.*

At wrestling camp, the coaches had talked to us about goal setting and writing down what we wanted to accomplish. I read these words every single day because I knew one thing about words—if you didn't believe in them, then there wasn't much chance of them coming true.

Before we were told to close our journals, there was another word that came to my mind. It was Asher's word. Again the other day, he had pointed at the backyard and said "My-my." I wanted to know what he was trying to say.

After ELA everyone hurried out to their lockers to dump

off books and supplies in a rush to get to lunch. By sixth period, you were starving. I hung back and gave Anna a hand opening her locker. I wanted to give her my hand to hold, but it'd been a long time since that last happened. I didn't know if she would want me doing that, and I wasn't brave enough to ask her. It took a lot of courage to share your feelings, especially with a girl.

Once Anna had her things put away, we headed to lunch and joined everyone else. Jessica was waiting for us when we got there. "We haven't even been in school for a day, and already I miss Mr. Terupt," she said.

"Don't feel bad," I told her. "We all miss him."

"Then as soon as we find Lexie and Luke, we need to make plans to go and see him," she said.

Even though we all liked her idea, finding a time to go and see Terupt wasn't going to be as easy as we'd thought. The same way I always gave myself an excuse for not taking Anna's hand, we would always have reasons to keep us from going.

Danielle

School was school. It wasn't terrible, but it wasn't anything exciting, either. The only thing that had happened worth mentioning was Anna and I joined the junior high yearbook committee. We figured this was a way for Anna to put her camera and newfound photography interest to work, and for me to add my art skills. But other than that, without Mr. Terupt, there wasn't anything else to report. Most of the stuff worth talking about was happening outside the classroom rather than in it.

My English teacher, Mrs. Reeder, who also served as our yearbook coordinator, was nice enough. I wanted to tell her that I shared lots of important words with God, but school and religion mix like oil and water, so I kept that to myself, like I did all my personal matters.

Lately, I'd been having days when I felt really worn out and not very hungry, and then there were other days when I felt fine. I figured seventh grade was just stressful, so I tried not to show it. I told myself it would pass once I got in the swing of things. But when you're exhausted, your body drags instead of walks.

"Danielle, are you feeling all right?" Mom asked me one afternoon. "You look tired."

"Just a little under the weather," I said, sounding like any good farmer.

"Go lie down and get some rest," Mom said.

I was happy to take her advice, and after that I made sure to look brighter around her so she didn't keep worrying about me. Whenever one of the girls said something, I blamed my tiredness on my period. I actually wondered if that was part of it. My clothes were getting looser, so maybe it was growing pains, too? In school, it was easy to deal with not being hungry. I simply threw my lunch out. No one ever noticed. But at home, Grandma was a different story.

"You didn't eat much at dinner," she said to me while doing the dishes one night. "What's the matter? Don't like my cooking anymore?"

"No, Grandma. I still love your cooking. Just too much on my mind with school, I guess."

"Everything all right without Mr. Terupt?" she asked.

"I guess so. I miss him, but things are okay. We keep talking about going to see him, but we haven't managed yet."

"You should, before time gets away from you."

"We will," I said.

"Well, I know what you mean about not being able to eat when your mind won't slow down. How do you think I've stayed thin all these years? Your grandfather has my mind going crazy. Goodness, he's even got me talking to myself these days. It's a wonder I've got any meat on my bones."

Grandma and I shared a good laugh. She wasn't exactly a

frail old woman. Plump was more like it. I took after her with my body type. I'd been thinking about our similarities these days. The truth was, school did have my mind busy, thanks to my new science teacher, Mr. Brobur. He kicked our year off by talking to us about genetics.

"Offspring inherit traits from their parents. You are all offspring," Mr. Brobur said. "Some of you might resemble your mother more than your father, while others might resemble the old man more. Some of you might be a nice mix. It all depends on how their information came together to make you. Those of you who look nothing like your folks should talk to the milkman."

The class erupted in laughter after Mr. Brobur made that comment. Not me. I sat in my seat motionless. Shocked. Mr. Brobur was joking about sinful behavior. He was an old man, a teacher who could've retired years ago, but he wasn't ready for that. He told us so. "I've got a few good years left in me yet," he said. "I'm in no rush to just sit around growing older. I'll know when the time comes."

Mr. Brobur reminded me of Grandma, an old person not ready to slow down, and one who could be free with his words. Grandma might have been conservative in some regards, but she'd never hesitate to tell you what she thought. Maybe the courage to say what you mean comes with age—and in Mr. Brobur's case, so did some absent-mindedness. He stood before us with his fly undone. Had anyone else noticed? For his sake, I hoped they hadn't. I said a quick prayer for him.

"Then there are times when traits seem to skip generations." Mr. Brobur continued with his lecture. "And other instances when random changes occur in our DNA, leading to brand-new traits that no one else in our family has ever exhibited. These random changes help explain how creatures have evolved into new ones over millions of years."

Mr. Brobur sure knew how to make me pay attention. First he teased about sinful acts, and then he started talking about evolution. Evolution and the church weren't always the best of friends. Evolution and Grandma didn't exactly see eye to eye, either. If you asked her, the mystery of life was the work of God. Evolution wasn't a topic we talked about, so I was secretly sort of excited to learn a little bit about it from Mr. Brobur. It was thanks to my new science teacher that I got to wondering, if no one else in my family was feeling sick or run-down like me, did that mean I had one of those random changes in my DNA? Or just some virus that I'd get over in time?

The one thing I did know was that whatever was going on with me—whether it was some sort of random evolution twist or the work of God—would stay between God and me for now. I needed to be tough. There was no way I was going to see any doctor. No one in my family went to the doctor unless it was serious. And this wasn't serious.

The only person I intended to visit was Mr. Terupt. Grandma was right about time getting away from you. It seemed there was always a reason why the gang couldn't go to see him. It was either too much homework, detention for Peter, or some other after-school commitment that one of us had. But I'd had enough of the excuses. With or without the gang, I was going.

Dear God,

I've got two things for you tonight. First, I'm hoping you will help me feel better soon. Please. And second, I'd appreciate it if you could help me get the gang to go and visit Mr. Terupt. Even though I'm prepared to go alone if I have to, I'd rather have everyone with me, and I think Mr. Terupt would like that, too. Thank you.

Amen.

L

It's no secret that I like math and numbers, but I'd never given much thought to the number zero before. Zero is a wonderful value. It's a natural number, a rational number, neither positive nor negative, a whole number, and a complex number, and it holds a significant place in science as well. Zero was also the number of friends I had in seventh grade. Zero can be a horrible feeling.

I was excited when school first began. Being in all the advanced classes offered was something I'd always wanted, but it wasn't at all what I'd expected. The one kid I planned on having in class with me—Theo from last year—had apparently moved away over the summer. By the end of our first two weeks, my new classmates still weren't including me. Even though it was the accelerated bunch, raising my hand and answering all the questions wasn't cool and didn't make me popular.

Lexie and Peter and Jeffrey and the rest of my old friends never hated me for knowing the answers. Even Jessica, who was the smartest person I knew when it came to books and writing, didn't ever get annoyed. I missed her. I missed all of

he old gang. They knew I loved school and projects, and hey liked me the way I came. But not my new classmates. I got used to eating my lunch alone. I thought of Peter and how lonely he must've felt after the snowball accident that sent Mr. Terupt to the hospital back in fifth grade. Unfortunately, James, our friend with special needs from the Collaborative Classroom we used to visit, wasn't there to help me like he did Peter.

If seventh grade had us hunkered down in the same classroom all day long, then I think I would've felt better, but this changing rooms and teachers every time the bell rang had me off balance. And the halls were the worst.

LUKE'S SEVENTH-GRADE SURVIVAL GUIDE
TIP #3: Do not carry your books loosely at your side. Failure to heed this warning will lead to the same results as failure to abide by Tip #2.

The same pack of hyenas had knocked the books out of my hands every day so far. It happened at all different times, so I never knew when to expect it, and they never failed to get me. Like clockwork, Zack would reach out and smack whatever I was holding, and his buddies would jeer and jostle me. Each time, they sent my books and papers flying all over the place. Then they'd stand there laughing at me while I scurried around like a little mouse trying to gather my stuff. Of course, they always had something nice to say.

"Dork."

"Geek."

"Nerd."

"Loser."

I had inherited all sorts of names in seventh grade, but "friend" was not one of them. I would hear them cackling as they walked away, giving each other high fives. "You got him good today, Zack."

Science proved to be the one highlight in my day. It was my last-period class, so the thought of it helped get me through everything that came before it. I was naturally interested in the subject, but the fact that it was also taught by my favorite teacher—not including Mr. Terupt!—made it all the better.

Mr. Brobur was a much older man than Mr. Terupt. He was bald on top with the exception of a few white hairs that sprang out in all different directions, and he had wisps of hair just above his ears—and coming out of his ears, too. He was on the smaller side, wiry, but he was big on personality. I liked him from the start.

"We'll begin our year with a unit on genetics even though it's not in the textbook," Mr. Brobur announced. "Why? Because these old books are falling apart and are seriously outdated, and the school can't seem to buy us any new ones, so the heck with them. I'd much rather talk about something that is wildly exciting and certain to be in your future. There are three billion steps that make up our DNA. What's DNA?"

I raised my hand before reminding myself not to. I couldn't help it. Old habits die hard.

"Luke?"

I heard grumbling around me. "The instructions that tell our cells what to do and how to make us," I said.

"That's a very good answer." More grumbling. "Would

you believe that you and any other person on this planet are said to be ninety-nine point nine percent identical when it comes to those three billion steps?"

I thought of Lexie. She and I were supposed to be 99.9 percent identical in our DNA? I didn't think so. We had to be the exception.

"I know Mrs. Reeder loves to talk about words, and she'll have you thinking about them all year long," Mr. Brobur said, "but that isn't something only reserved for the English classroom. Science is full of wonderful vocabulary. *Genotype,* for instance, is the word we use when referring to the actual steps in your DNA. *Phenotype,* however, is the word we use when talking about the traits you physically express: white skin, brown skin, blue eyes, green eyes, big muscles . . . no muscles." Mr. Brobur pointed at me, trying to be funny.

My classmates got a kick out of his joke. Mr. Brobur didn't realize I needed no help when it came to being made fun of.

"Now," he continued, "who can tell me what your phenotype is the result of?"

"Your genotype," someone up front answered.

"Yes," Mr. Brobur said, "and?"

We were quiet. No one knew. I had a good idea, but I didn't voice it.

"Ah, no one wants to offer an answer. That's okay. This is actually a question that you will be exploring all year long. That's what seventh grade is largely about. What is your phenotype?"

The bell rang.

LUKE'S SEVENTH-GRADE SURVIVAL GUIDE
TIP #4: Don't answer all the questions—even if you know you're right. Failure to heed this warning will leave you lonely, unpopular, and without the company of friends.

Was there anything that could make me feel better? I knew the answer to that question, too—Mr. Terupt. I was so happy when I found out we were going to see him.

Alexia

Things at school were way better after my nightmare first day. A week in, I bumped into Reena and Lisa, the high school girls I had met last year, and they complimented me on my outfit. And then those same older boys from day one came cruising by, but instead of making fun of me, I heard the guy named Zack elbow his buddy and say, "Who's that girl over there? She's hot."

He didn't even remember me! Like, I was looking that good. I was back in the game. Of course, that jerk didn't stand a chance with me, but I decided to let him think differently. It'd be fun to string him along only to crush his heart later—he deserved it.

So like, things were good. I had my wardrobe working for me—which was key—and classes were fine, too, but my favorite part of the day was lunch. That was our chance for the old gang to hang out. We'd laugh and joke, and at some point we always got back to talking about Teach. Jessica was the first to mention going to visit him, but it was actually Danielle who finally put her foot down and made it happen. She can be tough when she wants.

"We keep talking about it, but haven't done it yet," she said one day. "Well, enough is enough. I'm going tomorrow, and you guys can come with me or not."

"Whoa! You're not going without me," Peter said.

"Count me in," Jeffrey said.

"And me," Anna said.

"I'll make sure Luke knows," Jessica said.

That settled it. We were going, and we were excited. We were also in for a surprise.

The next day we met in the lobby after school.

"It's exactly one point two miles from here to Snow Hill School," Luke said. "We should make it in fifteen to twenty minutes." He started the timer on his wristwatch.

"Piece of cake," Peter said.

"Hate to break it to you, but that's not happening in these babies," I said, lifting my foot and wiggling a stylish shoe. The guys looked at my feet and just shook their heads. They had no concept of fashion.

We made it eventually, but like, when we got there we couldn't find Teach. It was Mr. Lumas, the faithful Snow Hill custodian, who found us poking around the halls, looking for him.

"He's not here today," Mr. Lumas said.

"Where is he?" Peter asked.

"Don't know. Mrs. Terupt was out today, too. I'd tell you to check in with Mrs. Williams, but she's off to some meeting with the district big shots," Mr. Lumas said. "You picked the wrong day to stop by, kids. No one's around."

"Great," Peter said. "Just great."

"Sorry," Danielle muttered.

"It's not your fault," Jessica said.

"Why would they both be out?" Anna asked.

"Who knows?" Peter said, annoyed. "Now what?"

No one had an answer, so I just said the first thing that popped into my head. "We can walk to the restaurant."

"Are you crazy?" Peter said. "Do you know how far that is?"

"Yeah, I do," I said. "It'll be fun. C'mon."

"What about your *shoes*?" he asked, mocking me.

"I'm not the one crying," I said. "Now, c'mon. Vincent will take care of us when we get there."

"Who's Vincent?" Peter asked. He had more questions than a two-year-old.

"He's the owner and cook at the restaurant, the guy who made the awesome food for Teach's wedding."

"Oh, yeah."

"What do you mean, take care of us?" Jeffrey asked.

"Give us some free food and drinks."

"Why didn't you say so?!" Peter cried, suddenly all excited. (Boys love food.) "Let's go!"

Even though the walk was more than two miles, it didn't stop us. When the gang was together, we were capable of anything.

Once we made it to the restaurant, I had everyone hang back in the waiting area while I went and found Mom. I was surprised to see her taking a break. She was everyone's favorite waitress, which meant she was always on the go, so to find her sitting down was unusual. She said it was because she had a headache, but even so, she didn't stay there for long because Vincent got after her.

"No sitting down on the job," he teased.

"You're right," Mom said, getting back to her feet. "Just a little tired today for some reason. And I don't mean tired of you, 'cause that's an everyday thing." Headache or not, Mom still outwitted Vincent. It was like me and Peter.

"So, to what do I owe this lovely surprise?" Mom asked.

"We tried to go visit Mr. and Mrs. Teach," I said, "but they weren't in school today."

"Neither of them?"

"Nope."

"Humph."

"So like, we ended up here instead," I said.

"Well, it's great to have you," Mom said. "Take your friends over to the big table, and I'll get Vincent to put some snacks together for you."

"Okay."

As I had promised, Vincent took care of us. He put three pitchers of lemonade and two large platters of nachos and fries on our table.

"Awesome!" the boys cheered.

"Thanks," the girls said.

Vincent winked at me.

We dug in. Peter sucked down so much lemonade he had to run to the bathroom before finishing his food. While he was away from the table, I decided it was time to get even with him for making fun of my shoes—and my pimple. I took the salt shaker and loosened the top. Then I carefully placed it back on the table. Everyone looked at me, but no one said a word. After Peter returned, we carried on like normal, even though we were all dying for him to get a taste of his own medicine. When he took a heap of fries, I slid the salt shaker toward him.

"They're better with salt," I said.

Peter never gave it a second thought. He grabbed the salt, tipped it over his plate, and gave it one hard shake. That was all it took. The top went flying and he was instantly left with a pile of white crystals smothering his fries.

We lost it. Jeffrey tried to hold it in, but he couldn't. He spit his mouthful of water all over Peter. The rest of us had tears coming down our faces after that. Even Peter was laughing in the end, but I should've known he would be looking to get me back.

It was great having the whole gang together.

Danielle

"I don't know what it is, Danielle, but men aren't very smart," Anna said.

We were in my bedroom after coming home from Lexie's restaurant. I was sitting on my bed with my sketchbook while Anna paced in front of me. She was as quiet as a mouse in school, and as wild as a caged lion at home. I loved that about her.

"Now you're sounding like Grandma," I said. That made her crack a smile, but just a quick one.

"What's taking Charlie so long?" she asked.

"Farmers are careful planners, Anna, not impulsive people."

"For crying out loud, how long does he need? If you ask me, it's about time."

"Patience, Anna. Patience makes the world go round."

"Now *you're* sounding like Grandma."

"Anna, c'mon, honey," her mom called from downstairs. It was time for her to go home. Anna stayed over sometimes, but her mother never did. She and Charlie wouldn't do that until they were married. Grandma might've loved Anna and her mother, but she wasn't going to allow that.

"Be right down," Anna called.

We knelt by my bedside and said our prayers, same as we did every night when we were together. We'd been doing it ever since we declared ourselves half sisters. I said the prayer this time, but sometimes Anna did the talking.

Dear God,

We thank you for a great afternoon. It was a lot of fun having everyone together, but now we have a couple things to ask of you. First off, please help the ignorant men of the world—like Charlie—figure out what they're supposed to do and say. And, if possible, we'd like that sooner rather than later.

"That was good," Anna whispered to me. I knew she'd like that.

And lastly, we'd also like it if you could check in on Mr. and Mrs. Terupt. Both of them being absent today has us nervous. Please don't let them ever experience anything bad again, like when Mr. Terupt was in his coma almost two years ago. Thank you.

Amen.

Anna gave me a hug and then headed home. I'd felt good today, so I thanked God for that, then went to bed.

OCTOBER

ANNA

I spent the night at Danielle's, so I got up early and went and found Charlie in the barn, just like I knew I would. He was already busy with the milking. He started every day the same way.

"Do you like spending your mornings with these cows?" I asked him. He was putting the milking machine on a pair of udders.

"I do," he said. (At least now I knew he could say those two words together.) "I like the quiet, and I know these girls are happy to see me." He was referring to the cows. "We enjoy each other's company without saying anything at all."

"Don't you like talking to people?" I asked him.

"Sure," he said, "but sometimes the quiet is nice, too."

"Jeffrey's like that at school," I said. "We do a lot of hanging out together, but he never says too much. Sometimes I wish he would, so I knew exactly what he was thinking or feeling."

"Maybe he's just waiting for the right moment," Charlie said, moving on to the next cow, which happened to be Bessie. She looked at me, and I smiled at her. Charlie sat on his stool.

"Or maybe he's too chicken to say anything," I said. I reached out and touched Bessie's tickle spot. She swung her tail around, and it slapped Charlie right across his cheek. Bessie was my special cow, but when it came to her tail, she was no different from the rest—that thing was disgusting. She left Charlie looking like he'd just been clobbered upside the head with a cow patty.

"Gosh darn it!" he hollered. I couldn't contain my laughter. "She got me good." He sputtered and spit, rising from his stool. He wiped his face on his shirtsleeve and marched over to the hose.

"Maybe she was trying to tell you something," Danielle said. She'd been standing quietly off to the side the whole time I was chatting with Charlie. I'd seen her, but I didn't let on.

Charlie waved at her but didn't say anything. He was more concerned with sticking his face under the hose.

"C'mon, Anna," Danielle said. "We don't want to be late. We're having that big assembly today."

"Bye, Charlie," I said. "It was nice talking with you. Bye, Bessie." I winked at her, and I swear she smiled back. I wished I could communicate with boys as easily.

"I wasn't talking about Bessie when I said that to Charlie," Danielle whispered.

"I know," I said. "Hopefully Charlie's smart enough to figure that out."

We exchanged the same smiles those twins in *The Parent Trap* did when they were up to no good.

Danielle

All seventh graders were required to meet in the gym following homeroom for a special assembly. I found Anna and Jessica and Lexie and sat with them.

"Like, what's this all about?" Lexie asked.

"I don't know," Jessica said.

They looked at Anna and me. "We don't know, either," I said.

Once the teachers had all of us seated in the bleachers, Principal Lee took over. He stood at a podium out in the middle of the gym, raising his hand. I remembered my second-grade teacher using the same tactic to bring us to attention, but it didn't seem to work as well with seventh graders. A few of us stopped talking, but most did not. To Principal Lee's credit, he recognized his shortcomings and put his arm down. I watched him reach under the podium. I couldn't imagine what he was going to try next. I'm glad I was paying attention because I was able to cover my ears in time. Principal Lee lifted an air horn high above his head and blasted it. The noise was deafening as it bounced off the walls. The kids around me started screaming and squealing while covering their ears. He had caused an even bigger ruckus, so he went ahead and gave that thing a second blast. Thankfully, that made everyone wise up, and our group fell quiet.

"I'd much rather have you go silent when I do this," he said, raising his arm in demonstration, "but if that won't work, then I will resort to other measures. This is our first gathering, so I trust you will get it right in the future."

"Yeah, get it right next time," some obnoxious boy on the other side of the bleachers yelled, and got plenty of laughs in response. I looked over and saw it was Peter. Seventh grade didn't intimidate him in the least. He was already Mr. Popular.

"Thank you, Mr. Jacobs. Now sit down," Principal Lee said, all hints of joking gone from his voice.

More laughter. Principal Lee probably didn't even know I existed, but he had Peter pegged.

"This is always one of my favorite events in the fall," Principal Lee said. "I encourage all of you to listen carefully and to take this opportunity seriously. Your social studies teacher, Mr. Smith, will now explain student government to you, and how you can get involved."

There were moans and groans all around me, but the mention of government had me thinking of my family's ongoing—though quiet—land war with the Native Americans. If I listened to Grandma and Grandpa, it was clear our government was one that couldn't always be trusted. I wondered if that was the kind of system our seventh-grade student government would be—one built on false promises. I was thankful that I had a group of friends I knew I could trust.

"Student government is your opportunity to get involved. To have a voice," Mr. Smith said.

For the remainder of the assembly, our seventh-grade teachers took turns explaining the various positions in student government. Before they got done, I started feeling blah and spaced out, so I didn't hear everything Mr. Smith had to say, but the gist of it was that we would need to elect a president, vice president, treasurer, and secretary. Those deciding to run would have to organize campaigns. There would be a need for speechwriters, artwork and posters, slogans and promises.

"We will reassemble in December to hear speeches, after which you will be able to cast your votes," Mr. Smith said. "Since seventh grade is your first year being all together, we like to hold our election later than the older grades so you have the opportunity to get to know your classmates beforehand. The last thing I'll say is that this should not be a popularity contest."

I was glad he was finished with things to say because I was beginning to feel even worse.

"I'm running for president," Lexie whispered to us.

Anna, Jessica, and I looked at each other, none of us surprised. Lexie still loved attention, and she was already popular among seventh graders. Mr. Smith could tell us it wasn't a popularity contest all he wanted, but we knew that was exactly what it was.

"Jessica, I'll need you to be my speechwriter, and, Anna and Danielle, you'll be in charge of my posters and that sort of thing," Lexie said. The three of us exchanged glances and rolled our eyes. Lexie was in charge. Everybody look out. Of course, we didn't object. We hadn't been given anything like this to work on together since Mr. Terupt's classroom. It was going to be fun.

"We need to tell the guys," Jessica said. "Maybe they'll help."

"Like, one day we'll talk about how this moment was the beginning of me becoming president of the United States."

Lord help us if that ever happened.

Jeffrey

I was hoping to sit with Anna during our assembly, but we didn't find each other in time. It ended up being just me and Peter and Luke. Even after we sat down, I kept looking around, trying to find her in the bleachers. She was good at making herself invisible. It wasn't until Peter opened his big mouth and had everyone staring our way that I found her. I smiled, and she gave me a small wave in return.

I didn't hear much of what was said after that because I spent the rest of the assembly stealing glances at her. She caught me once. In my daydreams I always managed to ask her out, but I couldn't seem to find the courage to do it for real. I was afraid she might not give me the answer I wanted.

"Did you hear me?" Peter said, nailing me in the ribs with his elbow.

"What?"

"I'm running for president, and you and Luke are in charge of my campaign."

"What? I don't think so." We were on our feet and exiting the gym. I was searching for Anna so that we could at least walk out together, but thanks to Peter I'd lost sight of her again. I wanted to punch him. I was on my toes scanning the crowd.

"Who're you looking for?" Peter asked.

"No one," I said, putting my heels back on the ground.

"Anna?"

"No. Shut up."

"Oh, I see how it is. You can't help me become president because you're too busy being a lover boy."

Sometimes Peter didn't know when to stop. "I said shut *up*." I slugged him in the arm, hard enough that he knew I was done fooling around. Hard enough that he didn't exactly appreciate being punched like that.

If it weren't for good timing and Luke, things might've gotten out of hand between the two of us. If it weren't for Luke, things might've gotten out of hand between Peter and Lexie. And if it weren't for Luke, I wouldn't have been given the chance to hang out with Anna again like I did for our PowerPoint project last year. Boy, I loved that kid and his brain. We needed him around more.

LUKE

Besides not getting to see my friends in school this year, the other thing I'd been deprived of up to this point was any sort of project to work on. That was a Mr. Terupt specialty. I needed to get him over here to show these junior high teachers how it was done. But as I listened to Mr. Smith talk to us about student government, I began to think my opportunity for a project had finally arrived. The only issue I saw was that there was no way I could run for office. Mr. Smith could tell us it wasn't a popularity contest until he was blue in the face—everyone knew that wasn't the truth.

Only when we were leaving the gym and Peter mentioned wanting to run for president did it start to come together. Peter was a popular kid. This could work. I started racking my brain, trying to figure out how to make this one of those Mr. Terupt sort of projects. I wasn't paying any attention to Peter or Jeffrey, but something weird was going on that had them about ready to choke each other.

"There they are," I said.

"Who?" they asked.

"The girls." I pointed. Just in time, I thought. Thankfully, those two relaxed.

"I'm running for president," Lexie said, marching up to us. "The girls are in charge of my campaign. Do you losers want to help?"

I saw Anna smile at Jeffrey.

"Sure," I said.

"What?!" Peter cried. "No. *I'm* running for president and these guys are managing *my* campaign."

"You're running against *me?*" Lexie said, sounding surprised. "You don't stand a chance."

"We'll see about that. You best hope you don't have another mountain on your nose when it's time for your speech," Peter said.

"Okay, squeaky," Lexie retaliated.

Now I was getting really excited. This felt just like old times. And then it hit me. It could be exactly like old times. "Hey, I've got a great idea," I said. This was the first time I'd been fired up about school all year.

"What?" Peter and Lexie snapped.

"We should make Mr. Terupt's classroom our campaign headquarters."

They all just looked at me.

"What? This is a major project, and his classroom is project central," I said.

"But we're on opposite sides!" Peter protested.

"So we'll have two camps set up in there."

"But like, we don't even know if he'll be okay with it," Lexie said. "Or if he'll even be there."

"We all know he'd love to see us. And he'll be there."

"I miss him," Jessica said.

"Me too," Anna agreed.

"We already know we can walk there after school," I said, "at least, while the weather is nice."

"Our campaigns will work side by side," Jessica said.

"Just like old times," I added.

Jessica smiled at me, the same way Anna had smiled at Jeffrey.

"It's settled, then," Peter declared. "We'll go to T's classroom tomorrow after school and tell him our plan. Great idea, Lukester. That's why you're running my campaign. I'm sure to win."

Truthfully, I didn't care about winning. I wasn't convinced Peter or Lexie would make a good president. I was just pumped about being back with the gang and working on a project together—in Mr. Terupt's classroom.

LUKE'S SEVENTH-GRADE SURVIVAL GUIDE
TIP #5: Never stop thinking. No matter how dark the times, a great idea can give you a hopeful light.

Jessica

Dear Journal,

Luke's idea was perfect—some things never change. I was
so excited about it that I had to tell Mom. Somehow I managed to wait until we were seated at dinner, which was when
I knew I'd have her undivided attention.

"Luke came up with this genius idea today," I said.

"Luke again, huh?"

"Mom, stop it. I'm talking about his idea, not him."

She couldn't resist. She started in, repeating things I'd said
in recent weeks, and doing it in this high-pitched voice of a
girl dizzy in love. "Oh, I haven't seen Luke. I wonder how he's
doing?"

"Mom!" I banged my hands on the table, rattling our
dinnerware.

"Okay, okay. I'm sorry," Mom said. "Just having a little fun.
Tell me about this idea of Luke's that you're so excited about."

I filled her in on everything. I told her about missing having
everyone together in the same class and missing Mr. Terupt,
the student government elections, and our campaigns.

"And so you're hoping to visit Mr. Terupt once or twice a

week after school," Mom said, "to work on your campaigns in his classroom?"

"Yes! Told you his idea was brilliant."

"It reminds me of the book I'm reading, *Tuesdays with Morrie*."

"Why?"

"Well, it's a story about a guy who visits his old teacher, Morrie, once a week—on Tuesdays."

"Why does he visit him?" I asked.

"Because he's dying."

"Mom, that's not the same! That's terrible!" She should have known that was a sensitive topic after everything we'd been through with Mr. Terupt.

She took a sip of water. "I know—sorry. You're right. It's not the same. It's just that the mention of Mr. Terupt makes me think about books. He had a way of making the stories you were reading come to life in meaningful ways, through real connections. He always knew what to put in your hands. I miss that."

"Me too," I said, "which is why this is going to be great. It's going to be just like old times."

"I'm sure it will be," Mom said.

Eager for tomorrow,
Jessica

P.S. Still no invitation. I'm scared to ask Lexie if she got one. Would she tell me if she did?

P.P.S. Maybe I do have a thing for Luke, but don't tell.

Peter

The junior high got out forty-five minutes before Snow Hill School did, so we arrived a bit early. It's hard to wait when you're excited about something, and we were psyched to see Mr. T. Since we had time to kill, we decided to stop in and visit Mrs. Williams. That was my idea, and it was a good one because she was very happy to see us.

"Oh my goodness, if it isn't my favorite kids!" She sprang from her chair and hurried around her desk to give us hugs. "Come in. Come in."

We crowded into her space.

"Mrs. Williams," Lexie exclaimed, "I love your top! It looks great with those pants. And your heels are to die for."

Leave it to Lexie to comment on clothes, but even I had noticed Mrs. Williams's new look. Her fun shirt and pants were a big change from her old business-skirt-and-jacket getup.

"Well, thank you, Lexie," Mrs. Williams said. "I decided to do some school shopping this year and mix it up a bit. I probably should've tried wearing slacks when you guys were around here."

Mrs. Williams winked at me, and everyone started laughing. Who could ever forget her crash-landing in our classroom, falling over, and exposing her twisted underwear? And then there was my daredevil cart ride. That also might've ended better for her if she'd been wearing pants.

"Tell me, Peter, is my office better than Principal Lee's?" Mrs. Williams asked.

"Way better," I said.

"You mean to say you've already been in his?!" she cried. "I was only joking."

"Peter doesn't waste any time," Jeffrey said.

Mrs. Williams shook her head and chuckled. "I guess some things never change." She walked around her desk and sat in her chair. "So how is seventh grade?" she asked. "Is it so bad that you're back here already?"

"We're here for a project," Luke said.

"A project?"

"Yes," everyone answered together.

We took turns telling Mrs. Williams all about school and our plans for a campaign headquarters. She listened and didn't object to any of it. She'd always had faith in us. I realized then that I'd been missing her, too.

Once dismissal was over, she escorted us to Mr. T's classroom. We hid in the hall while she rapped on his door. "Knock, knock," she said. "I have a surprise for you."

Mrs. Williams barely had time to get those words out of her mouth before we rushed into his room. The girls—and Luke—mobbed him with hugs. I knew from experience, hugs with Mr. T ranked among the best feelings in the world, but

Jeffrey and I stayed back. We didn't want to overwhelm the poor guy.

"Wow! This is a surprise! What're you guys doing here?" Mr. T said.

"We're taking over your classroom," I told him.

"Really?" He looked at Mrs. Williams.

"I'll come back and check in on you later," she said. "Have fun."

We were so excited that we tried telling T all about Luke's idea and our hopeful plan in a single breath. After he got us to slow down, we were finally able to explain everything to him so that he understood.

"This sounds awesome!" he said. "You know, I've been thinking about you guys. Wondering how you were doing. I'm so proud of you. All of you. I knew you didn't need me. You've stuck together and come up with this incredible project idea all on your own. And the best part is, I get to have you working on it here."

That was it. We got started. And Luke was right. It felt just like old times, especially after I spotted the new toys T had in his room. I couldn't resist trying one out.

Jessica

Dear Journal,

After we got past all our hugs and pleasantries and caught our breath and explained everything to him, Mr. Terupt told us how proud we made him.

His praise felt wonderful, like it always had, but I wasn't so sure we didn't need him anymore. Maybe we didn't on a daily basis, but we needed him in our lives. I liked knowing he was still there for us.

Once we got started on the campaigns, Mr. Terupt approached our project time the same as he did when we were his students—he made the rounds, checking in with each of us. I was busy trying to craft Lexie's speech when he came over to visit with me.

"I see you're carrying your journal around instead of a book," he said.

"Yes. I like my journal quite a lot. Thanks again." I rubbed my hand over your Moroccan cover. "Our English teacher, Mrs. Reeder, has us thinking carefully about words. I like to keep it with me in case I end up with a few to write down."

Mr. Terupt smiled. "I'm sure you will," he said. "What're you reading these days?"

"In class we've been reading ghost stories and stuff like that, not my favorite. But on my own I just finished *Tuck Everlasting*."

"That's a good one," he said. "It's full of beautiful language."

"Yes," I agreed, "but did you think it was a happy ending?"

"Sometimes you have to find the happiness in situations, Jessica. It all depends on how you look at things."

I was quiet after he spoke those words. He'd given me much to ponder—just like old times. I found myself wishing there was a way I could make my time with him become everlasting. Being back around him and discussing literature felt wonderful. I fantasized about Luke whipping together a magical concoction to make my daydreams a reality.

"How about you?" I said. "What're you reading?"

He paused, almost as if he didn't know what to tell me at first, like he had to think about it. "Oh, Mrs. Terupt and I are reading a few different nonfiction books together. The sort of stuff young married couples read to learn what to expect when starting their lives together."

Peter interrupted our book talk at that point, squawking from across the room. "Hey, T! Where is the missus, anyway?" He must've heard Mr. Terupt mention his wife.

"She didn't make it to school today. She was sick this morning."

"She caught that stomach bug, huh?" Peter said. "You better not be sucking face with her, then."

" 'Sucking face,' Peter?! Seriously?" Lexie cried.

"What do you want me to say?"

"How about 'kissing' or 'smooching'? Anything's better than 'sucking face.' You make it sound so disgusting."

I remembered when Bud Caldwell referred to it as "busting slob" in the story *Bud, Not Buddy*. I thought that sounded even worse than "sucking face," but I wasn't about to get involved in a debate on kissing, not with those two.

Mr. Terupt walked away chuckling and shaking his head. I'm sure it was beginning to feel like old times to him, too. Too bad we didn't remember to watch out for what good old times always entailed when it came to Peter.

Elated to be back with Mr. Terupt,
Jessica

P.S. I didn't tell Mr. Terupt about the important writing I did over the summer. I hope to tell him about that after the invitation arrives.

P.P.S. I hope Mrs. Terupt feels better soon so we can see her, too.

LUKE

It didn't take any time at all for that magical feeling to come back. There was no place like Mr. Terupt's classroom. It was like going home. We were stationed all around the place, surrounded by project materials, working and having fun.

I was doing my best to come up with Peter's speech, and he was providing little help—no surprise there. He was like a little kid in a candy shop when it came to Mr. Terupt's classroom. He was over by the windowsill area checking out the catapults Mr. Terupt had his students building. I was incredibly jealous.

"I see you've spotted our catapults, Luke," Mr. Terupt said. "It's a fun project. After they're built, we're going to fire them off and do lots of math and science. We'll measure the mass of different objects and the distance that each gets thrown. We'll also pull the catapult back at varying lengths and measure how far a certain ball gets tossed each time. Once we get all that data, we'll do some graphing and see what predictions we might be able to make about the relationship between mass and distance launched—all sorts of cool physics."

Cool physics indeed, I thought. This was a classic Mr. Terupt project. Listening to him made me wish I was back in sixth grade, but he had also given me an idea for our campaign.

I planned to conduct a wide range of surveys and then use the results to construct a series of graphs and charts showing Peter's climb in the polls. These statistics would convince many of our voters. The same thing happened in real life all the time.

"What are your new students like?" I asked Mr. Terupt. I wanted to know a little about the lucky kids who'd get to fire off catapults.

"Well, I have a boy named Kevin who's a bit like Peter. He needs some reminding every once in a while, but he's got a tough old grandma to keep him in line, and she does a pretty good job of it.

"And there's Marcus, who's a bit like you." Mr. Terupt leaned closer and in a hushed voice said, "His catapult will perform the best."

I smiled.

"And I have Suzi and Olivia and Maya, who are quiet girls but lovely readers." He looked at Jessica and Anna and Danielle when he said that.

"Who do you have who's like Lexie?" I asked.

"No one, Luke. There's only one Lexie. We all know that."

"And she's going to be president," Jessica said.

I glanced at Peter to see what he had to say about that, but he wasn't paying attention. My eyes almost popped out of my head when I saw what he was up to.

LUKE'S SEVENTH-GRADE SURVIVAL GUIDE
TIP #6: There's nothing like a good project. This is a surefire way to bring friends together and make everyone happy.

Peter

Luke was all into the math and science Mr. T had planned with those catapults. They were busy talking some crazy physics stuff when I spotted an irresistible target. The way I saw it, I was doing everyone a favor. What better way to make it feel like old times than by adding a little excitement?

I took the biggest, baddest-looking catapult, the one built by some kid named Marcus, and quietly moved it from the windowsill area to a nearby desk. No one was paying any attention. Next, I prepared my ammunition. I found a sheet of loose-leaf paper sticking out of the same desk and stuffed it in my mouth. For stunts like these, there was nothing better than the old-fashioned spitball. I chomped two different pieces of paper and then mushed them together, forming one heavy, wet bullet.

I won't lie, Lexie's easy on the eyes, but pretty or not, she was giving me the perfect target. I couldn't resist. She was on the other side of the room, squatting next to Danielle as they chatted about poster ideas. From behind, Lexie's low-rise jeans left her looking like a plumber, if you know what I mean.

I'm sure Luke would've given me a very complicated formula to follow to operate the catapult, but I didn't find that necessary. I placed my bullet on the launching pad and yanked that beauty back as far as it would go. I bent down in a crouch, hiding behind the desk and holding the trigger mechanism in my hand. I waited for Lexie to shift to the left just a tad, putting her in my crosshairs. I was waiting, holding my breath, when suddenly Mrs. Williams sprang into the classroom and yelled, pulling a Mr. T move on us. She thought she'd be funny and scare us, like he used to do. Well, she did just that! I jumped and whacked my knee on the underside of the desk. I lost hold of the catapult and sent not one, but two spitballs soaring across the room. That's right, they didn't stay plastered together like I had planned.

The first disgusting wad of paper flew like a missile locked on its target. It hit Lexie square on the lower back and slid down her crack and into her pants. Bull's-eye! She let out a wild squeal and jumped to her feet, wiggling and shaking her hips and butt, doing a crazy dance, sort of like Principal Lee's hot-coffee jig.

What about the second bullet? That spitball landed just under Mrs. Williams's chin and slid down inside her fancy new shirt. Mrs. Williams's eyebrows almost jumped off her face while her jaw just about touched the floor.

I hid behind the desk, but they didn't need to see me to know who was behind that prank.

"Peter, I swear I'm gonna wring your neck!" Lexie shrieked.

"I need to wear a hazmat suit around you," Mrs. Williams said, plucking the wad of gunk from inside her shirt.

Lexie's dilemma was a bit trickier. She had to go to the bathroom to remove the bullet that had snuck its way into her pants. If I fired that sucker off another million times, never would I be able to repeat what had just happened. It was like the impossible had a way of occurring in T's presence.

I stood up, and everyone stared at me, shaking their heads. "Just like old times," I said, and smiled.

ANNA

Even though Jeffrey and I were on opposing campaigns, we found a way to work near each other. He was busy making signs for Peter, and I was whipping up flyers for Lexie. It felt like a good opportunity for him to ask me out, but he didn't. If he was anything like Charlie, I knew I could be waiting awhile.

"Check this out," he said.

I glanced at his newest poster, which said VOTE FOR PETER, THE PROMISE MAN. We looked at each other and started cracking up.

"You know," Mr. Terupt said, standing behind us and surveying our work, "*promise* is not the P-word that first came to my mind for Peter."

"Us either," Luke said, "but *prankster, problem child,* or *pea brain* are not terms that will get you elected."

"How about *pathetic?*" Lexie said. "Or *puke-face?*" She was still steaming mad at Peter because of the spitball he had catapulted down her backside. But I knew she'd find a way to get even. Those two never stopped.

"Funny," Peter said, "but *promise* is the right word. I've

never broken a promise. I promised T we'd stick together, and look at this." He spread his arms wide.

Jeffrey and I made eye contact, and he smiled, which made the butterflies in my tummy flutter. I knew it wouldn't happen with everyone around, but I still found myself wishing he'd just ask me. Instead, I got to listen to him and Mr. Terupt talk about wrestling.

"You must be getting excited, Jeffrey. Wrestling season's right around the corner."

"I know," Jeffrey said. "It's hard to think about anything else."

That hurt. No wonder he wasn't asking me.

"I want to go undefeated," Jeffrey said. "I've been running before school, like you used to."

Mr. Terupt smiled. "Going undefeated is a lofty goal, but that's how it should be. Without the risk of failure, there is no challenge."

"Asher's excited, too," Jeffrey said. "You should see his wrestling stance and double-leg takedown."

"Maybe I'll come and watch one of your matches?" I said. They both looked at me in a startled sort of way. Mr. Terupt cracked a slight grin. "I mean, I'd like to see Asher."

"Sure. Okay," Jeffrey said, shrugging and nodding.

"Having Anna there won't make you nervous, will it?" Mr. Terupt asked Jeffrey. I didn't know if he was teasing him or being serious.

"No," Jeffrey was quick to say, staring at the floor. Would it? I wondered. Maybe Jeffrey *did* like me, and he just couldn't get himself to tell me.

I caught Mr. Terupt smiling at us again. As he got up to leave, he said to Jeffrey, "You better keep your buddy out of trouble so he can enjoy the season, too." He nodded in the direction of Peter, who was working with Luke now that he'd had his fun with the catapult.

"Yeah, like at camp?" I heard Jeffrey mumble.

"What happened at camp?" I asked him after Mr. Terupt had left.

"Nothing."

Now he was sounding like Danielle. If Charlie ever got his head out of his butt—excuse my language—then she and I were going to be half sisters, and yet she was trying to hide something from me. She could hide it from her mother and Grandma, but not me. She was all over the place. Happy one minute, exhausted or miserable the next. Whenever I asked her about it, she'd either get annoyed or blame it on her period. You get your period once a month, not every day.

Danielle

"I see you've got your sketchbook with you," Mr. Terupt said, sliding up next to me after he'd finished visiting with Anna and Jeffrey.

"Yes, pictures come to me in the same way words do for Jessica. I like to put my beginning works in here and play around with ideas before I decide to put my piece on official paper."

"Do you mind if I take a peek?" he asked.

I shook my head. Normally I didn't like to share my stuff, but Mr. Terupt was different.

"Looks like you were inspired to draw a storm front," he said, thumbing through the pages. He glanced up at me.

"You know us farmers," I said, and shrugged. "Always thinking about the weather." He chuckled. "Actually, I was thinking I might make a poster for Lexie that says to vote for her because she's"—here I made quotation marks with my fingers—"'Taking Seventh Grade by Storm.'"

"Ooh, I like that," Mr. Terupt said.

"That sounds awesome," Peter agreed. He'd been eavesdropping. "Why can't you make me posters like that?" he complained to Jeffrey.

"Keep whining, and I'll make you one that says 'Vote for Peter the Crybaby.'"

Peter walked away grumbling under his breath while Mr. Terupt and I tried not to laugh at the two of them.

"Your work looks great, Danielle," Mr. Terupt whispered. "And Peter's right. The storm idea *is* awesome."

"Thanks," I said.

Dear God,

I'm nervous. I didn't tell Mr. Terupt, but that poster image came to me because I have this eerie feeling we're in the calm before the storm. Like bad news is looming. Farmers can sense things, same as animals can. I just have a funny feeling. Keep an eye on us. Please.

Amen.

Alexia

We'd been working for a few weeks on the campaigns. Luke's idea to use Teach's place as headquarters was so smart. We had a blast getting together and chillin' with Teach. The girls and I kept hoping to see Ms. Newberry—I mean Mrs. Teach—but like, she hadn't made it to one of our meetings yet. She was either feeling sick or had an appointment or some other thing. Bad timing, I guess. Still, we hoped to see her soon. Teach told us we would.

Running for president required all the same stuff from theater camp that I loved doing. In the end, I'd need to dress up, stand onstage, and play the part. Fun, fun, fun. But, like, Anna and Danielle made these dazzling posters and flyers for me, and Jessica wrote the most amazing speech, and so, like, it turned into something more serious. The girls wanted me to get elected. They were working hard. I started thinking I actually had a chance. I'd never won anything before.

When we had only a few campaign meetings left at Teach's place, Jessica decided we needed to put in extra time, which meant getting together on our own. Meeting once a week until Election Day wasn't going to be enough. Jessica had the speech written, so now it was time to practice my delivery. This was something I wanted to do in private, and she agreed, so we made plans to do it at my house.

This was where all our theater camp lessons came in handy. Jessica planned it out so that during my speech there were times for me to turn to the left, to the right, to pause, to talk softly, and to raise my voice. Of course, I added my own flair with different hand movements and head tilts. We had the performance choreographed and rehearsed to perfection. I was ready to win an Academy Award along with the election. We were good, Jessica especially.

"The only thing left for us to do is design my outfit for the big day," I said.

"Oh my goodness," Jessica said, and sighed. "We'll be here all night."

"Will you relax? This is important stuff. What I wear plays a role in how I do my hair, which influences my earring selection, my nail polish color, and my shoes. This is real science, not that junk we do in school that Luke gets all giddy about. Besides, you know just looking good is going to get me half the votes."

"You're probably right about that," Jessica agreed.

I went to my closet and pulled out my first option. We spent the next hour going through some of my wardrobe. I'd hold up a possibility, and Jessica would give me her opinion: "Too risky . . . Boring . . . Too conservative . . . Now, that's hot."

It was fun showing her my choices. Her reactions made me laugh. And like, there was no way I could've made any of these important decisions without her help. We were about halfway into my closet when she said, "I sure hope we get invitations to the retreat."

I knew getting invited was like, a huge deal for Jessica. "Stop sweatin' it, girl," I said. "You will. You were made for this stuff." I meant what I said.

"Thanks. You're pretty good at it yourself, Lex."

I swung around with another outfit in my hand.

"Let's promise to tell each other if we get one," she said.

"One what?"

"An invitation!" she yelled.

"I know. I was just playing with you. Keep your pants on." I stuck out my pinky, taking us back to fifth grade. "Pinky swear," I said.

We locked fingers and made a solemn promise to tell. Then I lifted the outfit I had in my hand and held it out in front of me. Jessica didn't get a chance to say anything this time, though, because that was when my mom came crashing into the house. I heard her car keys and purse slam down on the counter. It was like, way out of the ordinary for Mom to come home early. I tossed my outfit on the bed and walked out into the kitchen to see what was up.

"Mom, what're you doing home?"

"I've got a migraine coming on," she said, tossing our mail on the table. I saw the envelope immediately.

"Hi, Jessica," Mom said.

"Hi. Sorry you're not feeling well."

"Just a headache. You girls keep having fun. I'm gonna go lie down."

I stepped between Jessica and the table, blocking her view

of the envelope that rested on top of the pile. I didn't want her to see it in case she didn't have the same thing waiting at home, but, like, I didn't see how that was even possible. Still, there was no way I was going to tell her I got one. She would need to tell me first. Sometimes you do less harm by breaking a promise than by keeping it.

NOVEMBER

Danielle

We arrived at Mr. Terupt's room for another Campaign Day—what was supposed to be our second-to-last one—but before we got busy, he told us the news. "Listen, gang, I won't be here next week. I have an appointment after school. But I think your work is just about complete anyway."

"What kind of appointment?" Peter asked. He didn't think twice about prying into Mr. Terupt's personal life.

"*We* have an appointment, is what he meant to say."

We'd been waiting to hear that voice since our first visit. Mrs. Terupt stood in the doorway—glowing. She had one hand on her belly and a smile on her face. I'd been around these situations enough times on the farm that I knew. She wasn't showing, but her mannerisms told me everything I needed to know.

Jessica, Anna, and Lexie all rushed over to her. I watched Mrs. Terupt wrap one arm around them while keeping her other hand on her belly—a mother's instinct. When the girls let go and realized I wasn't there with them they turned around and looked at me with puzzled expressions.

"Danielle, is everything all right?" Anna asked.

I looked at Mr. Terupt and then back at Mrs. Terupt. She knew I knew, and couldn't hide her smile. "Can I tell them?" I asked, looking back and forth between the two of them again.

They nodded.

"Mrs. Terupt's pregnant," I said.

The girls gasped and spun around to face her again.

"Really?!" Lexie shrieked.

Mrs. Terupt nodded.

"Oh!" the three of them squealed. Then they hugged her again, gentler this time. Luke was speechless. I think he was actually trying to figure out how this could've happened. Peter and Jeffrey gave Mr. Terupt high fives, and I couldn't stop smiling.

"Danielle, how did you know?" Jessica asked.

I shrugged. "Farmers have a way of feeling these things. It's like an extra sense."

"What're you going to name the baby?" Anna asked them.

"Lexie!" Lexie yelled.

"Peter!" Peter shouted.

"Um, no," Mr. Terupt said.

"Are you having a boy or a girl?" Jessica asked.

"We're waiting to find out," Mrs. Terupt said, walking over to Mr. Terupt's desk and wrapping her arm around his waist. "Billy likes surprises." It was funny to hear her call Mr. Terupt by his first name—and his nickname, at that.

"When are you due?" I asked.

"In June," Mrs. Terupt said, "which gives us plenty of time to think about names."

"We'll have a baby-naming contest," Lexie said.

"Or Sara and I will decide on our own," Mr. Terupt said, calling his wife by *her* first name now.

"You're going too fast," Mrs. Terupt told us. "Billy needs to take his time with big decisions like these."

"Don't all men?" Anna said.

Mrs. Terupt couldn't help but laugh.

"Back to the matter at hand," Mr. Terupt said. "I won't be here for next week's Campaign Day because Sara and I have an appointment with our obstetrician."

"Your *what?!*" Peter said.

"The doctor who will be delivering their baby," Jessica explained.

"Oh."

"That's right," Mr. Terupt said, "which means you guys will need to get together at one of your houses to finalize things."

"We should have a party!" Lexie exclaimed. "All campaigns end with parties. Plus, we have baby news to celebrate."

"That's a great idea," Peter said.

"Of course it is, you moron. I'm full of great ideas, which is why I'm going to make a fabulous president."

"Whatever," Peter grumbled.

"Where're we going to have a party?" Jeffrey asked.

"We can have it at my place," Peter said. "My mom and dad are going to be away on a business trip, so it'll be perfect."

"My parents aren't going to let me come over if your parents aren't home, Peter," Luke said.

"Ugh," Lexie groaned. "They won't find out if you don't tell them."

She'd said the same thing to me before stepping foot in that frightful store. I knew how Luke felt.

"Ahem." Mr. Terupt cleared his throat and raised his eyebrows. I'm not sure he approved of Lexie's advice.

"Oh, fine," she said. "Just tell them everyone is going to be there. That's the truth, and that always works with parents."

I wasn't sure that sounded much better.

"Our au pair, Miss Catalina, will be there," Peter said. "You can tell them that. She'll make us some fancy party food, and we can hang out in my brother's room. He's away at school, so he won't even know. We can use his TV and video game console, his stereo, and he's even got a foosball table."

Peter and Lexie were scheming together, and that was scary.

"I'm in," Lexie said.

"Me too," Jessica agreed.

"Okay," Jeffrey said.

Anna and I looked at each other and shrugged. I knew she was thinking what I was thinking. Going to Peter's couldn't be any worse than walking into Victoria's Secret, and we'd left there unharmed. "We'll be there," Anna said, meaning the two of us. We came as a package deal these days.

That just left Luke. We all looked at him.

"Okay," he said. "I'll tell my mom everyone's going to be there."

"Attaboy, Lukester!" Peter yipped. "I can't party without my main campaign guy there. It's not like Jeffrey did anything."

"Maybe I'll get started by rubbing your face across the mat at practice in a couple of weeks," Jeffrey said.

"Okay then," Mr. Terupt said, cutting those two off. "You guys better start working if you're going to get anything done today. And before these two start going at it right here."

On that note, we got busy. I grabbed my poster. There were a few minor details I wanted to address before it would be finished. Looking at it made me wonder if all this good news meant we'd missed the storm I'd been expecting. Or was it about to begin? I couldn't seem to shake that funny feeling.

Dear God,

I should be happy for Mr. and Mrs. Terupt. I am. But their wonderful baby news has given me something else to worry about. I've seen pregnancies on the farm end in a mother's death and with stillborns. I pray that everything goes smoothly for Mr. and Mrs. Terupt.

I'm also a bit on edge about this campaign party. When Lexie and Peter are in charge of something, you never know what to expect.

All this fretting can't be good for me. Grandma nearly died last spring because of all her stressing, but I can't seem to help it. Maybe you can give me a hand with that? Thank you.

Amen.

LUKE

Campaign Days were the thing I was most excited about. I so looked forward to my afternoons in Mr. Terupt's classroom each week. We all did. But now it was over. It was late November. Election Day was right around the corner, and Mr. Terupt had told us he wouldn't be able to meet with us next week, which came as a shock at first, but after learning that he and his wife were expecting their first child and had an appointment, it was understandable. That big announcement had everyone distracted for the remainder of the afternoon. The rest of our time was spent with groups either gushing over Mrs. Terupt and her baby on board or discussing details about a party that had all of a sudden been scheduled. Me? It felt good to hear Peter's excitement when I told him I'd attend his party, but all I could wrap my brain around was the fact that this was it.

"I can't believe it," I said. "Campaign Days are over."

"These afternoons have been my favorite, too, Luke," Mr. Terupt said. "You guys have done a great job of sticking together. Being around you makes me very happy. Just remember, though, there might also come a time when you need to stand up for yourself."

I thought about that for a minute, and then Peter added his two cents. "All good things come to an end, Lukester."

I nodded. He was probably right about that, but I was still secretly wishing for another project to come along so we could stick together.

LUKE'S SEVENTH-GRADE SURVIVAL GUIDE
TIP #7: Be careful what you wish for.

Alexia

Miss Catalina had snacks for us, but, like, I brought the party—and the knockout hors d'oeuvres that Vincent whipped up for us. Peter's house was sick, but we spent the whole night hanging out in his brother's room. The girls and I played foosball while Luke and Jeffrey and Peter battled at video games. When we got bored with that, we started jamming different tunes and playing DJ. The boys couldn't dance or sing to save their lives, so I had to show them how it was done.

After a while all that partying and going crazy made us thirsty. Danielle had been guzzling water all night long, but now the rest of us wanted some. Luke must've been out of his mind, 'cause he grabbed one of the soda bottles and chugged it like nothing I'd ever seen. He tipped his head back and downed it—the whole thing! Then two seconds later he let out a belch that was worthy of a Boy Scout badge.

"Whoa! Lukester!" Peter yelled. "Attaboy."

"Oh my goodness!" Jessica cried, her eyes wide.

She wanted to be grossed out, but she couldn't keep from laughing. None of us could. Luke had us on the floor, cracking up. That's how we landed on the carpet with an empty two-liter bottle between us.

I didn't even hesitate. Like, bringing the party means providing the fun and games—the excitement. There are some things that will never get old. Those things are classics, and this game was a classic.

I gripped the bottle and gave it a spin. Round and round it went. Then I did it again, and by that point I had everyone sitting still and paying attention. The laughing stopped. Things went from funny to serious in a heartbeat. The looks on their faces were priceless.

"Let's see who's first," I said, giving the bottle another spin. All breathing stopped. Round and round the bottle went until it landed, pointing at Jeffrey. "And who's the lucky girl?" I gave the bottle a final spin. Round and round it went until it stopped on Jessica. "Two minutes in the closet," I announced.

"What?!" Jessica said, sounding alarmed.

"I thought they had to kiss," Peter said.

"No, that's so last year. It's two minutes in the closet," I said. "That's more mysterious." I pulled Jessica over, and Peter nudged Jeffrey along. We pushed them inside, and then I shut the door and locked it. There was no escaping until I decided to let them out. I loved being in charge. I was going to make a fabulous president. "Start the timer," I said. "And turn up the music."

It was meant to be fun.

Jeffrey

This was all bad from the start. I had vowed not to get involved in Peter's bright ideas, and I knew better than to go along with Lexie's brilliant games, yet here I was, inside a dark closet with Jessica. Somehow, no matter what I intended, I got roped into this stuff. I had saved Peter's butt at camp, but this closet stuff was a lot more complicated than a wedgie.

I knew we weren't supposed to be whispering in there, but I couldn't even see Jessica.

"Lexie's such a troublemaker," I said.

"I know."

"I can't believe she's got us locked in here. I'm not going to try anything, Jessica."

"I don't want you to. Anna likes you."

"Really?"

"Yes. And if you can't tell that, then you're a dope."

All of our breathing and talking was making me hot. I could feel my face turning red, and it wasn't because of what Jessica had just said. "It's like a sauna in here."

"I know."

"Do you think they can hear us?"

"No, Lexie's got the music turned up to add to the 'mystery.'"

We were quiet for a moment, and then I asked her something else. "Have you ever told anybody about Michael?"

"Never," she said.

"Then can I ask you something else without you telling?"

"Okay."

The closet door flew open. Two minutes was up.

Jessica

Dear Journal,

When Jeffrey and I stumbled out of the heat and darkness of that closet, the first thing I saw was Anna's face. That's when I knew this was bad. Then I looked for Luke, but he was already walking out of the room. That's when I knew it was really bad. I thought of my mother and felt like my father. It was awful. Just awful.

I feel so guilty. Everything changed in that moment, just like it did on that terrible day back in fifth grade when Mr. Terupt had his accident, only this time it was all of us who were hit by the devastating snowball. It was like whatever trust we'd built over the last two years was suddenly gone.

Full of remorse,
Jessica

P.S. What difference would an invitation make now?

I was tired of people asking me that. I felt sick. I grabbed the doorknob and gave it a violent twist.

"Danielle?"

"I need to get out of here."

"We'll be out in just a minute," Peter said.

I could hear in his voice that he was only trying to calm me down, but there wasn't anything he could've said or done to make that happen. I snapped. "Get me outta here!" I yanked at the doorknob again, but it was no use. I fell back in a heap, hot and exhausted. I needed something to drink.

"Danielle?" Peter whispered.

I didn't say anything.

Peter leaned across the darkness and wrapped his arms around me in a hug. He was only trying to help, but once again his timing was absolutely terrible, because that's when the closet door flew open. I had to shield my eyes from the burst of light, but once my pupils readjusted I could see very clearly that Lexie wasn't giggling and carrying on anymore. It was game over.

I walked out of the closet, damp with sweat. My shirt was all twisted and partially untucked. It didn't fit right anyway. It was too big. I felt out of sorts. I headed straight for Anna. "It's time for us to go."

"Yeah, it is," she said, her voice cracking. "Hope you've had your fun like everyone else."

Her words hurt me more than anything that night.

Dear God,

I'm sorry if I've disappointed you. I just don't know what to do. Peter really is a great friend. But if I stick up for him, then

anna

They came out of the closet all red in the face, acting like some big secret had just happened in there. My heart was broken, and nothing I'd learned last year volunteering with Jeffrey at the Center for Love and Care was going to help it heal.

Wasn't it funny? All this time I'd wanted Jeffrey to make me feel like he cared by using his words, but he didn't have to say anything to make me feel terrible.

LUKE

I didn't need my compass. I knew where I was headed. I didn't belong here. These weren't my friends. This wasn't how friends treated each other—stomping on each other's feelings without even giving it a second thought. Taking what you thought you had and throwing it away like it was nothing. Being downright cold-hearted.

I called Mom. It was time to go home.

LUKE'S SEVENTH-GRADE SURVIVAL GUIDE
TIP #8: Seventh graders are like chameleons. They're always changing, but give them time, and they'll show their true colors. Don't let your guard down.

Danielle

I was ready to leave. Lexie's closet game wasn't a good idea. As soon as Jeffrey and Jessica came out all red in the face, you could see people's feelings getting hurt. But Lexie was having too much fun to notice.

"Oooh," she teased them. "Naughty-naughty." Then she gave the bottle another spin without even hesitating. It stopped on Peter.

I got up to get Anna. It was time to go.

I had walked a couple steps around the circle when Lexie gave the bottle another spin. It stopped on me! I should've stayed put. I would've been safe. She grabbed me by the hand and pulled me over to the closet. Then she shoved me inside with Peter. The door closed and locked.

"Two minutes," she called out. Then I heard them crank up the music.

It all happened so fast. I couldn't believe it. *Please forgive me. Please forgive me,* I prayed. And then I lost it. I had to get out. I needed to go to the bathroom. I didn't feel good. God was mad at me. I started rocking back and forth.

"Danielle, are you okay?" Peter asked.

everyone will think I'm only doing it because I'm trying to hide the truth about what really happened in the closet. What kind of friend does that make me? Anna's upset with me, and I don't know why, and I can't talk to Mom or Grandma about these things. I'm all alone. I need your help. Please.

Amen.

Peter

I'm all for pranks and joking around, but we had crossed the line. Lexie could dress up and hide things and make things look bigger or brighter or create any number of disguises, but she couldn't hide her anger when I stepped out of that closet. Her face was redder than mine, and if anyone else was looking, they would've noticed Danielle was white as a ghost. Something was wrong with her. But we didn't try to find out what because none of us were talking. The party was over. Our friendships were over.

I'd promised Mr. T we'd stick together, but instead, we'd fallen apart. We weren't just a bunch of kids in grade school anymore. We were messing around with real feelings. We had *all* crossed the line. And I didn't know if we'd ever make it back to the other side.

I should've gone to boarding school.

PART TWO

DECEMBER

LUKE

Thanks to that dumb campaign party, I suddenly found a reason to like school and my schedule. Why? Because it kept me from seeing Jeffrey and Jessica and the rest of them. I didn't have to face my former "friends." I'm not sure I could've stomached it. At least I knew what to expect with the kids in my classes. They didn't like me. Fine. At least their behavior was consistent.

Besides my classmates, the other thing I knew I could count on was Zack and his pack of hyenas. Without fail, they'd be there to knock my books and folders to the floor. But in this case, consistency was getting old. Little did they know, Mr. Terupt had given me permission to fight back when he went ahead and said, "There might also come a time when you need to stand up for yourself." That time had arrived. I put my brain to masterminding a plan that would teach Zack a lesson—once and for all.

I thought about executing a sneak attack. Doing something to his locker that would've got him good, like gluing it shut or squirting a concoction of ketchup and mustard inside it. But the more I thought about it, the more I realized that wouldn't solve my problem. Zack never would've suspected me as the culprit, which meant he would've continued hammering my books to the floor. He needed to know it was me getting the best of him. I needed him to fear me. That was the only way I would ever get him to leave me alone. But how was I going to make that happen? Was it even possible?

I thought back to last year, when I studied the different methods and techniques employed by organisms throughout the animal kingdom who were attempting to attract mates. In the same way, I knew I could research and find effective hunting and capturing methods. I was the predator, and Zack was my prey. The hyena isn't the king of the jungle. That title belongs to the lion.

I envisioned myself lying low, stalking my hyena, and then pouncing on him for the kill—or, in my case, the prank—but those daydreams always ended with Zack getting up and eating me. Lions form prides and hunt in numbers. I was on my own, and Zack had the pack. As I researched, it became clear—I didn't need to be a lion. I needed to be an assassin bug.

I discovered that there are several different types of assassin bugs, but my personal favorite was the one that preys on web-building spiders. The assassin bug uses its forelegs to pluck the silk threads of the spider's web, thereby mimicking the behavior of a trapped insect. This attracts the spider and lures it out of hiding to survey its next meal. As soon as the fooled spider is within striking distance, the assassin bug makes the kill.

* * *

It was on the day of the long-awaited and highly anticipated student government speeches that I decided to execute my plan. I was both nervous and excited. Not because of that dumb election stuff—I no longer cared about that—but because the time to teach Zack a lesson had finally arrived.

On my way to first period, I held my pile of books out in front of me, in complete disregard of LUKE'S SEVENTH-GRADE SURVIVAL GUIDE TIPS #2 and #3, baiting the dumb spider. After class I did it again. And after second and third and fourth period. But there was no sign of Zack and his hyenas anywhere. I worried that my plan wasn't going to work if he made me wait much longer. It was all about timing.

Then, like a dim-witted spider, Zack came in for his infamous attack after sixth period. I was on such high alert that I actually saw him coming. For a second, I considered yanking my books out of the way, causing him to whiff in the same way Lucy always manages to do to Charlie Brown, but I resisted the temptation and held my ground. This was going to be even better.

Like always, Zack's right hand came down hard and fast, perfectly connecting with my books—and the special paper I had resting on top. Like always, my papers and folders crashed to the floor, and the surrounding bodies stopped and turned to see what had happened. Same as always, the crowded hall filled with laughter. It was oh-so-funny to see wimpy old me get his books dumped. But then things took a turn from the usual course of events.

Zack started waving his hand around, yelling and freaking out. "What'd you do, you little dork?" He grabbed at the paper with his other hand. He couldn't get it off. He tore at it. Then came the foul odor. "What's going on?" His pack of hyenas backed away, plugging their noses.

You see, I had remembered from camp how sticky pine sap could be. Not only had I smeared a nice coat of it on the top of that piece of paper, but I had also used it to attach several leaves of skunk cabbage to the underside. This plant gets its name because, once its leaves are broken, they release a very pungent odor, like that of a skunk. I knew Zack would rip and tear at the paper once it was glued to his hand, thus opening the leaves and releasing the foul odor. And that's just what happened.

"Way to go, Zack!" somebody from the crowd called.

"Zack, you stink!" someone else chimed in.

The idiot tried rubbing his hands against his shirt and pant legs. He was in a panic, desperate to get the paper off, but the only thing he accomplished was spreading the pine sap and skunk scent to his clothes. Even his buddies started laughing, which put him over the edge. He reached out and grabbed the nearest one by the back of the neck, and—you guessed it—that kid's hair stuck to Zack's hand. When Zack finally released his grip he ripped the hairs right out of that kid's head. The whole spectacle was ridiculous. They looked like fools. It was better than I had imagined.

And then Zack snapped.

I saw him look over at me with red in his eyes. Of course, I knew this was a possibility, so I was ready. That's the Boy Scout motto: Be prepared! He stomped toward me. But then he came to an abrupt halt.

"Good thinking," a voice behind me said.

I turned and saw that it was Mr. Brobur. When I spun back around, Zack was already storming off, pushing his way through the ring of onlookers. He'd been defeated, out-smarted, and he knew it. Slowly, the crowd dispersed.

"What is your phenotype, Luke Bennett?" Mr. Brobur said. "And what is it that determines one's phenotype?" He paused. "With courage like that, perhaps you should join our wrestling team."

For the first time I noticed Mr. Brobur's ears weren't just a bit hairy, they were gnarly, too. He had a condition known as cauliflower ear, a true mark of the wrestler. "Mr. Brobur, are you one of the coaches?" I asked.

"Yup. Have been for over thirty years. I don't get up and down like I used to, but I still have a few tricks I can teach the boys."

"My old teacher was a wrestler too," I said. "He had me try the sport last year, but it didn't go so well. I'm afraid it's not in my genotype. Two of my former classmates were good at it, though."

"Who would they be?" Mr. Brobur asked.

"Peter and Jeffrey."

"Ah, yes. They're on the team. And doing quite well, I might add. You know, Zack is a wrestler too. He's on the var-sity squad."

"That's nice," I said without interest.

"That old teacher of yours must be Mr. Terupt."

"Yes, how'd you know?" I perked up. Now I was interested.

"He's been to a few of our practices," Mr. Brobur said. "A

very nice man, a wizard on the mats, and from what I hear, a truly special teacher."

"Yes," I said. "Very special."

"He's the sort of guy we need to keep around here."

I wasn't sure what Mr. Brobur was talking about. Mr. Terupt wasn't going anywhere. He was getting ready to welcome a baby. Mr. Brobur was showing his age.

"Well, Luke, I'd help you with this mess, but my old knees have enough trouble bending at practice, and besides, it looks like you've got some friends to give you a hand. I'll see you in class."

"See you in class," I said. Then I turned around and found several of my classmates picking up my papers.

"Luke, that was awesome," Jimmy said.

"I can't believe you did that!" said Rachel.

"Did you see that? Zack didn't know what to do," Alex chimed in.

"That was awesome!" Jimmy said again.

I got my things cleaned up, and then, for the first time all year, I didn't walk to my locker all by myself. Suddenly, I had a group of kids with me. I dropped off my supplies, and then we headed to the student government speeches. Little did I know, more of the unexpected was yet to come.

LUKE'S SEVENTH-GRADE SURVIVAL GUIDE
TIP #9: Use your brain. There might come a time when you need to stand up for yourself. This can be scary, so remember, in the battle of brains vs. brawn, brains win. Use your brain.

Alexia

Like, what can I say? I went too far at our campaign party. Things didn't go the way they were supposed to, but, like, what was I supposed to do? I couldn't play chicken and cry stop. I *saw* that it wasn't going right when Jessica and Jeffrey came out of the closet, but it wasn't until we opened the door on Peter and Danielle that I *felt* it wasn't right. And there was no one to blame but me. There was a time when I wouldn't have thought twice about how other people felt, but that wasn't the case anymore. Like, I was really upset about the mess I'd created with everyone, which is why I decided to do something drastic. Who knows, maybe I would've tried to do something more to help us get back together, but I was about to be dealt another lump that would make me forget all about that.

Peter

All of seventh grade gathered in the gym after sixth period to hear speeches from those of us running for student government. Mr. Smith started things off, stepping up to the podium. "I've been doing this for over fifteen years," he said, "and I can honestly tell you these were the best-run campaign efforts I've ever seen."

Luke and Jessica would've been the best for any of the positions—including president—but rather than enter the race, they had spent all their time helping Lexie and me. They were the real reason Mr. Smith had said that.

When Mr. Smith concluded his remarks, the kids up for treasurer, secretary, and vice president went next. I didn't listen to a lick of what the other candidates had to say. Not only did I not care, but I was busy rehearsing the words I was about to speak—and they weren't the ones Luke had come up with. I was ready to say some things that even Mrs. Reeder would've qualified as important—and they were my own words.

However, before I got my chance, Lexie took hers. And when she got up there it was a different story—I wasn't too distracted to listen. We hadn't said a word to each other since

the party, but one thing you can say about Lexie is that she commands attention. She stepped up to the podium, adjusted the microphone, and dropped the bomb. "I'm withdrawing my name from the ballot," she said. "Thank you." And with that, she walked out of the gym, never once looking back.

You could've heard a mouse fart after she did that, but as soon as she stepped out the door, the student body erupted in whispers and chatter. Everyone wanted to know the same thing, teachers included: what had just happened? I couldn't believe it, either. I knew how badly Lexie had wanted the job.

Doing his best to regain order, Mr. Smith stepped to the microphone and introduced me as the next—and only other—candidate for president. Lexie had just handed me the presidency. There was only one problem. I didn't want it.

"Ahem." I cleared my throat. "The success of my campaign, the words I had prepared to speak today, all of it, was the work of Luke Bennett, my campaign manager. Luke's the best person I know when it comes to projects—or anything in school for that matter. He works hard, and he gets the job done.

"That's why Luke's the person you should all write in as your vote for president. I'm not your guy. Luke is."

LUKE

I sat there, dumbstruck. Had Peter just told everyone to vote for me? My jaw dropped, and I couldn't move. That's when my new friends started patting me on the back. My luck had officially changed.

The story of me getting the best of Zack had already spread like wildfire throughout all of seventh grade, making me instantly popular. And since we all knew this was a popularity contest, I was the guy. Everyone went ahead and voted for me.

LUKE'S SEVENTH-GRADE SURVIVAL GUIDE
TIP #10: Despite what your teachers might say, student government elections are a popularity contest. If you want to win, you better do something that makes you popular.

I should've been feeling happy. Happy to have this honor, happy to have my classmates as allies, and happy that Zack had decided to leave me alone—for now. But what I felt was sad—sad that I couldn't celebrate any of it with the gang.

Shortly after the election, I attended my first student gov-

ernment meeting. It was nothing more than a chance for Mr. Smith and the current members to formally congratulate and welcome the new people, so we had a second, more official meeting only a few days later.

This meeting was an opportunity for us new people to observe how the older students conducted business. There were special rules to learn called parliamentary procedures, things like motions and seconds and calls to order. It was all very interesting, but in the end nothing substantial got accomplished. Why? Because we didn't have any money in our class accounts. That was one thing our school didn't have—extra money.

I wasn't feeling very confident. A president is the person you are supposed to be able to count on to rally people together and get things done. The person who is in charge and can save you, will keep you safe. I didn't know how to do any of that. I wasn't at all like those great figures I studied in Washington, DC. Mr. Terupt was the only one I knew who could do those things, and I didn't know when we'd see him again.

Peter

To my surprise, Luke actually got the job. After hearing about what had happened, his victory not only made perfect sense, but it also gave me something to smile about.

There were stories going around about the epic trick Luke had pulled on Zack. It wasn't hard to believe Luke could outsmart that buffoon, but some of the things I was hearing sounded a bit farfetched. There were kids claiming Luke had unleashed scary karate moves—which I definitely knew wasn't true—and then others were talking about the secret substance Luke had smeared on his papers. Supposedly, whatever it was got all over Zack's hands and made them stick together so he couldn't pull them apart, which made him defenseless. According to the stories, that was when Luke made him get down on his knees and beg for forgiveness. I didn't know what really happened, because even though I'd helped him win the election, Luke wasn't talking to me, but I would've paid money to see him getting the best of that moron.

Other than these tall tales, the only thing I had to feel good about in December was wrestling, which had finally started in November. That was the only time I could forget about everything else. When I wasn't on the mats, I walked around feeling lost. The gang was no more.

We saw each other across the classroom and passing in the halls, but we never spoke. I wasn't mad at anyone, but they seemed mad at me. I felt bad. Even though only a few of us had gone into that closet, we'd all been hurt. And worse, hurt by each other. How do you get over that? I didn't know. I was good at messing things up, not fixing them.

I glanced at Lexie every time I walked past her locker, hoping she might look back at me, but she never did. It was like I was invisible. Instead, what I found one day was Zack leaning on the wall of lockers, flirting with her.

If I had Luke's guts, I would've marched over and told Zack to get away from her—but I don't. So I watched him lean in closer, flexing his biceps and stroking his mustache as if to show Lexie he was a man, not a boy with peach fuzz like me. And then I saw her sheepish smile. I felt like I'd just been punched in the gut. There it was again, a girl falling for the bigger, older guy, just like with those field hockey girls at camp. I gave up walking by Lexie's locker after that.

Even Jeffrey and I had little to say to each other. We talked at practice, but that was about it—and only about wrestling, never the gang. The Central Connecticut Holiday Wrestling Invitational, which we hosted, was fast approaching, and that was all anyone on the team could think about. This was going to be our first time seeing Scott Winshall, who, according to legend, was the toughest, meanest kid we would come across all year. I heard he'd all but torn the limbs off three of our guys last year at the junior high competitions. He finished the season unbeaten, with all his victories coming by pin. This was impressive and scary, because it meant Winshall had tossed his opponents around like rag dolls until he'd decided to put an end to the match by gluing their shoulders to the mat.

"You better hope you don't get Winshall," Chris warned us. "Winshall wins them all. He's nasty. The kid's pure muscle."

No one knew what weight class he would be in this year, so everyone on the team hoped he wouldn't be in theirs.

"Winshall had a beard as a seventh grader," Mark said. "The kid's an animal!"

"I heard he got a tattoo this year," Adam said.

"I heard he eats raw meat for breakfast," Mark added.

Jeffrey and I just listened. Chances were, one of us would have this Winshall kid in our weight class. Neither one of us had lost a match so far, and we beat Chris and Adam and Mark every day at practice, but Winshall sounded legit. I shrugged like I didn't care, but I had all sorts of crazy images in my head. I kept picturing this muscle-bound kid with a beard and tattoos, and I thought about Zack with his mustache and Lexie's smile. Having facial hair instantly elevated your status with girls, and it scared your opponents on the mat. It was an advantage in both arenas. So was having a tattoo, but my mother would've killed me if I showed up at dinner with one of those. Leaving practice that night, I made a bold decision.

"I need you to stop at the store," I told Miss Catalina on

our way home. "I need to get some more energy bars and high-performance drinks."

"Okay," she said.

Miss Catalina never questioned me. She knew I was serious about wrestling, so asking for these foods made perfect sense. I did need more of them . . . but there was something else I really wanted to get.

"You can stay in the car," I told her. "I'll be right back."

"Okay."

I found the health food section and got the bars and drinks first. Then I went to the men's care aisle. That was where I found what I was really looking for.

When we got home, I went straight to my bathroom and carefully read all the directions on the box. I read them twice! Luke would have been proud. And I followed them step by step—except for the preliminary forty-eight-hour skin-allergy patch that was recommended. I skipped that. The only other thing I did differently was use a little more than it suggested, but I wanted to make sure it worked, and fast.

It tingled a little bit, which I figured was a good sign. But by the time I went to bed later that night, my face was starting to burn. I looked in the mirror and could see my upper lip and chin were redder than normal. I told myself it was just mat burn from practice. Or windburn and chapping from the cold winter air. Or anything else that would be better after a good night's sleep. But that wasn't the case.

By morning, there was no more hiding the truth. When I awoke, my face felt like it was on fire—and it looked like it, too! Whatever ingredients were in the beard and mustache dye had caused my skin to have an unpleasant reaction. I only wanted to make my peach fuzz look darker, like a real goatee, but instead I ended up with chemical burns all over my face. This was a hundred times worse than having Mount Everest on your nose!

The last thing I wanted to do was go to school, and Miss Catalina actually asked if I wanted to stay home, but if I skipped, then I couldn't go to practice, and I had to go to wrestling practice. The Holiday Invitational was right around the corner.

There must've been fifty kids who asked me what had happened before first period even started. I had to get creative because there was no way I could tell anyone the truth. I told everyone Miss Catalina had bought a new soap that caused the reaction. People seemed to buy it, but it didn't make everything better.

"If my dog had a face like that, I'd shave its butt and make him walk backwards," one of Zack's losers crooned.

"It looks like you've been sucking face with a toilet plunger," Zack said.

His followers started cracking up. I didn't think it was possible for my face to grow any redder, but I could feel the heat rising in my cheeks. And there was no one around sticking up for me. No one who had my back.

"Is that what you do since you can't get any girls?" Zack said. "You make out with the plunger?"

I made a beeline for the nurse, where I probably should've gone in the first place. She gave me some cream and a lecture.

And then she handed me a note so I wouldn't get penalized for missing practice—I wasn't allowed to go. What a waste.

This disaster ranked right up there with the world's worst wedgie. The results did not make me a heartthrob *or* intimidate my opponents on the mat *or* help me with Lexie. Turns out it would take something way worse than chemical burns to get us talking again.

Jeffrey

Wrestling was my outlet. It was how I got out all my anger and frustration. I wanted to forget about Anna and Jessica and everything, so I worked my tail off. I was undefeated, a perfect 5–0 entering December, a perfect 8–0 heading into our Holiday Invitational. There were twelve teams participating in the event, and it was one of the biggest competitions on our schedule. I had been preparing for it all fall, rising early to run and do my hundred push-ups and crunches before school each day.

The tournament took place on the third Saturday of the month. It was held in the high school gym because our junior high gym didn't have enough space to put down four full-sized wrestling mats. Matches ran nonstop throughout the day. I won my first bout pretty easily. After a quick takedown, I cranked the kid over and pinned him with a strong half nelson. In my semifinal match I met tougher competition, a kid from Madison. We were tied going into the third period, and that was when all my extra work paid off. My opponent got tired. I escaped from the bottom and then hit a quick single-leg, which I finished by tripping him to his back, leading to another pin. That sent me to the finals against Scott Winshall, the kid who wins them all. The eighth graders on our team had been telling stories about "Wins All" since day one. He had kicked the tar out of three of our guys last year. I tried watching him in one of his earlier matches, but he ended that one in twenty seconds. I didn't get to see much.

I did my best not to get nervous, but that was impossible, especially after Coach Terupt showed up. Anna didn't come. She had signed up to be a volunteer at one of the scorer's tables weeks ago so she'd be able to see Asher, take yearbook photos, and watch me, but she had obviously changed her mind about all that. I was still upset about the party, and I guess she was too. I was mad for even thinking about any of that at a time when I needed to focus on my finals match, but my mind kept wandering, and that did nothing to calm my nerves.

Sometimes when you really want something, you're scared to go for it. You're scared to let go and try. You hold on too tight. That was what happened in my match. That was why I didn't execute my moves. I let my nerves get in the way. I lost 6–3 to Winshall. It was the closest match he'd had in two years, but I didn't get up and run all those mornings before school so I could take second. I lost, and it hurt.

Peter won his weight class even though he'd had to miss practice recently. He was great. He had to attach this awful face mask to his headgear because of his burns, but that didn't seem to faze him one bit. He took first place, while I finished in second and had to kiss my perfect season good-bye. The older kids on our team tried to tell me what a great job I had done by going so close with "Wins All," but that didn't make me feel any better.

Peter worked hard, but I had trained harder. Even he would have told you that. I wished he had lost. I didn't want to feel that way, but I did. I wondered, what kind of friend did that make me? What kind of friend was I to Luke, to Anna, to the whole gang, when I went into that closet with Jessica? I sat on the lowest bleacher holding my second-place trophy that I didn't want.

"You did a good job, Jeffrey," Mom said, rubbing my back. That's what your mom is supposed to say. Even if you stink, your mom is going to tell you that you did a good job.

I shrugged.

"You'll get him next time," Dad said. That was a little better than telling me I'd done a good job. I was definitely hoping for a next time.

"Bye, Ree," Asher said, hugging me. "I wuv you."

I couldn't help but smile. He was the first person to make me feel better. "Bye, buddy. I'll see you when I get home." He and Mom left, and Dad went to wait in the lobby for me.

That was when Coach Brobur plopped down beside me. "Well, Jeffrey, you may have lost the battle, but you can still win the war."

I looked at him sideways. I had no idea what he was talking about.

"Doesn't Mr. Smith teach you anything in that social studies class? Wars consist of battles. Today you lost the first battle, but you'll see Mr. Winshall again before the season's over. You still have a chance to win the war."

"Really?"

"Yes. Now you've got something to look forward to, so stop feeling sorry for yourself and keep your head up. No creature won in its struggle for existence by wallowing in self-pity." Coach Brobur smacked me on the knee and then rose to his feet just as Coach Terupt came over. The two of them shook hands, and then Terupt took a seat next to me.

"You know the old guy's right," Terupt said.

I nodded.

"I heard what he was saying to you. He was talking about attitude. Losing is supposed to hurt, Jeffrey. You care a lot about this. But I can tell you I learned more from my losses than I did from any of my victories. The hard times like these make you better—on and off the mat—as long as you have the right attitude about things." He wrapped his arm around my shoulders and gave me a squeeze.

I stayed there for a bit, sitting and thinking. I thought about how Old Man Brobur was growing on me, and how I was already looking forward to my next shot at Winshall and my chance to win the war. I thought about how I hadn't even told Peter congratulations. I thought about the sad look in Coach Terupt's eyes when he mentioned hard times on and off the mat. I thought about the gang and wished there was a way for things to go back to normal.

anna

Last December I witnessed a truly romantic moment when Mr. Terupt dropped down on his knee and asked Ms. Newberry to be his wife. I hadn't given up on Charlie yet, not like I had my so-called friends. I held out hope that this December could take hold of his heart and move him to do something special.

I'd managed to find Charlie alone on a few different occasions in the weeks leading up to Christmas. Not to my surprise, each of those occasions happened out in the barn around milking time, and I was glad for them. It wasn't like I was looking to spend any extra time with Danielle. She was as moody as ever, and we still hadn't talked about the party. But Charlie always liked my company, though he did keep me away from Bessie when it came to milking her now.

"I've been saving up my allowance money to get something for Mom this Christmas," I said to Charlie one evening. I was standing in the alleyway, near the stall where he was milking.

"Really?" He took the machine off the cow, grabbed his pail, and moved on to the next udder.

"I was thinking maybe some jewelry," I said. I followed him, and this time I stepped into the stall beside him. "You know they have that stuff on mega sale around the holidays."

"You don't say." Charlie wiped the cow's bag clean and then slipped the machine on her.

"Really. I guess a lot of men buy it for their wives—or soon-to-be-wives," I said.

"Humph."

I stood next to the cow, petting her neck as I kept talking. "It was this time last year when Mr. Terupt popped the question. Betcha he got a good deal on that ring."

"I'm sure he did," Charlie said.

"Are you planning on getting Mom anything?" I finally asked him. "I think this Christmas should be a night we remember forever. Hint, hint."

"As a matter of fact, I have been saving up to get her a little something," he said.

My eyes widened as I bent forward. "Really?"

"Of course!" Charlie exclaimed. He touched the cow's tickle spot and ducked. Her tail came whipping around and almost caught me. "She just wants to make sure you're paying attention," he said, grinning.

Apparently I wasn't, because I hadn't even realized it was Bessie that he was milking and I was petting.

"Ol' Bessie here knows all about it," Charlie said. "You should ask her. She and I've been talking about it for a while. Haven't we, girl?" He patted her on the side and then took the machine and moved down the line.

I stood there with Bessie, looking her in the eye. She didn't say anything, but she told me what I wanted to know. I think I was starting to develop that farmer's extra sense Danielle had mentioned, because I had a feeling Charlie was finally going to do it!

Danielle

Christmas Eve is a very important day in our family. Dad, Grandpa, and Charlie work all morning to take care of the cows and get the farm settled, while Mom and Grandma prepare the house and the feast. I usually like to help in the kitchen, but I was feeling wiped out and nauseated, so much so that I actually stayed in bed. I couldn't even try to hide it and make out like I was fine.

"Your mother and I can handle the kitchen," Grandma said. "We've done it for a number of years. We don't want you around the food if you're feeling crummy anyway. Get some rest so you're refreshed for church later."

"I hope it's not the flu," Mom said.

"A little rest, and she'll be better," Grandma promised.

I didn't argue (not this time). I slept until after lunch, which was when Anna and her mother showed up. I could hear the two of them getting busy right away, helping with the meal preparations downstairs. I decided to get out of bed. I was tired of being tired. I kept my distance, though. Staying out of each other's way was something Anna and I had been doing a good job of ever since that party.

It took a lot out of me, but I managed to get candles

arranged in each of our windows, and I swept the floor in our entryway. Right about the time I finished with those two tasks, we all commenced getting ready for church. The glorious meal that Grandma and Mom had slaved over all day would be ready for us when we got back.

There were a lot of us going to mass, so we took several cars. I rode with Grandma and Grandpa. Terri rode with Mom and Dad. And Anna hitched a ride with Charlie. She was up to something, I just knew it, but I didn't get to spend much time worrying about it because Grandma showed me how smart and aware she was yet again.

"Danielle, it's important we remember that all this hoopla is because we're celebrating the Lord's birth. This is a time for us to be grateful and generous. Not a time for us to be moody, and especially not a time for us to be bickering with those we hold closest."

"Yes, ma'am." She had noticed the distance between Anna and me.

"Whatever it is, I'm sure the two of you can work it out. If I haven't showed you how to do that, then at least I know Mr. Terupt did."

"Yes, ma'am." She was right—about everything.

Grandpa pulled into the church lot and parked. "Your grandmother's a smart old lady, Danielle, even if she can be stubborn as a mule sometimes."

"You hush up, Alfred."

Grandpa looked back at me and smiled. "That's why we love her," he said. Then he leaned over and pecked Grandma on the cheek. "Merry Christmas, sweetums."

"Oh, all right," Grandma huffed. "Let's go, you two."

Church was torture, and I know Grandma would have another heart attack if she ever heard me say that, but it was true. Lying down all morning hadn't done me much good. I felt horrible sitting in that pew. I couldn't wait to get back home. In the midst of the service, I actually did something I never thought I'd have the nerve to do. I got up and went to the bathroom, which just so happens to be one of Grandma's biggest pet peeves.

"People should use the bathroom before church so they don't have to get up in the middle of it," she'd say. "I think they do it on purpose, so they have a reason to take a break. Well, the Lord knows what they're doing."

"A man's got to go when a man's got to go," Grandpa would say, egging her on.

"Then a man should tie a knot in it until after church!"

To hear Grandma talking like that almost gave *me* a heart attack. But she was serious, the bathroom could wait until after church, so it took no small amount of courage for me to get up in the middle of Christmas Eve service. It was either that or risk my bladder exploding during the second reading. I didn't dare look at her as I made my way out of the pew. The mere thought of her angry stare was enough to terrify me. Instead, my gaze landed on someone else in the congregation—Mr. Terupt! And Mrs. Terupt was with him. What a surprise. As yucky as I felt, I still managed a small smile and a wave. Mr. Terupt could do that to a person.

After the Mass concluded, my family stopped to say hi to them. "With a baby on the way, we knew it was time to find the right church," Mr. Terupt told us. "We figured what better pick than yours."

"There's a lot of old birds in this bunch," Grandma said, "so it's nice to get some good-looking young blood in here for a change."

I should've been laughing along with everyone else after Grandma said that, but I wasn't. Instead, I turned and headed to the bathroom—again. I had to go, plus I was dying of thirst, and the only place to get a drink was either from the holy water or the bathroom sink.

By the time I returned, Mr. and Mrs. Terupt were already gone. The only person waiting for me was Grandma, and she didn't say a word, which meant she was madder than the dickens.

ANNA

After that night in the barn, Christmas Eve and Christmas Day couldn't come fast enough. I know for most kids, the excitement is about what you might get, but for me it wasn't about that at all. I couldn't wait for my mom to get *her* present.

Too bad Danielle prevented that from happening. And that wasn't even the worst of it.

Danielle

After excusing myself from the table one too many times during Christmas Eve dinner, Mom got up and followed me. I had tried to tough it out like Grandma, I had tried not to ruin everyone's holiday, but I couldn't keep it up. One close look at me, and Mom knew. It wasn't her farmer's sense, but her mother's sense that told her there was something more going on with me than the flu.

Mom and Grandma brought me to the hospital straightaway. The good thing about going to the emergency room on Christmas Eve is that it isn't too busy. I only went to the bathroom once while waiting. Then a nurse came out and called my name. Mom and Grandma and I followed her to an empty room on the other side of the double doors. She asked Mom a series of questions, but I didn't do a very good job of listening. My body was too tired for that. I was too wiped out to even care when she took my hand and did a finger stick. Then she left us alone, and I got up to use the bathroom again.

When I returned from the restroom, I found the nurse was already back and waiting for me. "The doctor will be here in just a few minutes," she said. "In the meantime, he's asked me to start an IV and get more blood."

She stuck the IV in the back of my hand, pumping liquids inside me, and at the same time pulled the extra blood out of my arm, but I still didn't care. Just as she was finishing up her poking and prodding, the doctor entered. He waited for the nurse to leave, and then he sat down and wheeled his stool closer to Mom and Grandma. I knew then he was about to tell us something that wasn't the best news or easy to hear. And for the first time since arriving at the hospital, I actually did a good job of listening.

"Danielle has type one diabetes," he said.

Silence. No one said a word. Neither Mom nor Grandma moved an inch. They sat there like stone statues. And since they didn't have anything to say, the doctor started talking again, telling us more about my situation. But by then, I was done listening. All I remember is that when he stopped the next time, Mom *and* Grandma began to cry. For Grandma to shed even a single tear made me wonder if the doctor had just told them I was going to die. I'd heard of diabetes, but I still didn't know what in the heck it meant to have it.

Well, for starters, it meant having two bags of fluid pumped into my body through that IV. And after that I wasn't so darn thirsty. It also meant spending the night in the hospital. And it meant sitting through almost six hours of diabetes education with Dr. Barnes, the endocrinologist, on Christmas Day. I imagine she wasn't hoping to spend her Christmas at the hospital, either, but she didn't complain. Dr. Barnes put on a Santa hat and a cheery face and we made the best of it. Mom and Grandma stayed by my side the whole time. Dr. Barnes told us there was a lot everyone in the family was going to have to learn—and she was right. She talked to us about my pancreas and glucose and insulin and shots—I had to give myself plenty of those now.

"I just don't understand," Grandma said, shaking her head. "I think I had an uncle who had trouble with his sugars when he got older, but he's the only person I can recall who's had diabetes in the family."

"That would have been type two diabetes," Dr. Barnes explained.

"Oh. And that's different?" Grandma asked.

"Yes." Dr. Barnes continued, "With type two a person is still making insulin, but it's not working as well anymore. It is often linked with obesity. That type of diabetes can be helped with weight loss and a better diet. Danielle, on the other hand, has type one, which means her pancreas has pretty much stopped making insulin. Type one cannot be reversed. This is something Danielle will have to deal with for the rest of her life."

After hearing that, I understood why Mom and Grandma were upset. Dealing with something for the rest of your life does make it a pretty big deal, but the good news was that having diabetes doesn't mean you're going to die, not as long as you take care of yourself. The thing I had to be most careful about was not letting my blood sugars get too low or too high. The goal was to maintain a reading on my meter between 70 and 100. If it ever happened that I got too low, then I could pass out and even fall into a coma—and Lord knows we'd had enough of those with Mr. Terupt. My sugars going a little high wasn't quite as serious. If that happened, I was likely to feel weak and tired, maybe spacey, and probably irritable, but that was about it. However, I didn't want my sugars to stay high because, over the long run, that's bad for you. And if they ever got too high, I could end up in a coma that way, too. I think I spent most of my fall with my sugars going up and down, especially when I got locked in that closet with Peter. I'm pretty sure it wasn't the heat rising, but my sugars spiking that made me flip out.

Being diagnosed with type 1 diabetes was a lot to take in, but I wasn't angry, or even all that sad. I was actually happy to finally have an answer for what had been going on with me, and relieved to learn I'd be feeling better now that we did know. And here's something I realized. It was time for me to be strong like Grandma—for Grandma.

"Danielle, I just don't get it," Grandma said when we were back home. She knelt with me by my bedside. "Why you?"

"Because I can handle it," I said. "I'm glad it's me and not anyone else. Maybe I didn't get the diabetes gene from you, but I've still got a lot of you in me, Grandma. I can do this."

Grandma pulled me into another hug. "You're amazing," she said. And then she started tearing up again.

"Grandma, stop that crying already," I said. "If you keep it up, I might start to think you aren't all that tough anymore."

She sniffled and chuckled and then led us in a prayer.

Dear God,

Thank you for sending Dr. Barnes our way. She was a saint and helped all of us a great deal down here, but you be sure to keep an eye on Danielle. As long as you take care of her, the rest of us will be all right.

"Grandma, I'm fine," I whispered.

"Don't interrupt. I'm praying."

I sighed. "Don't forget the Terupts," I said.

"Ah, yes."

And, Lord, we also thank you for bringing Mr. and Mrs.
Terupt and their bundle of joy that's on the way to our church.
Do continue to take care of those wonderful people.

And lastly, I pray you help Danielle repair things with Anna,
because now is when she'll need her most.

Amen.

Grandma gave me a kiss on top of my head and then left
me alone. I used to think Mr. Terupt was the one who knew
everything, but Grandma wasn't any different. Maybe she
was beginning to show signs of forgetfulness, but she didn't
miss much. A minute later, there was a knock on my door.

"What did you forget?" I said, guessing it was Grandma
coming back to tell me something.

It wasn't Grandma. It was Anna. She walked across the
floor, but before she even got to me I met her halfway, and we
pulled each other into a hug that I won't ever forget. It was
one that took me all the way back to Mr. Terupt's hospital
room. I thought of Jessica and Alexia, and my arms ached to
hold them as well.

The storm had hit, but was it over? I hoped so.

Alexia

I was the first one awake on Christmas morning, which is how it's supposed to be—kids getting up early while moms and dads stay snuggled in bed—but normally, I like to sleep late. It's important for a girl like me to get her beauty sleep. But I decided to get up early and get the coffee going for Mom and me. I was ahead of my years with both my sleeping habits and my love for morning joe. I'm a sophisticated woman who was trying to be a nice and thoughtful daughter. I even baked a batch of muffins.

Mom and I only had a small tabletop Christmas tree. Since it was just the two of us, we didn't need one of those that you go and cut down. The small size worked just fine for us. We didn't have many ornaments, so I always made my own by doing kindergarten-style craft projects. This year I decided to make our tree a fashionista. On Christmas Eve, I wrapped white lights around her and then dressed her in one of my old feather boas. I bedazzled her with little designer purses, pairs of tiny sparkly shoes, and several fancy minia-ture evening gowns. Rather than placing a star on top, I gave her a pink bow. I even created a little skirt to put under her.

"I love her pink bow," Mom said. "That's the perfect touch. I guess we'll be having a pink Christmas through and through."

I smiled because I thought she was talking only about the bow.

After enjoying our coffee and muffins, Mom went to her bedroom and came back with a basket of gifts for me. In it there was an assortment of lotions, nail polishes, and bubble baths with a pumice stone. There were special face-cleansing scrubs to keep away any future Mount Everests, and a mani-pedi set complete with emery boards and nail clippers. I adored all that girlie stuff, but my favorite item was the fashion-designing manual. It was full of ideas and patterns for dresses, handbags and purses, and even shoes. I had taught myself how to use Mom's old sewing machine, and I was beginning to make some of my own things, nothing I dared wear to school yet, but maybe down the road. Fashion was my future.

I gave Mom a hug and told her how much I loved all of it, and then scooted to my bedroom to get what I had tucked away for her. I'd spent most of my money on school shopping, but I also hung on to some so I could get Mom a present. Early on I had ideas for jewelry or different accessories, but Teach had given me a photo of Mom and me at his wedding, and I decided that was what I wanted to give her. I found a charming mother-daughter picture frame to hold that special moment forever. Mom had to wipe her eyes after I gave it to her.

Shortly after exchanging our gifts, I heard the crunching

of gravel out in our driveway. Who could that be? I wondered. I went over to our window and pushed aside the curtains. "It's Vincent," I said, surprised.

"I told him to come over," Mom said.

"You did? On Christmas?"

"He's not with his girlfriend anymore. I didn't want him to spend the day alone."

I left the window and went to open our door. There, I was greeted by one of the biggest surprises I'd had in a long, long time. Vincent held the cutest little poufy-haired puppy I'd ever seen!

"Merry Christmas," he said, handing her over.

"Is she for me?"

"Well, who else would want a froufrou dog like this? Of course she's for you!"

"Oh, Vincent! Thank you! Thank you!" I squealed. My new puppy started giving me kisses. "Look at her hair!" I cried. "She's beautiful!"

"You oughta have fun styling her up," Vincent said.

He was right. I couldn't wait to make this little girl some outfits.

"Mom, look!" I rushed into the living room.

"Vincent, you shouldn't have done this," Mom said.

"There's no better way to keep a person smiling during tough times than with a puppy."

I stopped and looked at him. What was he talking about, 'tough times'? I looked over at Mom.

"Vincent!" Mom looked mad. She and Vincent exchanged glances.

"I'm sorry, I thought you told her—"

"What's going on?" I said.

Mom sighed. "Have a seat, Alexia. There are some things I need to talk to you about. I wanted to wait, but . . ."

I cradled my puppy and sat down on our couch. I was scared. This wasn't like Mom. And Vincent knew what was coming.

This year, I'd lost my best friends. In that next moment, I learned that I had to worry about losing even more. My entire world was about to fall apart.

Looking back, it's hard to believe I made such a big deal over a pimple. A lump on my nose that one of those boys had said looked like a tumor. Isn't that ironic? Had I known then about the lump coming my way, I wouldn't have even cared. I would have happily dealt with that pimple every day if it meant I wouldn't have had to worry about the other ugly mass that showed up.

Jeffrey

I entered December angry because of all that had happened with everyone, Anna especially. And then I suffered a heartbreaking defeat against Scott Winshall. The pain in my chest was heavy. But as time wore on, that weight began to lift—in one of those places, anyway.

Scott Winshall had not won the war, and I had Coach Brobur and Coach Terupt on my side. I had my little brother, who was always there for me, who loved ripping open his presents on Christmas morning, who squealed when he tore the wrapping off a silly Christmas board book and then patted the angel on the cover and said, "My-my."

Whatever that meant.

Jessica

Lexie and I had done little talking since our disastrous party and her surprise announcement at the student government speeches, but it wasn't like we were mad at each other. It was more like we didn't know what to say. But I decided to call her anyway—after all, it was the holidays—and to my surprise she asked me to come over. She was getting ready to go to the restaurant, but had something she wanted to show me first. I worried she'd received the invitation that I had not.

I heard the yipping before she even opened the door. Not only was I greeted by Lexie, but by her new companion as well.

"Who's this?" I said.

"This is Margo," Lexie said. "Margo, quiet. Yipping is not very ladylike."

Lexie had her little dog's poufy hair fashioned with pink and purple bows. "I didn't know you wanted a puppy," I said.

"Vincent got her for me. She was a surprise."

"Looks like you're having fun dressing her up already."

"Yeah. He gave her to me because he said puppies have a way of making people happy no matter what."

"That's why he got her for you?"

"Yeah. Come in. We need to talk."

I followed Lexie into her small living room. I sat in the chair adjacent to the end table that held a fashion tree, not a Christmas tree. It was perfect for Lexie, just like little Margo. I looked around to see what else I was missing, and that was when I spotted the envelope sitting on their coffee table. Lexie hadn't even tried to hide it. It was sitting out in plain view, like she wanted me to see it. I thought Margo was what she had to show me, but guess again. I knew we had pinky-sworn to tell each other if we got an invitation, but I didn't think she'd rub it in my face like this.

"Did you get one?" Lexie asked when she saw my eyes locked on it.

"No." I wondered if my voice sounded like I felt.

"I'm sorry," Lexie said. "I can't believe it."

I turned away and stared out the window. I didn't want her to see me. My eyes were already watering.

"Jess, I'm not going to go."

I shrugged, pretending I didn't care, when we both knew the truth—I cared so much.

"Jessica, Vincent got Margo for me because my mom has breast cancer."

I turned to face Lexie, my hands covering my mouth. All this talk about words with Mrs. Reeder, and I couldn't find one thing to say.

"Mom was having more headaches than I bothered to re-alize," Lexie said. "I was too wrapped up in myself to even care. Vincent's the one who noticed and made her find a doctor. Mom hadn't been to one in a long time 'cause they cost money, but Vincent told her not to worry about that and convinced her to schedule a physical. Her headaches have nothing to do with her cancer, so we're lucky they found the lump when they did the physical. If it weren't for Vincent, Mom never would've gone, and then . . ."

I still didn't know what to say. My eyes spilled silent tears, tears for Lexie mixed with tears that had previously welled up in self-pity. I felt horrible that I even had those. Who was I to be feeling bad for myself?

"Mom says they caught it early, so her chances are good," Lexie said.

A car horn honked out in the driveway, and Margo sprang to life, yipping out the window.

"That's Vincent," Lexie said, standing up. "He's here to pick me up for work. Mom's already there. He can give you a ride home."

Slowly, I rose from my chair.

"So I won't be needing this," Lexie said, handing me the envelope from the table. "I don't know if you want it, but it's yours to take."

I stepped forward and threw my arms around her. We pulled each other tight and squeezed. And I knew what mattered most was what I held in my arms and not in my hand.

Margo jumped up, placing one paw on Lex and one on me. We knelt down and rubbed her little head, and she started licking our hands, which made us smile, just as Vincent had promised Lexie.

So here I am, dear friend, sitting in my bedroom, staring at an envelope that I have yet to open, thinking not of it but of my friend Lexie—and her mom. Yes, I'm still upset about the invitation. I had wanted to go so badly, but it's just no longer the most important thing in my world, and I'm upset to even think I once thought it was. The person reading a book in our living room—my mother—is the most important, and I'm on my way to join her.

Sad but grateful,
Jessica

P.S. I hope everyone else in the old gang is enjoying a happy holiday, and not one like Lexie.

P.P.S. I voted for Luke, and not because of the stories going around.

JANUARY

Alexia

"After a breast cancer diagnosis, there are decisions to be made, Lexie—decisions about how best to treat it," Mom said. We were sitting on my bed. Mom was behind me, brushing my hair while Margo snuggled in my lap. "I gave my options a lot of thought. One was what's called a mastectomy," she said, then paused. We looked at each other in my mirror. "That's a procedure where they remove your breast in surgery."

"You mean cut it off?" I asked.

"Yes."

All this time I'd been wishing my chest would grow. I'd stuffed my bra—more than once—and purchased a special push-up bra so it looked like I had something. And here Mom was talking about having them take hers away. A-cups or D-cups, flat or voluptuous, none of that mattered anymore.

"Another option was a lumpectomy," Mom continued. "That's where they go in and surgically remove the lump, and you keep your breast."

I swallowed. "Which one did you decide to do?"

"My doctor is confident she can get the tumor because

we caught it early, so I'll be having a lumpectomy next week. Hopefully then I won't need a mastectomy."

"That soon?!"

"Yes, honey. We can't wait, otherwise we risk letting the cancer grow."

I stood up from my bed, handed Margo to Mom, and took the brush from her. It was my turn to play with her long strands. I needed to hold part of her while she went on telling me these scary things.

"Shortly after my surgery I'll begin chemotherapy," Mom said. "That might make me sick, but hopefully not for too long." She looked back at me. "And I'll probably lose my hair."

I took a scarf from my closet and tied it on Mom's head. "You'll still be beautiful," I said.

She spun around and pulled me into a hug. "I love you."

"I love you, too."

Margo immediately weaseled her way in between us, and we giggled together. My little puppy was doing her job.

Later that night, Margo cuddled next to me in bed. As I lay awake, I thought back to Mr. Brobur's science class and our lessons on genetics. He had told us how important this stuff was when it came to our health and family history, especially with things like heart disease and cancer. I'm not one for praying, but I took a page out of Danielle's book and asked God to heal my mother, and I told him I didn't care what size boobs he gave me, I was only asking that he'd keep me from getting cancer. I prayed for Danielle and the rest of my friends who I missed, and for Margo, who licked the silent tears from my cheeks before they could even fall to my pillow. And then I prayed for Mrs. Terupt, and asked that she never end up sick and need to tell her child news like this.

The funny thing is, no matter how much praying you do, bad things can still happen.

Danielle

This diabetes thing was a total shock to me and my family, but somehow, it was even more shocking for my school. Can you believe the junior high had never had a diabetic student before? So naturally, when they got the news about me, it put everyone in a tizzy. Principal Lee had an emergency meeting with Nurse Sharon and every teacher on my schedule. He wanted everyone to know what was going on. For a girl who's used to handling stuff on her own and keeping personal matters to herself, this took some getting used to.

It didn't stop there, either. There was quite a bit I had to get used to at school. Like all the stares I kept getting in the hallways. You would think I had showed up with a new tattoo that everyone needed to see. My "tattoo" was the kit I had to carry with me everywhere. It wasn't stylish, that was for sure. It looked more like a lunch box than anything else, but it fit all my diabetes supplies that I needed with me at all times. Dr. Barnes gave it to me before I left the hospital.

I also had to adjust to my new routine, which had me visiting Nurse Sharon to do a finger stick for a blood sugar check after third period, before lunch, and again at the end of the day. The school didn't want me making that trip alone in case my sugars were low and I passed out on my way there—they mentioned something about liability—so my new routine also became Anna's new routine since we had the same schedule—and since we had made up. Anna was happy to be my sidekick, though I knew what she really wanted was to be my official half sister.

Mr. Brobur was the only person at school who wasn't all in a fuss about my new condition. He took a completely different approach.

"Danielle, if it's all right with you, I'd like to do a demonstration in class tomorrow that will help your classmates better understand diabetes. And maybe after that you can answer some of their questions. I think it will help reduce the number of stares you're getting and whispers you're hearing."

Again, this was something I had to get used to—the notion of me being on center stage and being the focus of a class discussion—but I gave Mr. Brobur my permission. He was right about the stares and whispers—there were a lot of those, so anything that might help them go away I was willing to try.

The next day in science class, Mr. Brobur showed up with a little guppy feeder fish. "This is Sally," he said. "As some of you probably know, or maybe you don't know, over Christmas break Danielle learned that she has type one diabetes. It is something she will have for the rest of her life—unless, of course, someone like one of you goes on to discover a cure for it.

"Rather than bore you with loads of information about

diabetes, Sally and I are going to show you why maintaining the correct blood sugar is important." Mr. Brobur held up a syringe. "In here I have insulin. Insulin is a hormone produced by your pancreas—except when you have diabetes. You need insulin because it helps the cells in your body take the sugars from your bloodstream to make energy. Without it, sugars will continue to pile up in your blood, making you very sick and then killing you. Adding *extra* insulin to Sally's water will cause her blood sugar to drop below normal. I wonder what will happen to Sally as a result?"

The class watched in complete silence as Mr. Brobur injected Sally's water with the insulin. The little fishy continued to bop around her bowl for the next couple of minutes. Just when people started to get restless and impatient, she flopped over on her side.

"Look!" Peter pointed.

Moments later, Sally recovered and started swimming again, and everyone clapped. But then she flopped on her side a second time and floated to the top.

"Oh my God!" Lexie cried.

Again, Sally recovered, but when she tipped over for the third time, she floated to the top and went belly up. There were no signs of recovery.

"You've killed her!" Lexie shrieked in horror.

"Not yet," Mr. Brobur said, "but if we don't get her immediate help, she will die. What do we need to do to save her?"

"She needs sugar!" several voices shouted out.

"Very good," Mr. Brobur replied. He pumped Sally's water with a sugar solution, and within a minute she was swimming around the bowl again. Everyone breathed a sigh of relief, especially Lexie. I didn't expect the near death of a feeder fish to upset her—not like this. Why was she so sensitive?

After Mr. Brobur's demonstration, I fielded lots of questions, but none from the old gang. They were quiet. Quiet can mean lack of interest or it can mean full of concern. My other classmates did the asking and stopped the whispering and staring after that. Mr. Brobur's idea helped—a lot. He had pulled off the sort of thing that I used to think only Mr. Terupt was capable of.

I don't know if that little fish could feel when she was getting low, but whenever my sugars dropped, I could tell. It was easy for me to recognize my lows. I always felt shaky. It would be hard for me to steady my hands and even my teeth would begin to chatter. I wasn't as good at recognizing my highs, though. People around me often knew before I did. When my sugars went higher than 400, I felt like Grandma's wet dishrag, with zero energy, but when my sugars hovered between 200 and 400, I had a short fuse and was ready to quarrel with anyone over anything.

"Nice lunch box," Zack said, referring to my kit. Anna and I were on our way to Nurse Sharon's when we met him in the hall. "A girl your size must need to eat a lot."

"A girl my size isn't afraid to put her fist in your mouth," I said, stepping toward him.

Zack hurried away without another word.

"Sometimes I like it when your sugars are high," Anna said, her face lit up with excitement.

"I've had enough of that kid."

"Me too," she said, "and I don't think you even need to worry about asking God to forgive you for that one."

177

ANNA

Nurse Sharon's office was simple. She had several rusted filing cabinets and a dresser along one wall, a sink area, and her old brown desk—all of which rested on the white-tiled floor. Off her work space there was a sickroom, which contained ten green beds for her visitors who weren't feeling well or her fakers in need of a nap or any excuse to cut class. Nurse Sharon wasn't all that naïve, though. She knew when she had a faker, and those kids were often sent back to class after a brief stay.

Opposite the sickroom there was a door and hallway that led to the main office. I could see how this design made sense, making it easy for the nurse to communicate with the office staff about any students who needed to leave early or had something else going on, but I also saw how the short hallway between Nurse Sharon and the school secretary, Betsy Rollins, made it easy for the two of them to get together and gossip. And Danielle and I would find them doing just that almost every time we showed up.

You would think our arrival would've signaled for them to stop all that gabbing, but instead, Danielle and her diamy locker and hurried off to my double period Reeder. Out of all my classes, ELA was the easiest one to pay attention in, but not on this day. My mind occupied. I began thinking about Thursday and our over to Snow Hill School in the bitter cold. That was when I decided I'd have Mom drive us. It was the perfect solution. Excited to tell Anna and Danielle, I took out a small piece of paper and jotted down my idea. I didn't realize passing a note in class required such stealth and precise timing. I thought I had it all figured out, but I was a beginner when it came to this stuff. The moment Mrs. Reeder turned around to list vocabulary words on the board, I leaned across the aisle and held out my note.

"I'll take that," Mrs. Reeder said. Like any good teacher, she had eyes in the back of her head. She caught me red-handed and marched straight over to my desk. "I must say, I'm surprised, Jessica. This isn't like you." She held out her hand, expecting to confiscate my note, but I didn't give it to her.

"Mrs. Reeder, you can trust that these are important words. I wouldn't have been passing the note otherwise. Could you please give it to Anna?"

"That's bold, Miss Writeman, but if these are such important words, you could speak them to Anna after class."

"Sometimes it's easier to say things in writing," I said. Mrs. Reeder gave me a thoughtful expression. Then she took my note and delivered it to Anna, telling her, "You can read it after class."

Feeling lucky, but nervous,
Jessica

betes brought out the best of that gossiping in Nurse Sharon. She was such a nervous wreck about Danielle's blood sugars and the mere thought of her passing out on the floor that, whenever we walked in, her mouth seemed to kick into overdrive. It was like Danielle was the medical expert and she was the one with diabetes. Nurse Sharon turned into a fidgeting and blabbering fool the whole time we were there. And heaven forbid if Danielle was ever low. The one time her sugars dropped down to 49, Nurse Sharon darn near fainted. She turned white as a ghost. Mrs. Rollins and I had to sit her in a chair and tend to her while Danielle drank some juice and took care of herself.

It's safe to say Nurse Sharon and Mrs. Rollins made for entertaining visits, and Danielle and I seemed to leave with a little more dirt each time. It was thanks to them that we made the decision to declare ourselves Spy Sisters. (We were done waiting for Charlie.) We were determined to get as much of the inside scoop on the junior high school as possible. Of course, we had no way of knowing that overhearing "innocent" gossip would lead to our discovering something so awful.

The only person who seemed to always know more than us was Mr. Terupt. We saw him and Mrs. Terupt at church on Sunday and he asked us how things with the guppy had worked out.

"Great," Danielle told him. She and I looked at each other, both of us wondering how in the world Mr. Terupt knew about that.

"Glad to hear it," he said. "Listen, I'd like to have the gang visit my class on Thursday. I'm hoping to try something with my sixth graders. If it works out, we could make it a regular Thursday thing. Do you think you could round everybody up and tell them for me?"

Danielle and I looked at each other again. Neither one of us had the courage to tell him we couldn't. So we said, "Sure."

"Great," he said. "I'll see you then."

Leaving the church, I asked Danielle, "Why do you think Mr. Terupt wants all of us to visit?"

"Because he can sense things even better than a farmer," she said. "He can say it's about his sixth graders, but I think he knows something's up with all of us."

"Well, he's right. So, how do you propose we tell everybody?"

"We're the Spy Sisters. We'll make secret notes and slip them into everyone's lockers."

Dear Journal,

I found the note in my locker after third period.

Thursdays with Terupt

Mr. Terupt requests your presence in his classroom this Thursday. He needs your help with a project. All members of the old gang should report to the lobby immediately following school. Do not let him down.

I could tell from the handwriting and the artistic flair in the title that the note was the work of Anna and Danielle. The last line was particularly powerful. We could let each other down, but not Mr. Terupt. I knew everyone would show up.

I slipped the note into my pocket. I wanted to keep it close. Just knowing that we were going to his classroom again made me feel better, but the words had me nervous. Thursdays with Terupt reminded me of *Tuesdays with Morrie*. Is there such a thing as a bad omen?

P.S. I am beyond excited to see Mr. Terupt, but why did he have to pick Thursday? Am I being ridiculous, or is there bad news coming? For Mr. Terupt? Mrs. Terupt? Their baby? The gang? Me?

Omen (n): a sign or warning of impending happiness . . . or disaster.

LUKE

Mr. Terupt was like our sun, and we were his planets. We weren't getting away from him. He was still at the center of our lives. When Jessica's mother pulled up in front of the junior high after school on Thursday, we were all there waiting for her.

"Hello, Ms. Writeman," I said, climbing into her SUV—on the opposite side from her heartless daughter.

"Hi, Luke. It's nice to see you. How are you?"

"Fine, thanks."

She seemed overly nice. I caught her casting a quick glance and smirk at Jessica, who stuck her tongue out in return. What was that all about?

It was a tight fit with all our bags and bodies squished together, but we made it work. We closed the doors and started on our way. This was the first time we'd all been together since the party, and it wasn't feeling anything like old times. No one said a word, except for Ms. Writeman, who was determined to be a friendly mother and kept asking about our days and our parents.

"How's your mother, Anna?" Ms. Writeman asked.

"She's doing well," Anna said.

"Tell her I said hi."

"I will."

"And how's *your* mom doing, Lexie?" Ms. Writeman asked next.

"Good," Lexie replied.

Jessica shot her mother a look and subtly shook her head. More signals between the two of them that I didn't understand. We didn't give Ms. Writeman much for answers, but she was the first one to get us talking around each other, if not to each other.

Once we reached Snow Hill School, we all said thanks and then jumped out of her vehicle. I had wondered what the moment of our arrival would look like, us knocking on the door and then a classroom full of eyeballs turning to stare at us, but that didn't happen. Instead, we found Mr. Terupt's sixth graders spread out all over the place—like we used to do. They were busy working on a variety of projects.

"It's great to see you guys," Mr. Terupt said, meeting us at the door. Not one of us was left standing there without a smile. (He was the first one to get us doing *that* around each other, if not at each other.) "Thanks for coming. I wanted my students to meet all of you so they have your friendly faces to count on next year when they arrive at the junior high."

"This sounds like another one of your exchange programs," Jessica said. "Like with Mrs. Stern's class from Woods View School last year."

"Yeah, I guess so. I'm hoping you'll come every Thursday."

"Okay," I said, speaking for everyone.

Wasting no more time, Mr. Terupt led us to different

groups of students and had us jump right in. It's normal practice for a teacher to start a session like this with some sort of icebreaker—an activity designed to help strangers get to know one another—so you become comfortable and then can work together on something more substantial. His students were prepared. Each group began role-playing, acting as if they were the reporters interviewing us on TV.

"Hello, this is Kevin Cross coming at you live from Mr. Terupt's sixth-grade classroom, and here with us today is one of his former students. Can you tell us your name, sir?" Kevin held his makeshift microphone out to me.

"Luke Bennett," I said.

"Great. Now, Mr. Bennett, why don't you start by telling us about one of your favorite memories from your days with Mr. Terupt."

"I have lots of them."

"Give us one," Kevin said.

"Well, back in fifth grade, we did this plant unit and . . ." I went on telling them about the crazy concoction I had created that led to a cloud of smoke and a fire alarm. As I shared the story, I found myself talking about Jeffrey and Peter and the rest of the gang, and laughing and smiling while I was doing it. And when I glanced over my shoulder I saw that other good times were being shared. We were talking about each other and laughing and smiling while doing it. Our storytelling made it feel like old times that afternoon, even though it wasn't. But this was an important first step. Did Mr. Terupt know what he was doing?

Before leaving his classroom that day, the two of us shared a moment off to the side. I was standing by the windows, waiting for my mom to show up, when he clapped a hand on the back of my shoulder. "Lukester, this is the first I've seen you in quite a while. Congratulations on becoming the seventh-grade class president," he said.

"Thanks. Does that mean you heard about Lexie and Peter, then?"

"I did. Must be they decided you were the best person for the job. Smart move on their part."

My gaze immediately left his eyes and fell to the floor. "Yeah," I mumbled.

"Have you had any meetings yet?" he asked.

"A couple, but we didn't accomplish much. There was just a lot of grumbling about the lack of money in our class budgets."

"Budgets are important. It's hard to get anything done when you don't have the money," he said.

"Tell me about it."

"Do me a favor, Luke. Don't mention anything about a lack of money and budgets around Mrs. Terupt. It gets her upset whenever she hears things like that, and that's not good for her right now—or the baby."

"Okay," I said, not thinking anything of it.

"I know you'll make a terrific president, Luke," Mr. Terupt said. "It's your phenotype."

I looked up at him again. He smiled and pointed out the window. "Your ride's here."

LUKE'S SEVENTH-GRADE SURVIVAL GUIDE
TIP #11 (courtesy of Mr. Terupt): Budgets are important.

Jessica

Dear Journal,

Stories and books provide me comfort—and so does Mr. Terupt. During our first Thursday afternoon with him, he had us sharing stories with his sixth graders. Luke was a main character in my tale about our *Westing Game* competition. And then for our second afternoon meeting he had Lexie and me join a literature circle with two girls and two boys (Suzi, Olivia, Jarrod, and Seth) who were in the middle of reading *The School Story* by Andrew Clements.

Lexie and I were familiar with literature circles from our days with Mr. Terupt, and this book was one I had read when I was in fourth grade and still living in California. It was one of the titles Dad had given me because the plot twist had to do with writing and acting.

"This is a good book," I said, sitting down with the group.

"You read it?" Jarrod asked.

"There aren't many books that Jessica hasn't read," Lexie said, plopping down across from me.

"I read it a while ago, so I don't remember everything about it," I said, "but I know I liked it."

"We like it, too," Olivia said.

"So how far into the story are you guys?" Lexie asked, thumbing through the pages of the copy Mr. Terupt had loaned her.

With ease, we began a conversation about the book. Initially, I listened to what the sixth graders had to say, only adding a comment occasionally. They were insightful readers with lots of thinking recorded in their journals; they had plenty to share, and as their discussion moved along, I was struck by a thought.

"Have you ever pretended to be someone you weren't?" I asked them. "Like Natalie does in this book?"

As soon as those words left my mouth the unimaginable popped into my head. I don't even recall what the sixth graders had to say because Lexie and I locked eyes, and I knew she was thinking the same thing. I never thought I'd say great minds think alike when referring to the two of us, but that was exactly what had occurred in that moment. Besides, when it came to these sorts of wild ideas, Lexie was the expert. Having the same thoughts as her meant I'd just conjured up something truly crazy and dangerous.

The School Story was a bit easier than the novels I'm reading nowadays, but it spoke to me in a way that books always seem to in Mr. Terupt's presence.

When I sat down to do my homework later that night, I found a different book resting inside my backpack. Mr. Terupt had placed The Giver in there when I wasn't looking, along with a note.

Dear Jessica,

Here's an important story. I <u>chose</u> it because it's good timing. Pain, suffering, and struggle are all a part of life, and it's because of them we can find celebration in what we have. We have <u>choice</u>, and sometimes we get to choose how things end.

With a dangerous idea and an important book to read,

Jessica

P.S. Farmers might have a special sense, but so do teachers, especially Mr. Terupt. He has a way of always knowing. What would we ever do without him?

Alexia

Thursdays with Terupt turned out to be the medicine I needed. Don't ask me to explain it, but just being with Teach made me feel better. And after our second rendezvous with his sixth graders, I was like, given something else to think about other than cancer—and it came at a time when I needed it most.

Mom's lumpectomy was scheduled for a Friday morning. I didn't want to go to school, but she made me. She wasn't about to have me hanging out by myself in the hospital and worrying. She talked to Jessica's mom, Ms. Writeman, who happily agreed to bring me after school. I was good with that because then Jessica got to come with me. I would've been fine with Vincent bringing me, but I needed him to keep Margo for the day. The hospital was one place she couldn't go.

Mom was already out of the recovery room and in a regular room when we got there. She wasn't looking her best, but hospital bedsheets and gowns certainly aren't the most stylish accessories, either. Her doctor met us and explained that the surgery had gone well, but that the lump was a bit larger than they had previously estimated.

"That's not any cause for alarm," she told me, "but your mother's blood pressure has been low since the surgery, and because of that we'll be keeping her overnight as a precaution—merely as a precaution," she promised.

So we made arrangements with the doc to meet her the next morning. She told us she'd go over some instructions with us at that point, and then we'd be able to take Mom home. I took the flowers we'd picked up on the way and placed them by Mom's window, giving that drab room a splash of color. Then I kissed the top of her head and watched her heavy eyes fall shut.

Jessica's mom wasn't about to leave me alone in my house all night, so she told me I was staying with them. It's not like I had a choice, but I didn't object. We swung by my house so I could pack an overnight bag, and then we popped by the restaurant so I could get Margo. (She *had* to come with me, but Ms. Writeman was cool with that.) Vincent asked about Mom and told me he planned to go over later to check in on her. Then he gave me a hug—and it felt like one of those that only Teach used to be able to give me.

At Jessica's house, her mother got busy with dinner while the two of us—and Margo—got busy planning Jessica's daring adventure. This was what I'd been given to think about thanks to yesterday's visit to Teach's classroom. In that book his sixth graders were reading, one of the girls pretends to be someone she isn't. Jessica was going to pretend to be someone she wasn't in order to attend the retreat. She was going as me!

The weekend retreat started the next Thursday afternoon and ran all day long on Friday and Saturday, with an official off-Broadway production hitting the stage on Sunday. It stunk that I was missing my chance to be a star onstage, but I couldn't leave Mom, not now, and like, I was excited about helping Jessica. She loved talking about the characters from her novels, and how they were always there for her, and how she wished she could be like them. In my book, Jessica *was* one of those characters. That was why I was determined to help her get to New York City and to that retreat.

Once we put our heads together, we came up with a plan in no time. It was almost too easy. I don't even think Luke could've thought up something better. I felt a little bad about taking advantage of Vincent, but was able to get past that by telling myself it was necessary and for a good cause.

We knew Mom needed to take it easy after her surgery, so I had already convinced Vincent to give me a ride to school each morning. I told him the last thing I was about to do was ride the bus with all those smelly and obnoxious kids. I had Vincent wrapped around my finger, and he never told me no. So I made plans with Jessica to have Vincent pick her up each morning as well. On Thursday we'd get her earlier than usual because we weren't taking her to school, but to the train station. As long as Jessica and I acted normal, and told Vincent where she was going, he wouldn't think anything more of it. Once we got her there, she'd be on her own, but Jessica knew what to do because she did the train thing last summer. Once we got her there, she'd be on her way to the city—as me!

During dinner, I took care of the last detail that needed attention. I told Ms. Writeman that Vincent would be getting the gang to Teach's classroom after school on Thursday because he was already planning to pick me up each day before going to check on Mom.

"Are you sure?" Ms. Writeman asked.

"Yes. Vincent already said it was all right." (That was a lie.)

"Okay, but you tell him to let me know if he can't do it."

"Okay, I will," I said, then I winked at Jessica. She kicked me under the table because she was a nervous Nellie, worried to death about her mother finding out what we were up to. I had to bite the inside of my cheeks to keep from giggling.

Following dinner, I sat Jessica on her bed, along with Margo, and then I dove into her wardrobe. If she was going to the city as me, then she had to look good. We were in no rush, so I took my time going through her things. It was fun. Jessica had some cute clothes. Things she needed to wear more often, and Margo agreed with me. My pup had good taste. She yipped once when I held up something she liked, and barked a bunch when it was something she didn't approve of. She had us laughing our heads off.

The only thing we didn't think through with our plan was what would happen when Ms. Writeman finally found out that Jessica was missing. Jessica wasn't going to get to see that, but I would.

Peter

It was Thursday again, our favorite day of the week. We weren't exactly getting along, but we were slowly starting to talk. We were hanging in the school lobby, waiting for our ride.

"Where's Jessica?" I asked. "And where's her mother?"

"They're out of town," Lexie said. "Vincent's giving us a lift today."

"Who?"

"Vincent."

"You mean the guy from the restaurant? Is he your mom's boyfriend?"

"Don't talk about my mother!" Lexie snapped. "And don't talk to me!"

She'd turned into that spider Luke had told us about during his PowerPoint last year, and she'd just bitten my head off. I wasn't trying to be a jerk, but Lexie made it pretty clear she didn't like me. In fact, I'd say she hated me—and, I was about to find out, so did her dog.

Vincent pulled up in front of the school, and when he came to a stop this pint-sized critter leapt up from the passenger seat onto the dash. If ever there was a Lexie dog, this was it. The thing was fashioned with a pink bow and clips in its fur, and was wearing a purple sweater with poufy cuffs and neck.

"Margo!" Lexie squealed. Other than T—and Zack—this pip-squeak hairball was the only thing I'd seen that had made Lexie smile since our party. As soon as it saw her, the dog started yipping and crying.

We piled into Vincent's ride, and Margo started going nuts, bouncing around like a pinball and running all over us. She was an excited little devil. She jumped into Lexie's lap and did a series of donuts before slowing down enough to give Lexie's hands all sorts of licks. Just when it looked like she was finally going to settle down, Lexie's fingers must've run out of flavor because that little mutt hopped into *my* lap and started kissing my hands. I was fine with it—until that same warm and wet sensation I was feeling on my fingers suddenly showed up in my lap. I grabbed that fur ball and hoisted her in the air as the last of the pee dribbled from her.

"Margo!" Lexie cried, taking her from my clutches before I popped her like a balloon.

The car filled with laughter. Lexie's rat-dog peeing all over me had everyone cracking up, including Lexie. It was the first time I'd heard her laugh like that in over a month. It was the first time I'd heard everyone laughing together in over a month. And even though they were laughing at me, that warm sensation in my lap spread through the rest of my body.

When we reached the school, Lexie put Margo in a bag and climbed out of the car with her.

"You're bringing that purse-dog in with you?"

"Yes," Lexie said. "Teach met her at the restaurant and asked me to bring her today. But, like, don't talk to me."

Maybe Margo gave kisses, but her owner was still in the mood to bite. I let Lexie go ahead of me, leaving plenty of space between us. Besides, I had to hit the bathroom to wash up and dry off before going to T's classroom.

Jeffrey

"Whoa, nice shiner," Peter said to Terupt.

It wasn't a dark-purple one, but a less obvious yellow-green color, so I hadn't noticed it. But Peter saw it the moment he entered the classroom, finally arriving from the bathroom. The truth was, I'd been busy trying to look into Anna's eyes, not Terupt's.

"Did the missus give that to you?" Peter asked.

"It's true my darling bride is not afraid to put me in my place, especially when I start acting like you," Terupt said, "but no, she's not the one who gave this to me. I actually got it at wrestling practice the other day when I was rolling around with Brandon." Brandon was a high schooler we met last year through Lexie. He'd seemed like bad news at first, but Terupt had helped straighten him out.

"You went to the varsity practice?" I said.

"I did, and I was thinking I'd take the two of you today when we get done here," Terupt said.

"But we have our own practice to go to today," I said.

"I know. We'll go to that first, and then when you're finished, we'll scoot over to the varsity workout. Your practice gets done right about the time the varsity is finishing with warm-ups and conditioning, so we should make it just in time for the scrimmaging—unless you don't want to go. We don't have to. It was just an idea."

"No, I want to go," I was quick to say.

"Who will we pair up with?" Peter asked.

"They have a few kids your size, but one in particular who I think will make a great partner for both of you."

I was excited, and so was Luke—but not about wrestling practice. Luke had suddenly come up with another one of his famous ideas.

LUKE

At this point I had attended exactly three student government meetings, and the third was no better than the first two. I was beginning to think the whole thing was a joke—as were my classmates. They were saying things like, "Luke, when're you gonna get us something?" or "Student government is stupid. You guys don't do anything."

Instead of feeling privileged to be president, I felt frustrated. I didn't want to be the guy who got nothing done, but without money there wasn't much I could do. Mr. Terupt had said the same thing. What we needed was a fund-raiser. But what kind? And then it hit me. I always did my best thinking in Mr. Terupt's classroom.

LUKE'S SEVENTH-GRADE SURVIVAL GUIDE
TIP #12: When things aren't getting done or going your way, you can sit around and complain, or you can choose to _do_ something about it. The trick is to find a solution that makes both students and teachers happy.

I stood up. "Mr. Terupt, I have a proposal."

"Uh-oh," Peter said. "He's got another idea. Brace yourselves."

"I'm listening," Mr. Terupt said.

"I've got an idea—"

"Told you," Peter blurted out.

"Zip it, Peter," Mr. Terupt said. "Go ahead, Luke."

"We would call it the Everything Fair," I began, "and it would be just what its name suggests, a fair that includes everything, not just your typical math and science stuff, but much more. We would have tables set up where we demonstrate our skills, share our knowledge and passions, talk about our pets"—I pointed at Margo, and Lexie smiled—"anything and *everything*."

"I like it," Mr. Terupt said. "Keep going."

"Well, we'd have it at the junior high," I continued, "and it would be a fund-raiser for the seventh-grade class, so they'd have to do most of the work for it. But also, it would be a terrific opportunity for your students to be exposed to the junior high school before next year. We could charge a seventh grader three dollars to participate in the Everything Fair, and charge one-dollar admission to everyone else. Why would seventh graders pay to participate? Because it would get them out of classes for the day, and because the money earned would be going right back to them."

"That sounds awesome," Marcus said.

"Yeah," Suzi agreed.

Mr. Terupt's sixth graders were on board, and I saw the gang silently nodding—and even cracking tiny smiles.

"Well, Luke. If I didn't know any better, I'd say it's starting to feel like old times around here," Mr. Terupt said. He gave us a sly grin. "The only thing missing is Jessica. Where is she today?"

"Uh . . . she's out of town," Lexie said.

"Oh. Well, I'm sold on this idea," he said. "Luke, I want you to go and present it to Mrs. Williams now, and then you'll have to clear it with Principal Lee at the junior high tomorrow."

So that was what I did, and Mrs. Williams loved it. In fact, she loved my idea so much that she got on the horn with Principal Lee right away. Principal Lee was hesitant at first, mostly because this meant we'd be missing a day of classes, but once he discovered how much learning and work our fair entailed, and that it was a student government initiative, he was easily persuaded. He even told Mrs. Williams that he was looking forward to it.

LUKE'S SEVENTH-GRADE SURVIVAL GUIDE
TIP #13: If you want to convince your teacher and principal to go for your idea, then make it a learning opportunity.

I had only one question: Was a good project also a surefire way to bring *former* friends back together?

Peter

I had more than enough to be mad about on our walk from the junior high gym to the varsity wrestling practice that day. First off, Lexie's fur-ball dog had whizzed on me, then Luke had to go ahead and get one of his brainiac ideas that meant I suddenly had a project to complete. The last thing I wanted was more homework, though his fair did sound pretty cool. As if all that wasn't enough, at our junior high practice Mark threw up all over the mat when I slapped a tight waist on him. His macaroni and cheese lunch came spilling out everywhere. Some of his nastiness even got on my arm. It was disgusting! It's safe to say I wasn't having the best afternoon, and believe it or not, it only got worse. The varsity kid that T had in mind for us to practice with was none other than Zack!

"Hey, Zack," T said when we walked into the gym.

"Hey, Mr. Terupt. How's it going?"

"Good. I brought you a couple of workout partners today. This is Peter and Jeffrey." T pointed to us as he said our names.

We didn't say a word. Who did Zack think he was, acting all cool with T? I might've been mad earlier, but now I was furious. Jeffrey didn't seem to care. He was too psyched about being at the varsity workout. He was willing to do whatever it took to beat Scott Winshall at the end of the year.

The varsity guys took a water break while Jeffrey and I got our shoes on. Exactly as T had said, we were just in time for the scrimmaging part of practice. The varsity coach told everybody to get in groups of three. That meant Jeffrey, me, and Zack.

While we waited for the rest of the team to get in groups, Zack tried being cool with us. "Have you guys seen that chubby girl in school who's always walking around with her lunch box? She's such a weirdo."

"Her name is Danielle, and it's not a lunch box," I said. "She has diabetes, and that kit she carries around contains the medicine she needs to stay alive, so don't make fun of her."

"One and two, on your feet!" the coach yelled.

Zack didn't get a chance to say anything back, which was good, because I'd already had enough of his fat mouth. He and Jeffrey were closer in size, so they went at it for the first minute, and Jeffrey gave Zack all he could handle. Neither one of them scored a point. I went in with Zack next, and even though I was a bit smaller, I was determined not to lose to that jerk. I went toe-to-toe with him. After those first two minutes, Zack knew he wasn't going to have it easy with us. Of course, I was tired after my first round with Zack, so Jeffrey whipped up on me next, but I didn't care—Zack wasn't getting the best of me.

We spent twenty minutes scrimmaging in our groups and then finished practice with some hard conditioning. When it was all over, the three of us lay on the mat exhausted, but I felt great, and I could tell Jeffrey did, too. We had just worked out with the big dogs.

"You guys did a terrific job today," T said, sitting down next to us. "You wrestled hard and helped each other get better."

We nodded.

"What's the matter, old man, afraid to wrestle with me today?" It was Brandon. He gave T a friendly shove and then he reached out and slapped five with Jeffrey and me as he knelt down. He'd certainly come a long way since his days as Middle-Finger Boy. Mr. T could do that for a person. Was T helping out Zack, too?

"I wanted to keep an eye on the lightweights this afternoon," T said. "Besides, you need to recoup before I give you your next whooping."

"I'm not the one with the black eye," Brandon said.

Jeffrey and I laughed.

"It's good to see you guys," Brandon said. "I heard you've been tearing it up on the junior high mats. You going to come back and work with the Zack Attack some more? We need you to make him tougher."

Zack sneered at Brandon. Jeffrey and I shrugged and then looked at T.

"I think we'll be back," T said. "Jeffrey's got a big match to get ready for."

"Oh, yeah? Against who?" Brandon asked.

"Scott Winshall," Jeffrey said. "I lost to him at the Holiday Invitational."

"I lost to him last year," Zack said. "He's tough, but you can beat him."

What was this? Was Zack being cool?

"You better come back," Brandon said. "The Zack Attack needs partners, and the old man needs me to keep him in shape." Brandon gave Mr. T another playful shove and then stood up. "See you guys," he said, and then headed to the locker room.

"See you later," Jeffrey and I called.

"I'm going to hit the showers," Zack said, standing. "Um . . . thanks for coming."

"Good job today," T said.

Why was I surprised? I should've known by now, anything was possible with T.

After Jeffrey and I got cleaned up, T gave us a lift home. We dropped Jeffrey off first, then it was on to my house.

"You know, Peter," T said as we drove along, "it's one thing to have a friend's back when you're with them, but to stick up for them when they aren't around is a real testament to your character, and that makes you much more of a man than any whiskers—fake or real—ever will."

It helped to hear T say that because with the gang all messed up, I'd been feeling like a bad friend. But I wasn't. I still had everyone's back, like I had promised him. And that also meant looking out for T, so before climbing out of his car I asked him what I'd been wondering since first spotting his shiner. "T," I said, "is it okay for you to be wrestling with Brandon? I mean, with your head and all." I couldn't help worrying about T's head, even two years after his coma.

"Gosh, Peter, you're starting to sound like my wife."

I tried to chuckle, but I was serious.

"Yes, it's fine," he said. "Don't worry. I'm careful. Brandon's not that tough yet, though he's getting there. He's got a shot at a state title this year."

I nodded, but I still wasn't feeling all that good about his answer.

"And I'll tell you something else," T said. "You and Jeffrey are definitely better than I was as a seventh grader."

My eyes widened. Wow! Talk about a compliment.

"Thanks," I said.

"I wouldn't tell you that if it weren't true. Now, go do your homework."

When I reached my front door, I turned around and watched T drive away, and as he did, I stood there hoping he'd been telling me the truth—and I don't mean about how good I'd become at wrestling.

Danielle

Anna and I entered the kitchen one night after finishing up our homework and found Grandma and Mom and the rest of the family huddled around the table talking in hushed voices. My first thought was that there was something going on with the Native Americans' court case again. I was about to let the whole bunch of them have a piece of my mind for keeping me out of the loop, but Grandma stopped me before I could even get started.

"Danielle, don't you go and get your hair all in a dander now," she said. "I'll fill you girls in on what we've been talking about, but first get your sugars under control. I can tell already that they're running high."

Anna let out a small giggle because Grandma had read me like a page out of her Bible, but I was still angry. I gave myself a shot with the correct amount of insulin, and then Anna and I followed Grandma back up to my room.

"I want to know what's going on," I demanded.

Grandma plopped down on my bed. "If you give me a chance, I'll tell you. Boy, they need to make that insulin work faster."

"It's not my sugars that've got me acting like this," I said. "It's your blood in me."

Grandma glared at me, but then she cracked a big smile—and that helped my hair settle down. I was smiling too. We started laughing when we heard Anna let out a sigh of relief. She must've thought we were really going to go at it.

Once we managed to get ourselves under control, Grandma got around to telling us what was going on. "Tonight when I was leaving my meeting at the church, I noticed Mr. Terupt was there lighting a candle. I didn't stop to talk to him because it's not the right time or place to interrupt a man when he's having a word with God. All's I know is people don't tend to show up and light a candle unless there's something pressing in their life."

Anna and I exchanged nervous glances. Why would Mr. Terupt be doing that?

"Let's pray," Grandma said. "That's the best we can do right now without knowing anything."

She was right, the Spy Sisters didn't have a clue. We closed our eyes and bowed our heads and then Grandma began.

Dear God,

I'm here with the girls, and we have something important to ask of you. I saw Mr. Terupt having a word with you tonight, and it's got us nervous. We know people come to you when nothing's wrong, just to ask for support and a watchful eye, but we also know people come to you because something's got them worried or scared. We're not sure what the case is for Mr. Terupt, but we're asking you to take care of him. Take care of his lovely wife and unborn baby, and keep all of them safe and healthy.

Amen.

Jessica

Dear Journal,

The last time my body felt this way was when Mom and I climbed into the car and started our trip from the West Coast to the East. We had a destination, but what lay ahead after that was a mystery. It was the most frightening ride of my life.

Sitting on the train today, I raced toward the city, but what waited for me after that was another mystery. My mind kept going back to Mom, and how I had deceived her. When we made that trek across the country, Mom had traveled beside me. Today, I was on my own, and I worried I could be without Mom forevermore if she didn't forgive me for what I was doing. My heart beat faster than the train carrying me.

I reached for my book. I needed comfort. I opened the novel Mr. Terupt had given me, and as I read about this young boy, Jonas, I found myself pondering the power of memories along with him. I was reminded of happy times and sad times. My thoughts drifted back to Mom, and to what used to be my friends. As I turned the pages, Jonas and I grew to understand that we had a choice and that this was something wonderful. His dilemma was different from mine, but we both had something we could do—it was our choice.

Before I could finish Jonas's story, my train slowed to a stop. I slid *The Giver* back into my bag and then continued on my way. When I reached the building where the retreat was taking place, I left Jessica standing outside and walked through the doors as Alexia. Inside, I glided through the registration process with ease; I was off to a good start as an actress. That was about as far as my talent carried me, though. During our first theater session, it was obvious that I was out of my league. I don't want to make it sound as if I'm a terrible actress—I'm not—but in the company of such gifted students, I stuck out like the ugly pumpkin. I had our extraordinary instructor talking under his breath, and my classmates whispering to each other. I feared that I would be asked to pack my bags and head home early because the fact that I had even received an invitation was most definitely a mistake, so I didn't return to my acting class after taking a bathroom break. Instead, I snuck my way into the writing group and found the biggest surprise of my life. Standing before me was the last person I thought I'd ever see again. He stopped midsentence when I stepped into the light. . . .

Alexia

"Alexia, Ms. Writeman's here," Mom called out in a weak voice.

I was hiding in my bedroom, dreading this moment. I hugged Margo. Mom had been napping in her chair when Vincent dropped me off, so she had no idea. She'd started chemotherapy earlier this week and it had left her wiped out. I walked into the living room, cradling Margo.

"Hi, Lexie," Ms. Writeman said. "Where's Jessica?"

I steadied myself. "Um . . . she's not here."

"What?" our moms said together.

"Where is she?" Ms. Writeman asked.

I swallowed, and then let the truth all out in one breath. "New York City," I said. "I like, gave her my invitation to the weekend drama retreat. I couldn't go, and she wanted to go so badly, so like, she went as me. We got the idea from a book we were reading. Ms. Writeman, she just had to go."

"Alexia, you were invited?" Mom said, showing the most energy I'd seen from her all week. "I didn't know. And honey, you didn't go? I'm sorry."

Ms. Writeman hadn't moved. She wasn't freaking out

about her daughter taking off. She wasn't demanding answers. She wasn't doing anything I thought she'd do.

I started to cry. My tears came out of nowhere, and I couldn't stop them. I was a designer bag of emotions these days, and after telling the truth to Jessica's mom, my bag ripped open. I spent every day worrying that my mother could be taken from me, and here I was telling Ms. Writeman that her daughter had taken off.

"Ms. Writeman, I'm so sorry. Jessica should've been invited. There must've been a mistake. I had to help her."

"She was invited," Ms. Writeman said.

My crying stopped just as quickly as it had started. "Wait. What?"

"She was invited. I hid the invitation from her."

I couldn't believe what I was hearing. "But . . . why would you do that?"

"Because her father is one of the professionals at the retreat."

Jessica

I couldn't believe my eyes.

"Dad?"

"Jess?"

"Dad?"

His room full of students stared at us. "Class, let's take a ten-minute break," he announced abruptly.

We waited for the room to empty, all those eyes pretending not to look at us when they were, all those ears pretending not to be listening when they were. My heart wailed against my rib cage. I didn't know whether to stay or run. I wanted to do both.

"Look at you," my father said. "You've grown so much. You're so beautiful, the spitting image of your mother when she was young." The man I hadn't seen or heard from in over a year started toward me, lifting his arms.

"Don't," I said, putting my hand out and taking a step back. "Don't."

He stopped. "I didn't think you were coming," he said. "I saw your name on the list, but you weren't signed up."

"What list?"

"The list of people who received invitations. I had no idea you were one of the recipients when I signed on to do this, but then when I got here I saw your name. I was thrilled, and then devastated when I learned you weren't coming. I thought you had declined because you knew I was going to be here."

"What are you talking about? I never got an invitation!" I said, my voice rising. Even after all this time, he was still lying to me.

"Jessica, I promise, you were mailed an invitation. I don't know what happened, but if you didn't get it, how are you here?"

I was supposed to have an invitation? And didn't get one? "How was I supposed to know you were going to be here?"

"There was a pamphlet listing all the instructors that was included with the invitations."

I never saw the pamphlet or the invitation. "Are you here with what's-her-face?" I said.

"No, things with what's-her-face ended shortly after you and your mom left."

"Then is there someone else?"

"No."

"You called for the divorce papers. That's all you cared about."

"I tore them up."

"What?"

"I tore them up. Your mother and I aren't officially divorced."

"Then what are you? You're not married."

"Technically, we are married; we're just not together. That's my fault."

"Then why didn't you ever call again? You just erased us from your life!"

His gaze fell to the floor. He couldn't even look at me. "I was ashamed."

"That's it? You were ashamed? That's the best you can do? You should be. You blew it."

"I know." He sounded choked up. His shoulders slumped. He looked so defeated.

"And you never tried to get us back."

"I wanted to," he said, looking at me. "I wanted to so badly, but I was afraid." His gaze fell to the floor again. "Your mother is a much stronger person than I am. I'm glad you've got more of her in you."

"Me too," I said. I turned and ran.

"Jessica, I'm so sorry."

His words chased me, long after I was gone.

Scared and confused,
Jessica

FEBRUARY

Danielle

Mr. Terupt's mysterious candle lighting had given the Spy Sisters something to think about around the clock, but Mom and Grandma hadn't forgotten about me. They were constantly checking in. Constantly asking me about my sugars.

I prayed to God every night and asked him to take care of Mr. Terupt and his family, and I asked him to help Mom and Grandma relax about my diabetes. I asked him to help them see that I was being responsible and taking care of myself and doing my best to keep my sugars under control. I wished Grandma would stop her worrying altogether because it wasn't good for her heart, but getting her to stop that was like asking the sun not to come up. To compromise, I asked God to consider giving Mom and Grandma something other than me to think about for a change.

I'm not sure if it was God answering my prayers, or Mother Nature, but one of them went ahead and cooked up a devil of a snowstorm, and if there's one thing we farmers never grow tired of talking about, it's the weather. The February blizzard that barreled down on us gave Mom and Grandma something else to think about for *several* days. We were hammered by snow. So much that it was measured in feet, not inches. Four times, Dad and Charlie had to get the tractors out to plow the driveways. School closed for not one day, but three. It wasn't until midmorning on the third day that the snow finally stopped falling. If ever there was a winter wonderland, we were in it.

"It's absolutely beautiful out there!" Charlie exclaimed, coming into the house having just finished the morning milking. "After I get cleaned up I'm heading over to get Terri and Anna, and we're going to enjoy being outside—all of us. This is a day to remember forever."

So after lunch that day, we went outside—all of us. Charlie had managed to plow a path to the back pond, which he had shoveled off. We got brooms down from the attic and managed to get Dad's old Arctic Cat snowmobile running for the first time in years. There was a good time to be had.

The February blizzard dropped a lot of snowflakes, but it also delivered one big surprise. Not all of our snow memories need to go back to Mr. Terupt's accident—not anymore. It turns out a winter wonderland is more than just beautiful, it can also be romantic. Now I sound like Anna.

anna

With people trapped inside because of what the news was calling the Valentine's blizzard, there were thousands of roses never getting picked up or delivered, hundreds of restaurant reservations being canceled, and who knows how many hearts broken. It was sad. There was to be no romantic story this year—or so I thought.

For two days, Mom and I hunkered down. We made the best of our situation by having a mother-daughter movie marathon. We cuddled and cried our way through sappy girl flicks like *Sleepless in Seattle, Titanic,* and *The Notebook.*

On day three of the storm, our knight in shining armor came to our rescue. The roads were finally clear enough for Charlie to reach us. He arrived, waved at us, and blew Mom a kiss from across the snowdrifts, then unloaded the snowblower he had on the back of his truck and got busy digging us out. Mom was at the door waiting for him once he finished. They hugged like they hadn't seen each other in years.

After their movie embrace, Charlie told us to bundle up because everyone was waiting at the farm. "It's a winter wonderland out there," he said. "You don't want to miss it. It's the sort of day you'll want to remember forever."

Mom and I got our stuff on, and then we climbed into Charlie's red truck. Never had I experienced so much snow. The roads were lined with white mountains, making it feel like we were visiting the North Pole. It was incredible.

Once we reached the farm, Charlie told me to hop out and get on the snowmobile that was parked nearby. "I'll be back to get you in just a minute," he told Mom.

Charlie gave me a ride on that machine that I won't soon forget. He bounced me out across the pasture over and through waves of snow. I squealed and laughed and held on to him tighter than Mom did during their hug. The only thing going faster than that snowmobile was my heart—and Charlie would make that go faster still before the day was through.

After reaching the pond, I discovered that *everyone* didn't mean only Danielle and her mom or dad, as I was expecting, but the entire family—even Grandma and Grandpa. Charlie dropped me off and then zoomed back to get Mom.

"About time you got here," Grandma Evelyn barked. "My old bones were getting cold from standing around and waiting for you. Let's get playing."

Danielle walked over and handed me a broom.

"What's this for?" I said.

"Broomball!" Grandma cried. "A Roberts family tradition. You ready for this old lady to show you a thing or two?"

Grandpa snorted. "You better save all that hot air you're spewing," he told her. "You're going to need it once we start sliding around."

"You hush up," Grandma told him.

The two of them had all of us laughing again.

"Broomball is a game we sometimes play when winter rolls in like this and the pond freezes over," Danielle explained to me. "We haven't played it the last few years, but Charlie told us this was a day to remember forever and that we had to get out here."

"He told me the same thing," I said.

The Spy Sisters looked at each other, each of us wondering if there was anything more to that, or if it was just a coincidence.

"Broomball is just like ice hockey," Grandma said, "except you don't need skates, and we knock around a ball with brooms instead of a puck with sticks." She passed the ball and shuffled out onto the ice. "Let's practice while we wait for your mother," she said.

I slid around on the ice and batted the ball back and forth with Danielle and Grandma. A short while later we heard the whine of the snowmobile engine approaching, but instead of parking alongside the pond as he'd done with me, Charlie zoomed past us and stopped farther out in the pasture. We all turned to see what in the world he was doing. We watched as he took Mom's hand and led her over to a nearby snowman—a snowman I hadn't even noticed until then. A snowman with one arm raised and extended straight out. And Mom seemed to be taking something from its palm.

I gasped when the object she held sparkled in the sun. And then Charlie pointed toward the hill at the back of the field. Written in the snow in huge letters were the words I'd been praying for him to say: *Will You Marry Me?* It was so romantic. They kissed and hugged—and it blew those movie ones away.

After all this time, I could hardly believe it. We were going to be a real family now.

Danielle might tell you it was God or Mother Nature that dished out that Valentine's blizzard, but I think it was Cupid. It was a sweet and lovely storm, one full of romance and snowflakes—and a diamond ring!

Jessica

Dear Journal,

It's taken me a while to tell you this; I've been scared to write about it. The memories and feelings you keep inside are yours—and yours alone. But if you only keep them in your head, you are bound to lose pieces of them over time. Memories swirl around like colors mixing on a painter's palette. After enough swirling, they begin to change, and a once-clear image can become blurred. Then one day, you might find it is gone forever.

Our memories are important for the future, which is something the Giver shows Jonas. I can't pass my stories on to others like the Giver does in that book, but I can put them down inside you. By putting myself down on your paper, I have a place to take root and become permanent. My memories and feelings will be there for you until the end of time, and for all those that come after us. And maybe if I share myself with you first, I'll find the courage to tell Mom.

I didn't stay for the drama retreat. I didn't belong in the acting class—pretending to be Lexie—and I couldn't stay where I belonged—pretending the teacher wasn't my father.

That would've required better acting than impersonating Lexie. As much as I ached to be there, I needed to go home. I called Mom.

The thought of calling her had me shaking uncontrollably, but I knew I could do it. Mom had made sure I was listening when she told me I could always call her if I ever ended up in a situation where I needed help. "Maybe you wind up at a party and find out there is alcohol there and you want to leave," she said, "or maybe you and your friends end up drinking at that party and need help getting home."

"Mom, that's never going to happen!" I'd said.

"I hope not, but it's not always easy, and sometimes people make mistakes," she had told me, "and I need you to know that you can always call me—no matter what."

Remembering her words, I fought to steady my hands and pushed the numbers on the keypad. She answered on the first ring.

"Mom?"

"Jessica, are you all right?"

"Mom, I'm sorry."

"So am I," she said. "So am I. I should've told you."

"I want to come home."

"I'm on my way."

We didn't talk about it the whole ride home. We didn't talk about it after we got home. We still haven't talked about it. We haven't talked about *him*. There wasn't supposed to be anything Mom and I couldn't discuss, but we never talked about Dad.

The problem is, I can't stop thinking about him. If I hadn't heard the regret and sorrow in his voice, if I hadn't seen the pain in his face, if I hadn't felt the desperation and longing in his outstretched arms, then maybe I'd still have him out of my mind, but not now. Now I see his face everywhere.

Mr. Terupt was the first to show me how to forgive when he came out of his coma. He took Peter in his arms and told him it was okay, that he forgave him. But here's the thing: Everyone knew that Peter didn't mean for that snowball to hit Mr. Terupt, or for any of that terrible day in the snow to happen. It was an absolute accident. What I need to know is, how do you forgive someone who knowingly hurts you? How am I supposed to forgive my father when what he did doesn't chalk up to an unfortunate accident? And the even bigger question: How's my *mother* ever supposed to forgive him?

"It's February, people," Mrs. Reeder said today in class. "I'd like to remind you of your yearlong quest to do something of importance with your words. Your paper on this very topic will be due before you know it. Do not make your key word *procrastination*," she warned.

This much I know: If our old gang stands a chance, if the marriage that's still—by law—intact between my mother and father has any chance, then some of those important words that Mrs. Reeder keeps talking about will need to be shared. No procrastinating.

Complicated,
Jessica

P.S. When I gave *The Giver* back to Mr. Terupt, I told him I thought it was a happy ending even though it reads as ambiguous. He said I'd have to show him.

Alexia

Dorky/geeky Luke couldn't wait for his Everything Fair. And though he didn't know it, I could've kissed him for giving us that project to work on. It was a much-needed distraction in my life, because I spent every other second of every other day worrying about Mom, wondering if her cancer was gone, or still lingering. And, like, that wasn't anything we'd know for a few months still.

Mom had suffered through so much already. Every round of the chemotherapy drugs kicked her butt. When taking the medicine, she did nothing but sleep and throw up. I wished there was some way I could make her feel better, but, like, all I could do was help her in and out of the bathroom and hold her hair back while she was draped over our toilet. I had to scold Margo after every episode because she kept trying to lick Mom's face, which was incredibly gross, but it also made Mom crack a tiny smile. Vincent knew what he was doing when he got us that little angel.

Vincent was there for me and Mom every step of the way. Bringing us dinner on the bad nights, checking in on us every day, and keeping an eye on Mom at work. She'd been back waitin' tables for a week now. Mom thought the best way to get over the fatigue she'd been experiencing from all those drugs was to keep moving. Vincent made sure she didn't overdo it, but the regulars at the restaurant all understood anyway. They were like our family away from home. Of course, even strangers caught on right away when they saw a woman wearing a scarf on her head. Mom was still beautiful, though. I did her nails, and let me tell you, they were dazzling. And I made sure she had sparkling earrings and plenty of bling on her hands. She was still a knockout. There was no doubt about where I got my looks. And I had my looks working for me, too.

Zack was constantly at my locker, trying to hit on me. That was fun at first, but he was getting a bit annoying, like a mosquito I wanted to swat away. I needed to figure something out—and so did Jessica. She'd come back from the retreat with all sorts of complicated feelings, but she wasn't ready to talk about them. I told her I'd be there to listen when she decided it was time.

"Thanks, Lexie," she said. "Actually, there is something else I want to discuss now."

"Oh, yeah? What's that?"

"The book I just read."

"You've got to be kidding me. A book? Again? And after what happened with the last one?"

"Not just any book, a book Mr. Terupt gave me," Jessica said. "And I know he gave it to me for a reason."

"Sometimes I think you're crazy."

"Me too, but just listen."

She went on telling me all about that book and what it meant for us—and for the gang. She had me listening because what she was saying made sense. Like, who wouldn't want things back the way they used to be with all of us? There were glimpses of the old stuff whenever we were around Teach, and it always felt good. The way Jessica saw it, we had a choice. Either keep on being quiet or get busy using some of those important words Mrs. Reeder was always yapping about.

"Communication is one of the keys in a relationship, and in fixing one," Jessica said.

I wasn't sure if she was only thinking of the gang when she said that, or her mom and dad, too, but the plan was for us to try talking to the gang. We thought it wouldn't be easy. But then something happened that got us talking in no time—something that shook all of us awake.

LUKE

We scheduled the Everything Fair for the final Friday in February because then we had all of our Thursdays to prepare for it, and we needed every minute we could find, especially after the Valentine's blizzard flattened our town and took one of our Thursdays away from us. There was a ton of work to get done with advertising and organizing for our big event. Thursdays were my favorite day of the week by far—but it wasn't a Thursday that changed everything.

In Mr. Smith's social studies class, Wednesdays were most important. This was because we spent Wednesdays preparing for Friday's current events trivia game, and the team to win in current events trivia received an additional three points on their next quiz or test.

"Part of being a responsible citizen is knowing what's going on in the world," Mr. Smith had told us after the new year. "How are you supposed to go out and make the world a better place if you don't know what's going on in it? You need to be paying attention to the world, national, and local news. Therefore, we're going to make a habit of doing exactly that in this class."

I was excited by his declaration because I also knew part of being a good president was being knowledgeable about these things. I was always focused and eager to learn and absorb as much information as possible on Wednesday.

Mr. Smith would pass out the newspapers and give us the next thirty minutes to read. After reading, we would meet in our teams and discuss what we'd learned, giving us a chance to prepare for Friday's trivia contest. Mr. Smith always saved the last ten minutes of class to answer any of our questions.

This Wednesday, I pulled out the local section first, as usual. I liked to start with that because there was never much going on, so after a quick skim I'd be able to move on to the more important stuff—but that wasn't the case today. I grabbed my paper and bolted from my seat. I was on my feet and running down the hall.

"Luke, where do you think you're going!" Mr. Smith yelled.

I never slowed down. I booked it to the lunchroom.

"Luke, what're you doing here, aren't you supposed to be in class?" Danielle asked. She was the first one to spot me when I burst into the cafeteria.

"Where is everybody? I need to talk to you guys."

She gestured. The gang was scattered about the room, but once they saw me they got up from their places and started toward me.

"Are you cutting class?!" Peter asked, all excited by the idea of me doing something bad.

"Luke, what's going on?" Jessica asked, concern in her voice. She knew very well there had to be a good reason for me to be standing in front of them instead of sitting in social studies.

I led them over to a nearby table and spread my newspaper open. Then I pointed to the article previewing this year's upcoming school budget vote.

"Yeah, so?" Peter said. "The stupid budget. Big deal."

"The *stupid* budget failed by almost a thousand votes last year," I said. "They're expecting difficulty with it again this time around."

"It'll pass eventually. It did last year," Peter said.

"It only passed after cuts were made," I said. "If it fails again this April, more cuts will need to be made."

"What kind of cuts?" Jeffrey asked.

"That's the question," I said. "They've planned a special meeting for next month to discuss all of this—the potential cuts. We need to go to that meeting."

"I'm not going to any stupid school board meeting," Peter said.

"You're still not getting it. They've already made cuts when it comes to supplies and materials. Now they'll be forced to do something more. That could mean eliminating teacher positions."

"So they'll get rid of some of the old farts around here," Peter said. "That's not a bad thing. There are a few that need to go."

"Sure, except that's not how it works," I said. "It's all based on seniority. It's the low man on the totem pole who gets axed."

"You mean they could get rid of Mr. Terupt?" Anna asked, her voice shaking.

"No way!" Peter said, slamming his fist on the table. He looked at me for confirmation.

They all looked at me, hoping I would tell them that wasn't possible, hoping I would tell them Mr. Terupt was safe, but all I could say was "We've got to go to that meeting."

LUKE'S SEVENTH-GRADE SURVIVAL GUIDE
TIP #14: Know what's going on in the world, especially close to home. This is important for more than just current events trivia with Mr. Smith.

Danielle

I couldn't believe it. My fears had come true. The storm wasn't over. It was picking up speed.

Luke wanted us to go to the budget meeting.

"It says here the meeting isn't for another month, and then they're voting some weeks after that. We've got to do something right away. We've got to go see Mr. Terupt," I said. I needed to see him.

"We can't go to Mr. Terupt," Jessica said. "He's got enough to worry about without worrying about us, too."

"I don't think he'd want us to know his job was on the line," Anna said.

"You're right," Lexie said. "We've got to help him without him knowing."

"How?" Jeffrey asked.

"We've got to show everyone what a good teach Teach is."

"I've got it!" said Jeffrey. "Let's work on the Everything Fair like we planned, but let's make sure to tell everyone it's all because of Terupt."

"That's perfect," Jessica said. "They'll see how much he inspires us and what a good teacher and mentor he is."

I could see Luke thinking it over. "You know," he said, "it just might work."

"It's gotta work," Peter said.

Dear God,
Please make it work.
Amen.

Alexia

Even though we had a plan, we walked out of the caf like a bunch of zombies going through the motions of getting ready for our next class. I ended up in the girls' bathroom—the same one I'd started the school year in with my friends. Back then we were busy trying to hide something. Today was a different story.

I found Anna and Danielle in there already, and then Jessica came in a minute after me. For a second, the four of us just stood there. Then we let it all out. We were done hiding. Teach needed us—and we needed each other.

"Jeffrey really likes you," I blurted to Anna. Those words just leapt right out of my mouth. It was as if I had to say everything I'd been storing up over the last three months in the next three minutes. "Jessica and Jeffrey were talking about you in the closet. That's all that happened."

Anna had been silent before I said anything, but I swear, what came spilling out of me left her even more silent after that.

"I'm sorry," Jessica said next.

"Me too," Anna said.

"So am I," Danielle said. "Lexie, Peter was only trying to help me in the closet because I was freaking out. I shouldn't use my diabetes as an excuse, but I didn't know I had it back then. I wasn't feeling right, and I didn't know what was going on with me. I'm sorry."

"The closet was my stupid idea," I said. "*I'm* sorry. I'm sorry I haven't been there for you since learning you have diabetes."

"It's okay," Danielle said.

We inched closer and closer with every word we spoke.

"I missed you guys," I said.

"We missed you, too," Anna said to me and Jessica.

We threw our arms around each other. The bell rang in our ears, but we only squeezed tighter. There was never a better reason for being late to class. I felt a surge of strength that I'd been missing ever since the party.

There was still more that we had to say, but I knew now that it would happen. I love my friends so much. It made me so happy to have them back.

Jeffrey

The Everything Fair had been important from the start, but now it was a really big deal. We worked our butts off and told everyone we invited that it was because of what Terupt taught us that we were able to pull it off. If we could get everyone seeing what an amazing teacher Terupt was, then getting rid of him would be impossible.

Working on the fair took our minds off why we were working so hard. It really was going to be awesome. We had something for everyone. Anna and two of Terupt's sixth graders set up a photography and scrapbooking station. Lexie (plus Margo) and Jessica, along with two sixth graders, were working with makeup and face painting. Danielle had a sixth grader helping her run an art station where kids could sketch and paint or create name designs, and Luke organized an animal center (which is why Margo was allowed to attend) with the help of a few others. In addition to our stations, Terupt's students had a yoga center, an origami table, a baseball card shop, and more. Plus, we had another 153 seventh graders participating!

Peter was our DJ and MC for the event. Everyone who

was at Mr. and Mrs. Terupt's wedding last year would agree, Peter did a great job of DJing there, so we were excited to have him doing this. We knew music would add to the atmosphere and help make it a high-energy and fun environment.

For my station, those completing name designs (with Danielle's assistance) got to bring their creations to me, where we used the paper drawings as templates and cut the name out of a piece of wood. The cutting was done with a jigsaw, so my father was there overseeing the operation because (1) it was his jigsaw, and (2) Principal Lee and Mrs. Williams said his supervision was mandatory since the activity involved running a power tool. I didn't argue with them on that point. It made good sense. And Terupt and Luke used *their* good sense when they put Peter's station as far away from my area as possible.

On the morning of the fair, Terupt asked Danielle to make a name design for me while my dad and I worked to get our station organized. Terupt wanted me to practice before any students or other visitors started arriving. I thought that was a good idea. Once we had everything set up, I turned the saw on and did a few warm-up cuts on scrap wood, and after that, I told Danielle I was ready.

"Anna," she yelled over to a nearby table, "I made you a name design. Jeffrey's waiting to help you cut it out."

Anna looked at Danielle with the same surprise I felt. "What do you need me for?" Anna asked.

"Mr. Terupt wants Jeffrey to practice helping someone cut their name out so he's ready for today. He asked me to make your name so Jeffrey could help you."

My mouth went instantly dry. I couldn't even swallow. What was Terupt thinking? Things were definitely better with the gang now. Ever since learning about the budget, we had come together, no questions asked. But Anna and I still weren't back to where we were before things fell apart.

I watched her get up from her scrapbooking table. She walked over to Danielle, who handed her the paper design, and then she came over to me.

"Huh-huh-hi," I croaked.

"Hi," she said.

I stood there on my weak legs staring at her, full of more nerves than I had before any wrestling match.

"Aren't you going to help me cut my name out?" she asked after a minute of me not moving or saying anything.

"What? Oh, yeah," I said.

She giggled.

I took the template from her, and as I did, my fingers brushed against hers and sent a jolt of electricity racing through my core. I taped the paper onto a block of pine. Then I showed Anna the saw and explained the safety features to her. Dad's number-one rule was always "Safety first." After giving her the rundown, I demonstrated how to use it—safely—by making a cut alongside the first letter A in her name. Then I handed her the tool—carefully—so that my fingers brushed up against hers again.

I watched her getting started, and kept watching her. I wasn't even looking at the wood or her cuts. I couldn't take my eyes from the side of her face.

"Jeffrey, are you going to help her or just stare at her all day?" Dad said. "You're liable to cut one of your fingers off if you don't start paying attention."

Dad's teasing had me turning beet red, almost as bad as if I'd tried putting hair dye all over my chin. I looked down and noticed that Anna had the blade twisting. It was about to break. I took ahold of the saw—with my hands wrapping around hers—and helped her back it out of the wood so that we could start the cut again. I felt Anna's warm breath against my cheek when she giggled this time.

Together, over the next several minutes, we managed to cut her beautiful name out. Those were the best minutes I'd had all year.

"Thank you, Jeffrey," Anna said when we were all done. "Everyone's going to love your station today."

I nodded, not knowing what to say. She turned, starting back toward her table, and that was when I found my voice. "Anna."

"Yeah?" she said, stopping and looking at me.

"Um, well, so next weekend is our last wrestling tournament. I have this big match, and I was hoping you might come and watch. It's at Perry Falls, which isn't too far from here, and Asher will be there."

"I'll think about it," she said, "but only if you're going to win."

"I'll win."

"Then I'll be there." She smiled.

It was at that moment that I knew Scott Winshall didn't stand a chance—not this time.

"Well, you're not quite as smooth with the ladies as you

are with your wrestling moves," Dad said, clapping me on the shoulder, "but you're getting there."

Before the fair ended, Terupt came up to me.

"You did a terrific job, Jeffrey. All of you did."

"We never would have been able to pull it off without you," I said.

Terupt nodded, but he didn't look as happy as I'd thought he would.

Peter

The highlight of the Everything Fair had to be when Luke put on an exhibition of sorts with his snake, Stanley. Poor Luke was so determined to help Mr. T by making the fair the most awesome thing to ever have happened at the junior high that he got a bit carried away. He had his show scheduled for eleven o'clock, which was when the second graders were visiting. Had Luke known about that class and who was in it, I'm sure he would've held his demonstration at a different time, but hey, that's why they say hindsight is twenty-twenty. Lesson learned, I guess.

At exactly eleven o'clock, I dimmed the lights and announced Luke's surprise show over my microphone. "All right, boys and girls," I called out in my best ringmaster voice. "The moment we've all been waiting for has finally arrived. We need you to gather around the animal center for a special show. You're the only class that gets to witness this amazing thing today."

I added that last part so the kids would get excited, but as I soon found out, they didn't need any extra encouragement. The entire class went bonkers and clamored over to Luke's area. They were dying to find out what surprise awaited them.

Luke remained calm and asked all the young boys and

girls to sit on the floor. They did, and their teachers and everyone else (meaning us) sat off to the side. Then, continuing in his patient way, Luke asked all the boys and girls to stop talking. They did. So far, so good. Next Luke knelt by the tank that he had resting on the floor nearby. He had the tank covered by a blanket so the second graders were still unaware of what lay underneath it. Up to this point, things had gone perfectly, but that was all about to change.

"Inside this tank resides Stanley, my four-foot ball python," Luke told all those eager faces.

"Whoa!" several little boys exclaimed, already getting wound up.

"Eww!" several little girls cried.

"Shh," Luke whispered, holding his finger against his nose. "I have Stanley covered by this blanket to help keep him calm. We have the lights dimmed to help keep him calm. It is extremely important that everyone stay quiet when I lift the blanket off his tank."

"What's he gonna do?" one little boy yelled out.

"Shh. Quiet, Donnie," his teacher said. "Let Luke finish explaining."

"I want to see him!" Donnie cried out.

"Quiet, Donnie!" a little girl with braids shouted.

"Shh," their teacher urged, glaring at both of them.

Her shushing wasn't working, I could see that, but Lukester did a good job of continuing with his show. That was the only way to keep Donnie from jumping out of his pants.

"Loud noises will make Stanley nervous and stress him out, and then you won't be able to see him perform," Luke explained to the kids. "You must stay quiet. Understand?"

"Yes," a chorus of small voices answered, all their heads nodding.

"Good," Luke said, gripping the corner of the blanket. He looked over his crowd, pausing for dramatic effect, amping those second graders up even more, which wasn't necessary or smart. Then, in one swift motion, he yanked the cover away, revealing Stanley.

"Whoa, he's awesome!" Donnie yelled.

Luke smiled from ear to ear.

"Shush, Donnie," the girl with braids shouted.

"I want one of those!" Donnie yelled.

"Don-nie!" the girl with braids shouted.

"Missy, stop yelling! Donnie, that goes for you, too!" their teacher snapped. She was yelling now, too.

Luke's smile was beginning to disappear, but he pressed on with his show. I wonder, did he really think Donnie and Missy and the rest of those second-grade munchkins were going to stay quiet for this next part when they couldn't contain themselves after just *seeing* Stanley?

"If you can quiet down—and stay quiet—then I'll move on with the show," Luke said. "Stanley is waiting to perform." The soft patience in his voice was gone and had been replaced by a shorter, harder tone.

The second graders grew silent—even Donnie. Everyone wanted to know what Luke planned to do next. The entire gym sat holding its breath.

Luke reached into the backpack he had sitting on the floor behind Stanley's tank and pulled out a see-through container. Inside it, a white mouse huddled in one corner. The whole class let out a gasp. Donnie was already on his feet.

Luke didn't hesitate. He lifted the top off Stanley's tank and dumped that furry little critter inside. Pandemonium erupted.

"Whoa!" Donnie shouted. It was too much. He couldn't take it. He started hopping up and down and pumping his fist. "Get it! Get it!" he yelled at the top of his lungs.

Missy and several other girls in her class started screaming, "*Ahhh!*"

A group of boys joined in with Donnie. "Get it! Get it!" they yelled. They couldn't contain themselves.

"Quiet!" Luke shouted. "Quiet! You're scaring Stanley! You're stressing him out!"

Forget it. There was no stopping them—any of them. They were out of control.

"Get it! Get it!"

"*Ahh!*"

"Quiet!"

Stanley didn't budge. Even with the furry little mouse scurrying around all over the place, he had no interest in performing. Luke threw the blanket back over the tank. He was done. He'd had it.

Donnie was mad. "That's a stupid snake," he said.

"Maybe if you weren't yelling, he would've done something," Luke said, all out of patience and smiles.

"Maybe if you gave him something better than that dumb mouse, he'd perform," Donnie said. Then, fast as lightning, the little rat grabbed Margo off Lexie's lap and hoisted her in the air. "Something like *this!*" Donnie cried, yanking the blanket and top off Stanley's tank and dangling Margo above it.

"*Ahh!*" the girls screamed.

"Margo!" Lexie shrieked.

That was when I stepped in and grabbed that little twerp by the back of his shirt. "Hey, Donnie," I whispered in his ear, "how about I stuff *you* in that cage with Stanley?" His eyes popped. I knew how to talk to him. Let's just say he reminded me of someone.

I'm not sure if Margo was excited to see me, or if Donnie had scared the bejeepers out of her, but she started peeing all over the front of him. Donnie started crying, and his class started squealing and laughing, especially Missy. I took Margo from Donnie, and his teacher took him by the hand and escorted him out of the gym. I could feel Margo's little heart pitter-pattering against my chest as I cradled her in my arms. I carried her over to Lexie.

"Thank you, Peter," she said.

The way she said it, and the way she looked at me, got my heart racing faster than the dog's.

"You wait and see. Donnie and Missy will end up dating down the road," I said.

"Sometimes opposites attract," Lexie said. "We know how that works."

Now my heart almost stopped. I couldn't get any more words out, so I settled on a smile—one that Lexie returned. This was definitely the highlight of my fair.

LUKE

The only hiccup that occurred at the Everything Fair was during my show with Stanley, but Peter helped me out there, and Mr. Terupt talked to me afterward.

LUKE'S SEVENTH-GRADE SURVIVAL GUIDE
TIP #15: When planning a presentation or show of sorts, it's best to know your audience beforehand.

"I'm sorry Stanley didn't respond the way you were hoping," Mr. Terupt said. "I think our friends got a little excited."

"Yeah, just a little," I said.

"Don't let that get you down, Lukester. Look at this." Mr. Terupt swept his arms around the gym. "This is the result of your idea. It takes a great leader to dream this up, and a great leader to get people working together to make it happen. You should be proud. This fair has been awesome."

Mr. Terupt wasn't the only one to think our fair turned out awesome, either. I overheard several different teachers talking throughout the day, saying things like "This is incredible" and "I don't know how Mr. Terupt pulls it off, but I can tell you it wouldn't be happening without him around." Everyone who came through had a wonderful time. Mrs. Terupt and Mrs. Williams told me how much they loved it. Our superintendent, Dr. Knowles, even showed up and expressed the extreme pride he felt in our work.

"This is beyond impressive," he said to Mrs. Williams and Principal Lee.

"Mr. Terupt has a way of inspiring kids and getting them to do amazing things," she told him.

After hearing things like that, I thought for sure we'd done enough to keep Mr. Terupt safe, and I couldn't have been happier. Then Lexie went ahead and made my day even more wonderful.

"Luke, like, this fair has been a lot of fun," she said, taking me by surprise.

"Thanks," I said, "for helping to make it happen."

"There's something else I wanted to tell you," she said. "Nothing happened in that closet between Jessica and Jeffrey. They were in there talking about Anna the whole time. I think you're smart enough to see that those two like each other. If Jessica had it her way, it would've been you in the closet with her."

I stood there dumbfounded.

"And one more thing," she said. "I'm sorry that I even had us play that game at the party."

I never expected Lexie to be the one to make me feel so much better about the party and Jessica, but she did.

LUKE'S SEVENTH-GRADE SURVIVAL GUIDE
TIP #16: Sometimes it's okay to let girls do the talking.

The Everything Fair was a gigantic success. My popularity was instantly restored because I was the guy who got things done. We raised close to six hundred dollars, which our class had already voted to put to immediate use by purchasing a sno-cone machine for the cafeteria. The gang and I had other ideas about how to spend that money, but then I'd have lured my grade to the fair under false pretenses. I'd promised them the money we made would go right back to them, and I had to keep my promises. Besides, everyone there saw what an inspirational teacher Mr. Terupt was, so the fair had accomplished what it was supposed to—or so I thought.

It had been a terrific day for everyone, but that all changed the moment Anna and Danielle came rushing back into the gym from Nurse Sharon's office.

ANNA

Before the fair ended, Danielle started feeling shaky. She was out of juice in her kit, so I went with her to the nurse. It made me nervous whenever she got like that, especially when she didn't have sugar to treat herself with right away, but I was still nothing like Nurse Sharon. When we showed up unexpectedly and told her the situation, she got all frazzled.

Danielle and I remained calm. We knew the drill. Danielle sat down while I got her some juice. She drank it, and then we waited. After having a low blood sugar reading, Danielle was supposed to treat herself, and then wait until her symptoms went away. If her symptoms persisted, then she would need to do another finger stick to recheck, and continue to treat herself.

The waiting was torture for Nurse Sharon. She had some crazy fear that the juice wasn't going to work one of these times. Not surprisingly, her jitters spread to her mouth and she got going a mile a minute with who else but Mrs. Rollins.

"Did you go to that fair today?" Nurse Sharon asked Mrs. Rollins.

"Yes, I sure did."

"Wasn't it something?" Nurse Sharon said. "There was so much to see: origami, animals, knitting, wood burning, LEGOs—"

"It's a shame," Mrs. Rollins said. "Those poor kids really put their hearts and souls into it, and that Mr. Terupt seems like a wonderful man, but if push comes to shove, he'll still be one of the first people on the chopping block."

I'm not sure if Danielle's symptoms were gone, but she was right behind me, running down the hall. We rushed into the gym and found the gang as fast as we could.

"Luke was right," I said, fighting to catch my breath. "We just overheard Mrs. Rollins talking. . . . She said if push . . . comes to shove . . . Mr. Terupt . . . will be one of the first people to go."

"What does that mean?" Peter asked.

"It means what we feared *could* be true, *is* true," Luke said. "This fair hasn't changed anything. If the budget fails, Mr. Terupt is out. It's time for another campaign—Saving Mr. Terupt."

PART THREE

HONK FOR
MR. TERUPT !!

SAVE
MR.
TERUPT

Vote
YES!

MARCH

Danielle

Luke's not the only one who can come up with good ideas. It was my pancreas that had quit working, not my brain.

Anna had mentioned the wrestling tournament that she planned on going to for Jeffrey, and that got me thinking. Wrestling meant boys—lots of them. And adolescent boys must be among the hungriest creatures on the planet. I know because I watch them in amazement every day at lunch. There were also sure to be lots of hungry fans at such a big, all-day event. It seemed to me we could make a bundle if we were to have a bake sale at the tournament. If good teaching wouldn't change people's minds, maybe some cash would.

"That's a great idea!" Luke exclaimed. "And then we'll present our money to the Board of Education members at the meeting. It could be enough to keep them from making certain cuts."

"Let's do it," Peter said. "I'll get Miss Catalina baking around the clock."

"Vincent will make stuff for us too," Lexie said.

"We can call it the Budget Bake Sale so Mr. Terupt won't know we're doing it for him. Everyone knows about the budget issue, just not about which teachers might be cut," Jessica said.

It was decided. Everyone loved my idea, including Grandma. When I got home I told her all about it, and she immediately went to the cupboards and started taking an inventory of all the ingredients we had and those we needed to get.

Since I'd been diagnosed with diabetes, Grandma had been reading more and more about the different foods that were good for me. She'd always commanded the kitchen, but lately she had even more energy in there. She was determined to come up with some healthy options for me. Grandma was the best baker this side of the Mississippi, but all the different sugar-free recipes she was trying left much to be desired. For the bake sale, we agreed it was best to make the good old-fashioned stuff.

It was just the two of us knee-deep in flour when I got up the courage to ask her something I'd been thinking about lately. "Grandma?"

"Yes?"

"How old were you when you first took notice of a boy? I mean, noticed a boy 'cause you liked him. I mean, liked him more than just a friend."

"What's got you asking that question?"

"Well, all my friends seem to be liking each other in that more-than-friends way. And I was just wondering when that might happen to me."

Grandma stood up from the oven and turned around. She placed the warm tray of brownies on the counter beside me.

Then she wiped her hands on a towel and took a sip of her coffee. "Danielle," she began, "you shouldn't feel bad about this. There are plenty of women who don't get distracted with spending time on silly crushes, but wait until the real thing comes along and sweeps them off their feet. That's how it was for me. And that didn't happen until I was twenty. Nowadays, that sort of thing seems to happen even later, so don't be in a rush. There are some things in life worth waiting for."

"Grandpa swept you off your feet?" I said, and grinned.

"Now don't you go and tell him I said that."

Grandma and I spent the whole weekend making cookies and brownies, breads and pies. Mom helped, too. It was a lot of fun, and a lot of work, but we were willing to do everything we could to help protect Mr. Terupt's job.

The Budget Bake Sale was our second attempt aimed at saving Mr. Terupt, our first official one since we'd learned his job was indeed on the line. But it wouldn't be our last.

LUKE

I met the girls around midmorning at Perry Falls School to set up for our Budget Bake Sale. After Danielle came up with this brilliant idea, Mom called the principal there and got permission for us to hold our fund-raiser. I was worried they wouldn't want another school making money off their event, but they were understanding and said yes. The girls brought the signs and baked goods, and I was responsible for bringing the folding tables, cash box, and brand-new sno-cone machine. I felt better about having spent so much money on it now that it would be helping our cause. We had everything we needed. Peter and Jeffrey and Mr. Terupt had wrestling to focus on for the day, and that was good. We didn't want Mr. Terupt involved or worrying about us. He still didn't know we knew his job was on the line, and we wanted to keep it that way. Even though we weren't saying anything about him, he was Mr. Terupt, and if he were to go poking around the Budget Bake Sale, he might get suspicious.

By the time we arrived, the gym was already packed with people. Coaches shouting out instructions. Teammates yelling words of encouragement. Girlfriends biting fingernails.

Mothers and fathers either squirming in their seats or hollering at the referees. It was nothing like a Boy Scout meeting, that's for sure. It was nuts, but none of that was what Lexie noticed.

"What's wrong, Lexie?" Jessica asked after seeing her disgusted expression.

"I can't go in there. That smell isn't human."

"You'll get used to it," Anna said. "Trust me. I don't even smell the farm anymore."

"That's worse than a farm!" Lexie cried.

"I might have to agree with you about that," Danielle said.

"I'll have to wash my clothes a million times after sitting in there," Lexie carried on. "That stench will eat the nail polish right off my fingers."

"Don't worry," I told her. "You don't have to go in there if you don't want to. We're going to set up for the bake sale right there." I pointed to an area in the hallway a short distance from the gym.

Lexie let out a big sigh. "Good," she said.

It took us about twenty minutes to get the tables set up and arranged with all the food on display. In addition to Danielle and her grandmother's many delicious-looking treats, Danielle had also whipped up some fancy signs listing the various prices for our different items. At fifty cents a pop, we were set to make a couple hundred dollars on brownies alone.

Anna came prepared with her camera. She and I had talked about that ahead of time. She was going to be busy getting potential pictures for the yearbook, but we also discussed getting as many shots of Mr. Terupt as possible, knowing we might find a purpose for them later on in our campaign.

We had barely gotten ourselves situated when people started coming up to our tables and buying goods.

LUKE'S SEVENTH-GRADE SURVIVAL GUIDE
TIP #17: Should you find yourself in need of money, a well-organized bake sale—one featuring a variety of tasty choices—has the potential to be a terrific fundraiser, especially one that takes place at a wrestling tournament.

Alexia

Between Vincent, Miss Catalina, and Danielle and her grandma, we had a few hundred brownies and cookies, and another table loaded with pies and breads. We were busy selling all day long.

I hated leaving Mom alone, but she told me to go.

"You sitting at home isn't helping me get any better," she said. "If I can think of you as being happy, that *does* help, so go. Your friends need you, and besides, Margo will keep me company."

As much as I wanted to be there with the gang, it was only because of Mom's insistence that I ended up sitting outside that smelly gym full of gross boys. But I'm glad I did, 'cause like, the girls and I had a lot of catching up to do. In between all our selling, the four of us huddled together and got back to being besties.

"So, like, what's new?" I asked them.

The way Anna and Danielle looked at each other, it was obvious there was something new with them. Something they couldn't wait to tell me and Jessica. "What is it?" I asked.

"We've got another wedding coming up," Anna said, all

giddy. "Charlie proposed to my mom." She and Danielle went on, telling us all about Charlie's romantic proposal. ". . . and the ring . . . and a snowman . . . and words in the snow . . . and it was all just so lovely." She had us laughing. "I've got a dad now!" she cheered.

"I saw mine," Jessica said.

Things went from fun and light to serious real fast.

"You did?" Anna and Danielle said in total disbelief. "How? Where?"

Jessica told us everything. First, she filled Anna and Danielle in on the crazy plan we had hatched to get her to the retreat, and then she told us about running into her father, the divorce papers, and all that they said to each other in those few minutes.

"A couple of days after the retreat, his letters started arriving," she said. "I get one from him every day. He sends them to my mother, too, but she hasn't opened any."

"What do they say?" I asked.

"Nothing really."

She'd had enough. I understood. I could talk about Mom's cancer only so much. So when Jessica grew quiet, I reached into my purse and pulled out the surprise I had for Danielle.

"I made this for you," I said, handing her my creation. "It's a designer bag for your diabetes kit. If you've got to cart that thing around with you everywhere, you might as well do it with some style. Like, make it a fashion accessory."

"I love it," she said.

"And like, just so you know, I think the way you're handling everything is amazing."

"Thank you, Lexie," Danielle said.

"You should be around her when her sugars are out of whack," Anna said. "That's when she's amazing."

"Oh, be quiet," Danielle said.

The two of them carried on like an old married couple.

"Lex, you're really getting good with that sewing machine," Jessica said. "The bag is beautiful."

"I've been sewing more lately," I said. "Like right now I'm making a purse for Margo, but before that I made Mom a few different things. . . ." My voice trailed off.

Anna and Danielle looked at me without saying anything. They weren't stupid. They'd heard something different in my voice when I mentioned Mom. Like, I couldn't help it. It was hard for me to hide my feelings when talking about her. Jessica didn't say a word.

"I've been praying," I said, "but, like, I don't know if I've been doing it the right way."

"There is no right way," Danielle said. "As long as it comes from your heart, he'll listen."

I told them about Mom's breast cancer and her chemo and her recovery. I talked about it until I got tired of talking about it, like Jessica.

It was good having my friends back, and it was just in time. The Budget Bake Sale had gone smoothly, but things were about to get really rocky.

Jeffrey

The last time I squared off against Winshall I couldn't calm my nerves, especially after seeing that Coach Terupt was there—and that Anna wasn't. Her absence had me angry and upset, and anything but focused. I remember getting mad at myself for even thinking about her at that moment.

Today was a different story. Having Coach Terupt there made me excited. He believed in me, just like I believed in him. Asher was propped up on my dad's shoulders, cheering. And I found Anna sitting in the bleachers, smiling down at me. She'd taken a break from the bake sale so she could watch my match. She gave me a small wave and mouthed the words *good luck*. There were no nerves today. When I looked across that mat at Scott Winshall warming up, I knew I had everything on my side.

The amazing thing about a small school gym is if you put enough people in there, and give them a reason to scream and holler and go crazy cheering, the place can become deafening. You might as well be in a football stadium, that's how loud it can get. Still, when I zeroed in on my match with Winshall and visualized getting my hand raised in victory, the sounds all around me disappeared. I was ready. Peter had just won his match, capping off his undefeated season. I had trained with Peter, and seeing him win gave me even more confidence. Now it was my turn.

Every ounce of me felt strong, starting with our handshake. But Scott Winshall hadn't "won them all" for no reason. He was ready, too. And when the whistle blew, he came at me. We fought with our arms, pushing and pulling on each other, battling to get position. Winshall struck first. He darted in on a single-leg. I fought and fought to defend it, but he was able to finish the takedown as we rolled out of bounds. Winshall took an early 2–0 lead. On my way back to the center I glanced off to the side, and though I couldn't hear anything, I saw Coach Terupt and Peter hollering. I saw Asher clapping. And I spotted Anna up in the stands cheering.

I got set on bottom, and when the whistle blew, I exploded to my feet. Winshall couldn't keep me down. I escaped, making the score 2–1, and, with less than twenty seconds to go in the period, I found my opening. I snapped Winshall's head down, and as he fought to straighten back up, I blasted him with a hard double-leg, tackling him to the mat. The period ended with me in the lead 3–2. The gym was going nuts. Looking at Winshall, it was clear he knew he was in a dogfight.

The second period was more of the same back-and-forth struggle, and so was the third. It all boiled down to the end. With less than thirty seconds to go in the match, Winshall was up by one point. The score was 10–9, and we were on our feet. Takedown wins it, I told myself. I turned up the pressure, thinking of all my early-morning runs and extra push-ups. I went after it, knowing that if I didn't let go, there would be no happy ending. With time dwindling, I faked a shot to one side. Winshall reacted, setting up my single the other way. I hit it quick and got in on his leg. He fell over my back in a sprawl, and I immediately scooted my knees under me. As I lifted my head and came out the back door, I saw the final seconds ticking off the clock. I scored the winning takedown at the buzzer.

The gym went bonkers. Scott Winshall had been defeated! The referee raised my hand, and I sprinted off the mat and into Coach Terupt's arms. Coach Brobur and Peter were there to slap me on the back and congratulate me.

"You won the war, kid," Coach Brobur said. "Way to go."

"You were awesome!" Peter cheered.

"That's the first of many, Jeffrey," Coach Terupt said. "You looked terrific. Way to fight!"

I couldn't stop smiling. And what I found out is, after a win like that, there are a lot of people who want to congratulate you. I shook all sorts of hands and said lots of thank-yous—to teammates and even kids from opposing schools. Beating Scott Winshall made me an instant celebrity, but eventually, Asher got tired of waiting for his turn. He snuck by all those bodies and ran up and hugged me, wrapping his arms around my legs in his own double-leg attack.

"Yay, Ree!" he said. "You best!"

I bent down to his level. "Yeah, I did it. Thanks, buddy."

He took a step back and opened his hand to show me the candy hearts he was holding. We still had some left over from Valentine's. Dad had a dish of them sitting out in the house, and he was always picking them up and giving them to Mom in a playful way, flirting with her. After the struggles they'd had, I was fine with their displays of affection—at home. The letters on the hearts Asher was holding now were beginning to smudge from being squeezed to death in his sweaty palm, but you could still make out what they said.

"You want me to have one?" I asked him.

He nodded.

I took a red candy. "Thanks."

"Hi, Asher," Anna said, coming up behind him.

Asher turned to see who had just called his name. "This is Anna, buddy. You remember her?"

Anna's smile was quickly matched by the one on Asher's face. He looked back at me and showed me his candies again. "Would you like to give her one?"

He nodded.

I chuckled. Asher had clearly noticed how Dad liked to give the candies to Mom, and now it was his turn. "Go for it," I said, wondering if he was also planning to give Anna a squeeze or smooch like Dad often did with Mom. I couldn't wait to see this.

My little brother walked up to Anna with more confidence than I had just wrestled with and gave her his heart. Anna took the candy and said, "Thank you." Then she read it and burst out laughing. " 'Hot stuff'!" she exclaimed. Asher grinned from ear to ear. "You sure know how to talk to a girl," she told him. Then she bent over, wrapping her arms around him, and he planted his lips on her cheek.

I stood there wishing it was me sharing that hug with Anna. Then I realized Asher had just showed me how to do it. This was my chance. I had to go for it, like I did in my match, or else I'd lose out. I glanced at the candy heart in my hand. The perfect phrase was printed on it. I walked over to her.

"I have one for you too," I said, holding out my palm. The words BE MINE were faceup, staring at her.

She took my heart and looked at me. "I thought you'd never ask."

It was like I'd just won my big match all over again. I sucked in a breath so deep that it lifted me onto my tippy-toes. Before that moment, I hadn't been breathing, but now I felt like I could fly. When I exhaled, I came down and stepped closer to her. Our fingers found each other same as they had during the Everything Fair, except this time we didn't let go. There's no telling how long we would've stayed like that, holding hands and staring into each other's faces, if it weren't for Asher.

"My-my," he said, pointing.

I looked across the gym, but didn't see anything.

"My-ill," he said, this time with more determination, and still pointing.

"It sounds like he's saying 'Michael,'" Anna said. "Do you know anyone named Michael?"

Asher looked at us and nodded. I thought back to last year, to that night when I was working on Terupt's wedding gift with Dad, when I told him that I thought Michael had sent Asher to us. I thought about Christmas morning, when Asher had tapped the angel on the cover of his new Bible and said, "My-my." Michael had been with us all along. He'd always be with us. I squeezed Anna's hand.

"Michael taught me how to love and not to quit," I said.

I had a lot to tell her, and I knew now that I would.

Peter

The Perry Falls Wrestling Tournament was a day filled with much to remember, but it was what happened after my match that shocked me, and it was what I saw after it was all over that stopped me dead in my tracks—twice.

I capped off my undefeated season with a win in the finals. The kids in my weight class weren't nearly as tough as Jeffrey and Zack. Having the best training partners was a definite advantage for me. Mr. T knew what he was doing by getting us together.

After having my arm raised, I raced off the mat and got a big hug and congratulations from T and Coach Brobur. Then I slapped Jeffrey's hand and got set to cheer him on. I'd been more excited for his match against Scott Winshall than I had been for my own.

Jeffrey wrestled the best six minutes of his life and won it at the buzzer with one of the moves we'd learned at camp. It was awesome! I was so happy for him, and not at all surprised that he'd won. I was more shocked by what happened after that.

Zack came over to congratulate me on my win, which was cool of him, but then Lexie came over, too. I hadn't seen her all day, so she must have snuck in at the end. I thought she was coming to talk to Zack—and so did he. "Hey, Lexie," he said, reaching his arm out, expecting her to cuddle into him like she was his girl or something. But Lexie blew by him, and next thing I knew, she was hugging me—and it felt better than when I won my match.

"Great job," she whispered in my ear, squeezing me.

When she let go and turned back around, you could see in Zack's face that the score was even now. She'd just crushed him. And even though he deserved it, part of her must've felt sorry for him—he wasn't all bad—because she told him about some Meghan girl who supposedly had a thing for him, and then he left us alone to find her. But trust me, after our hug, I think he got the hint. It was more than a hug of congratulations.

"I thought *you* had a thing for him," I said.

"Are you kidding? You tried growing whiskers overnight. That's the sweetest thing anyone's ever done for me. Well, one of the sweetest. And dumbest," she said.

We stayed there for the next five minutes, laughing and talking together. Lexie filled me in on the success of the bake sale. Miss Catalina's brownies were gone, and so were Vincent's and Danielle and her grandmother's. The girls had made a killing.

"That's awesome," I said.

Then she told me all about Charlie's proposal and how excited Anna and Danielle were to be sisters and how romantic the proposal was.

"Charlie wrote the words *Will You Marry Me* in the snow," she said. "Isn't that so sweet?"

"Wow! He must've had to pee two or three times to write all those letters," I said.

"He didn't do it like that, you butthead!"

Things were getting back to the way they used to be, and I couldn't have been happier. It had already been an unbelievable day, but there was still more to come.

"My ride's going to be here soon," Lexie said. "Will you wait outside with me?"

"Sure," I said. I pulled my wrestling shoes off. "These are T's old ones," I told her, holding them up for her to see. "I don't want to get them dirty."

She plugged her nose. "It's a good thing we're going outside."

We were only out there for a minute or two before Vincent pulled up. I recognized his car. And then there was Margo going nuts in the window. She was standing on the lap of the person riding shotgun. It was when I finally saw who was sitting in the passenger seat that I was stopped dead in my tracks, my breath taken from me.

Lexie's mother sat there looking pale, with a scarf wrapped around her head. I knew Lexie was the queen of fashion, but something told me her mother's scarf wasn't only a stylish accessory. I might not know everything, but I knew Lexie's mom was sick.

I stared into Lexie's face. There was so much I wanted to tell her, but nothing came out. What do you say in a moment like that?

"It's okay, Peter," she said.

"Why didn't you tell me?"

"Well, let me think about that. How about, for starters, we haven't been talking until now, you stupid-head. But like, now that you know, I don't need you acting any different around me. Got it?" She jabbed me in the chest with her finger.

I nodded.

"I mean, don't joke about my boobs, because that's a sensitive topic, but other than that, I just need you to be Peter. Okay?"

"Okay," I said.

Lexie was so serious telling me how it was going to be that I didn't even notice when Margo escaped from Vincent's vehicle and made a beeline for us. I didn't realize until I felt my sock growing wet and warm. I jumped and yanked my foot away.

Now Lexie was giggling. She bent down and picked up her fur ball as I danced with my leg in the air. "She's just marking her territory," Lexie said. "She likes you."

"Great," I said. "I love it when she pees all over me."

Lexie was all smiles. And then, all of a sudden, she leaned closer and kissed me on the cheek. "That's *my* mark," she said.

Once again, my breath had been taken from me. I watched her climb into Vincent's car, and I waved to them as they drove away.

My head was spinning. The day had been a whirl, with more crazy twists and turns than Jeffrey's match against Winshall—and it wasn't over yet. The next thing I saw was T sprinting out of the school and across the parking lot.

"Mr. T, is everything all right?" I yelled.

No answer. He was already in his car and speeding away. What was wrong?

ANNA

I took photos of Peter and Jeffrey wrestling—action shots—and of each of them getting their arms raised in victory. (These were definite possibilities for the yearbook.) I got a couple of Mr. Brobur coaching, and I had several nice ones of Mr. Terupt. But my favorite picture from the day was the one of Jeffrey and Asher. This captured a special part of the afternoon.

Jeffrey had given me his heart and opened it up to me. His story of Michael, the brother he lost, blew me away. As I sat next to him on the bleacher, listening to him talk, I was on the verge of tears.

"Don't cry," he told me. "It's a sad story with a happy ending. Asher's here now. I've always thought Michael wanted me to find him, wanted him in our lives, and now I know I was right."

I snapped my photo of Jeffrey and Asher posing side by side after that. Their arms wrapped around each other with so much love between them that I could feel it. And with Michael's enduring spirit holding them and keeping them strong.

It was only seconds later when Mr. Terupt took us by

surprise. "I've got to go," he said. There was panic in his voice. Fear in his face. "Mrs. Terupt is on her way to the hospital in preterm labor."

Then he was gone, running out the door. I didn't even get to say anything, not that I knew what to say. I was scared for him—and Mrs. Terupt. It was then that I felt Jeffrey's hand take mine. But it wasn't a romantic gesture. It was just the two of us holding each other, because experience had taught us that was what we needed during scary times like these— and we were just getting started.

Jessica

Dear Journal,

The highly anticipated budget meeting was held in the high school cafeteria. The long rectangular lunch tables that normally occupied the space had been removed. The speckled tile floor had been swept and mopped and was now lined with chairs from wall to wall. Sitting opposite the chairs, behind a table and microphone at the front of the room, were the members of the school board and Dr. Knowles, our superintendent.

I'd never attended a school board meeting before, and from what I understood, that was true for most people. These meetings were often described as quiet and orderly, with few, if any, spectators. By all accounts, they were boring. But none of that was true tonight. Tonight's meeting was brand-new territory for our community.

It was a standing-room-only crowd. Mr. Terupt was not there, however; he was at home with Mrs. Terupt. They were able to stop her early labor with some medicine at the hospital, but she was now on bed rest until she delivered. There would be a long-term sub finishing the year with her students.

I sat on the floor along with the rest of the gang, our backs pressed against the cinder-block wall. We were there to listen but not be seen, like mice, huddled together in a corner. It was hot for March, and the room was packed with warm bodies. The windows were cracked open, but there was no breeze and no air circulating. It became stifling, like a sauna. Whenever we leaned forward, our sweat marks stamped the concrete, but it wasn't just the room heating up. The people attending were hot. The folks I'd seen at that wrestling tournament were nothing compared to this spirited bunch.

The men and women sitting behind the front table conducted routine business to start—and the room waited. Some people talked in hushed whispers with their neighbors, others sat with folded hands in their laps, and some busied themselves with their phones. After fifteen minutes of the boring stuff, we reached the point in the agenda that everyone had come for.

The man sitting in the middle seat pushed back from the table and stood. "Good evening. My name is Dominic Murphy. I am the president of your school board. I'd like to start by thanking all of you for your attendance and attention to this matter. Clearly, we find ourselves in a difficult position with this year's budget."

That was all Mr. Murphy managed to get out of his mouth. The word "budget" was almost enough to incite a riot. An old man sitting in the back row shot up from his chair. "If you'd make some cuts and stop hiking up our taxes, we wouldn't have this problem."

"Thank you, Harold," Mr. Murphy said. "We'd all like to keep our taxes from going up, but that's hard to do when we receive less and less aid from the state, and the cost of operating continues to rise."

"Then make cuts!" Harold roared back.

"Making cuts is not an easy thing to do," Mr. Murphy explained, somehow still managing to keep his composure, "and I'll remind you that we did that last year in order to pass the budget then. We eliminated a librarian position, three different modified athletic programs, and a custodial position. In other words, people lost their jobs and our kids lost opportunities. That's not a trend we're hoping to continue."

"My taxes going up year after year is not a trend *I* want to see continue," Harold retorted, followed by a chorus of "yeahs."

A woman in the middle of the crowd sprang from her chair and fired back. "What exactly do you want them to cut?"

"That's what those hotshots sitting behind the table are supposed to figure out, but they don't seem to be doing that. How about starting with the pay raise them teachers keep getting every year? From what I can tell, they're doing less and less, still enjoying their summers off, and getting paid more and more for it."

Again, Harold's remarks were met by a chorus of "yeahs," and that was when my blood started to boil. How dare this man speak negatively about teachers? Fortunately, I wasn't the only one feeling that way. Danielle's grandmother was right there with me.

"Stop your blasphemy, Harold," Grandma Evelyn snapped. I felt Danielle stiffen. "You didn't know enough to respect your teachers when you were in school, so I'm not sure why we'd expect you to show them any respect today, but disgracing them is not the answer."

There was a strong round of clapping after Grandma Evelyn said her piece. I don't know if it was her remarks, or if Harold was scared of her, or both, but for the first time all night he didn't have anything more to say.

Mr. Murphy seized this opportunity to interject and present the board's newest proposal. "Despite the extreme difficulties the board faced in doing so, we've gone ahead and made additional cuts to this year's budget," he explained. "Our new plan will reduce taxes *some*, but probably not as much as many of you would like. However, we're hoping you can meet us halfway on this."

Mr. Murphy took the next several minutes to talk numbers, and while he did, my mind wandered—all the way back to California, to when Dad was a part of my life, and he had me read one of his all-time favorite books from growing up. I still remember how he held the worn paperback out to me, and before letting go he looked at me and said, "I've been waiting for the day when I would give this to you. Take extra care of it, Jessica."

"I will," I promised.

I read *The Phantom Tollbooth* and loved it. As I read, I pictured my father as a little boy gripping the pages of the same wonderful story. Together we traveled with the character Milo to a magical place where there were peculiar characters and a thought-provoking feud. Fantasies rank with fairy tales for me; they aren't my favorite. But this particular story grabbed my attention because of the battle at its core. That battle, the one taking place in a magical world, suddenly seemed to be the very fight I was witnessing. For me, the question before our town was simple: Which is more important, numbers or letters?

Before finishing his presentation, Mr. Murphy explained to the packed room that if the budget failed, then the board would be forced to take more drastic measures—measures that would include the elimination of several teaching positions. Mr. Murphy stressed once more that the board was hoping to avoid these consequences. Then he listed the positions that were on the chopping block: a high school guidance counselor and business teacher, an eighth-grade technology teacher, and two different elementary positions. Because of seniority, we knew that meant Mr. Terupt.

If the budget failed, it was because numbers were more important in our community. Being the person I am, that did not sit well with me. That would not deliver a happy ending. Letters, words, and stories are my passion; it has always been that way. When I finished *The Phantom Tollbooth* and returned it to my father, he had asked me then, "Well, Jessica, which do you think is more important?"

"Letters," I said. "I can't imagine not being able to put letters together to tell a story or to express my thoughts and feelings."

Dad smiled at me. "Someday you're going to do great things with the letters you put together. I know it."

Whether I was ready or not, the time for me to do great things was upon me.

With letters to put together,
Jessica

P.S. Luke spoke at the meeting, and so did Lexie's mom. Their words didn't make me hot with anger; they warmed my heart. Because of them I left that meeting with hope—and with my hand itching to write.

LUKE

I never thought I had it in me. My parents took me on that trip to our nation's capital, and I spent the week reading all those famous quotes and speeches by our founding fathers and legendary presidents and other great leaders from the past, and I was convinced that wasn't something I could ever do—but I was wrong.

Mr. Brobur had asked us back in the beginning of the year to tell him what determined an organism's phenotype. I knew the answer then, but I understood it now. Other than one's genetic makeup (your genotype), it is the environment that contributes to what characteristics you ultimately express (your phenotype). You see, hydrangea flowers with identical genotypes can range from blue-violet to pink, depending on the acidity of the soil they're growing in. I was like a pink hydrangea waiting to become blue. I had the genes to be a dynamic leader, but I didn't know it because the environment had never been right to bring that out in me—that is, until now. I only needed a topic that I was truly passionate about. When Mr. Murphy got done explaining the school board's plan, and that Mr. Terupt would be out of a job if the newest proposal didn't pass, I became that leader.

"My name is Luke Bennett," I said, standing before all those people. "Mr. William Terupt was my fifth- and sixth-grade teacher. I was lucky enough to have him for two years.

"They haven't made a test yet that I can't ace. I like tests. I like how you get a definite score, a percentage, and an answer. I like numbers, how you can use them to calculate perimeters and areas—and test scores. We live in a world today in which a school's report card is based on student test scores, so you should like me.

"But try as you might, you'll never be able to measure the impact Mr. Terupt has had on us." All at once the gang rose from the floor and stood beside me. "His influence will be with us for the rest of our lives, helping us to make a difference in all that we set out to do. No test will ever reflect that.

"Mr. Terupt's one of the teachers who will be cut if you don't pass the budget. He's someone we should be bending over backwards to keep, not holding over a cliff. I hope all of you will remember that before casting your vote."

I walked to the front of the room and placed the money from our Budget Bake Sale on the table in front of all the school board members. "My friends and I have worked hard to raise funds for your budget," I said. "We'd like to give you this money to help. You should know, we're prepared to do whatever it takes to save Mr. Terupt."

LUKE'S SEVENTH-GRADE SURVIVAL GUIDE
TIP #18: What it is that motivates you to greater lengths than you've ever known, that brings qualities out in you that you never knew you had, might just show up unexpectedly, so be ready, for that thing is your passion, and you must pursue it.

There wasn't anything I was more passionate about than saving Mr. Terupt.

Alexia

Luke got to his feet and like, told that room full of people some of the nicest and truest things I could ever think to say about Teach. I was so proud of him. He spoke for all of us. I wished that Teach was there to hear him, but he was at home with Mrs. Teach.

After Luke got done with what he had to say, things got really quiet. It was the sort of quiet that you could hear. That was when my mother got to her feet. I'd tried telling her to stay home, that being around all those people and germs wasn't a good idea for someone in her condition, but she wouldn't listen.

"Alexia, you do these things when it's about someone who means something to you. And besides, these people need a good strong woman to tell them a thing or two. I'm going."

Danielle's grandma was more woman than that stupid Harold man could handle, but my mother still decided to stand up and say a little something too. She wore one of the knit hats I'd made her, and she looked tired, but somehow, somewhere, she found the strength. And when she did get up, she commanded attention like I'd never seen before. I thought I was good, but I had a long ways to go before I matched her.

"Someone who inspires our children to lead, like we just saw from Luke, is a person I want to keep around here as long as possible. Our children are destined to do great things in this world after having teachers like Mr. Terupt.

"These kids are here because they understand compassion and what it means to care for one another. What it means to put someone else before yourself. Mr. Terupt taught them that.

"Trust me, there will come a time for each of you when you'll want and need others to be there for you. I hope you do not find yourself alone when that time comes, because hating the world and everyone on the school board because your taxes are going up isn't going to make you feel better in the end. We need to be there for our teachers now."

The quiet that followed Mom's words wasn't just one you could hear, but one that you felt. I was proud of Luke, and beyond proud of my mother. She didn't just come to the meeting for Teach, but for all our teachers, and for me and the rest of my friends. And for all the kids coming after us who should have Teach.

The funny thing was, after Mom said her thing or two, I wasn't as scared of her cancer anymore, 'cause like, I knew she had too much love and fight mixed together inside her for it to win.

Danielle

Dear God,

There's a whole lot going on down here, and I know you know that, but I've got to tell you about it. First of all, thank you for taking care of Mrs. Terupt and her baby, and not letting anything real bad happen. Please stay with them. They still have a ways to go.

Now, for that meeting tonight. The only place I've ever been with that many people all lined up, sitting in rows and facing the front, was in church, when we were gathered there for you. It wasn't like that. People weren't showing any signs of peace or passing smiles to one another. People were on their feet and ready to fight—including Grandma. After that old man, Harold, got done blowing his top, Grandma sprang to her feet and let him have it. I was feeling shaky during all that, and it wasn't because my sugars were low. Of course, after Grandma got done, I'm pretty sure Harold was shaking more than me.

I'm shaking again now, God. The money we raised wasn't enough to change anything. Please make that vote turn out the way we need it to. I honestly don't think we could ever recover from losing Mr. Terupt. Please.

Amen.

Danielle

APRIL

LUKE

Mr. Terupt was in trouble. There was no time to waste. If the budget didn't pass, the best teacher in the entire world wasn't going to be our teacher anymore. He would be taken from us. Having him taken alive almost seemed worse than what we had feared as fifth graders. I wasn't letting him go without a fight, and the rest of the gang was right there with me.

"We can't just sit and wait, not this time," I said.

We were gathered around a table, whispering during silent study hall. I had recently managed to get my seventh and eighth periods switched. This was possible because it didn't involve any of my major classes. I only had to flip-flop my initial study hall block with computers, which was just starting since we were at the beginning of the final trimester, so it all worked out.

LUKE'S SEVENTH-GRADE SURVIVAL GUIDE
TIP #19: Know your schedule, but also know when and how to go about changing it, because that can make a huge difference in your life.

"This can't be one of those instances where we mean to do something, but then time gets away from us. We have to act—now!" I said.

"Shh!" Mrs. Cross, the meanest proctor who'd ever lived, hissed. The old woman was *cross*. She handed detentions out like candy on Halloween, but we didn't let her stop us.

"I'm ready," Peter said. "What're we going to do?"

"We need to do everything we can to get people to vote yes. We've got to get the word out about Mr. Terupt," I said.

"I'll write letters for the town paper," Jessica said.

I smiled at her. That was perfect.

"I can make posters," Danielle whispered.

"We'll help," Jeffrey and Anna said, keeping their voices low.

"What can I do?!" Peter asked a bit too loudly. Like the rest of us, he was eager to help. He just wasn't as good at keeping his volume down.

"Shh!" Mrs. Cross hissed again, this time staring at us.

"We'll need your place to be campaign headquarters," I said.

Everyone tensed. The last time we got together at Peter's house things didn't go so well.

"We'll need to meet almost daily, and we can't use Mr. Terupt's classroom for this project. We couldn't anyway, with Mrs. Terupt on bed rest," I explained. "So, Peter's place is our best option."

That was all it took. Peter's house was designated as our home base, and no one worried. With the most important project we'd ever known in front of us, there wasn't anything that was going to tear us apart or slow us down—not even Mrs. Cross, the evil shushing proctor woman.

"Shhh!" she hissed again, this time with such gusto that spit flew from her mouth.

I don't know what Peter was thinking, but the next thing we knew, he stood up and went head-to-head with the hissing lady. "Mrs. Cross, I apologize for our whispering, but we've been assigned a very important group project, and we must work on it. I'll talk to my friends about keeping it down. I love your hair, by the way."

"Your flattery won't work on me, Mr. Jacobs," she warned. "Keep it up, and you'll be hanging with me *after* school."

"No place I'd rather be," he murmured.

"What was that?" she snapped.

"I still like your hair," he said, taking his seat.

Believe it or not, Peter's crazy stunt worked—in a backward sort of way. Mrs. Cross rose from her chair and marched over to our table. She glared down at us like a fire-breathing dragon, her eyes scanning our area. I thought for sure she was going to slap each one of us with a detention.

"This project of yours, is it about Mr. Terupt?" she asked, nodding at my papers.

I swallowed. "Yes. Do you know him?"

"My grandson, Kevin, is in his class this year," Mrs. Cross said. "Best teacher he's ever had. It'd be a terrible shame if he lost his job. Don't you worry, I'll be voting yes."

Suddenly, we were all smiles. "Thank you," I said.

"Good luck, kids. I'm rooting for you."

That was the thing about Mr. Terupt. After meeting him,

even somebody as nasty as Mrs. Cross couldn't help but love him and want to keep him. If we got the word out about Mr. Terupt, people would *have* to vote yes.

It was strange doing the biggest Mr. Terupt project without the man himself, but that was the way it had to be. It wouldn't look good for him to be campaigning for his own job, and he had other things on his plate. It was time for us to look out for Mr. Terupt the way he always did for us.

LUKE'S SEVENTH-GRADE SURVIVAL GUIDE
TIP #20: Sometimes things sound simpler on paper than they turn out to be.

Jessica

Dear Journal,

If Mr. Smith thought our efforts during the student government elections were impressive, he'd find all that we've accomplished for Mr. Terupt's campaign unbelievable. But when the man you owe so much to is in danger, you're willing to go to great lengths to fight for him, to do whatever it takes. I wonder if that's how Dad feels? Is he willing to go to the end of the ocean for Mom and me?

Like Dad, I haven't slowed down. I've written one letter after the next for the paper. Recently, I've started writing multiple letters each day. I'm being creative. I've crafted letters from a concerned student, a concerned parent, a concerned community member, and on and on. I'm not the only one getting creative, either. Vincent is running a special at his restaurant—a sandwich called the Mr. Terupt. It's a bestseller.

Mrs. Reeder is doing her part to help, too. Don't tell me it was a coincidence that she picked now to begin a unit on persuasive writing.

"Ladies and gentlemen, it strikes me as an opportune time to begin thinking about persuasive writing," she announced. "Persuasive writing is about careful word choice. The goal is to get your reader to agree with your position by the end of your essay. Since we've been thinking carefully about words all year, this shouldn't be too difficult. In fact, let's take a few minutes to share some of the insights you've made about words thus far."

I raised my hand.

"Go ahead, Jessica," Mrs. Reeder said.

"Important words are the ones you feel," I said. "They can hurt or help."

Mrs. Reeder nodded. "Anyone else?"

"You need to be a good listener if you want to hear the important things people have to say," Jeffrey said.

"Whether spoken or written, they can make a difference," Anna said.

"Sometimes with beautiful language and complex sentences," I added, "whereas other times a single word can mean everything."

"Terupt," Peter said.

"Yes, exactly," Mrs. Reeder said. "Now let's take a look at persuasive writing so that we know how to choose our words carefully, and then our readers and listeners will decide to agree with our view on things."

Feeling persuasive,
Jessica

P.S. I know words can persuade, and I deeply hope the words we use on Mr. Terupt's behalf convince enough voters, but I'm also wondering something else—something I didn't ask Mrs. Reeder. Can words heal? And, on their own, are they ever enough?

Peter

Lexie and I were responsible for the flyers. We made mini-posters with VOTE YES printed in bold letters across the middle of each one, and right next to those two words we stuck a catchy picture of T, thanks to Anna's awesome photography skills. Once we had them made, we went door to door delivering them. We'd knock, and when someone answered we'd give them a short speech—using the persuasion skills Mrs. Reeder had taught us—to go along with the flyer we shoved in their hands.

We met all sorts of people. There were those who were happy to see us, and those who were so happy they offered us cookies and something to drink. We regretfully declined, as ordered by Lexie's mom. And then there were the ones who greeted us with mean, growling dogs that could've swallowed Margo whole, and others who slammed doors in our faces. And who could ever forget Mr. Harold Meezer, the old man who was so nasty he put Mrs. Cross to shame.

"Hi," Lexie said when he'd opened his door. "I'm Alexia, and this is Peter. We're here to kindly remind you to vote on the budget, and we encourage you to vote yes so we can save our extraordinary teacher, Mr. Terupt."

"You don't have to worry about me," the old man said. "I'll be voting, but I'm not about to vote yes. That Teenup man you're all trying to save is just another money-sucking teacher as far as I'm concerned."

"And you're just an old fart who doesn't know his head from his butt," I said.

"You get off my porch!" he roared.

Lexie grabbed my hand and got me away from there as fast as she could, before I said anything more. I didn't mean any disrespect to Mr. Geezer, but he didn't have the right to talk about T that way. I lost my head—and my tongue—after he said those awful things.

I don't know anything about it, but somehow Mr. Geezer woke up the next morning with his house and car gift-wrapped in VOTE YES flyers. He even had SAVE MR. TERUPT written in huge black letters across his garage door. From what I understand, it was written in washable marker, but it was still there several days later. That's what I call karma!

Danielle

With Anna and Jeffrey helping me, we made close to a hundred posters. By using a wide range of big, bright block letters, we made sure each one was an attention grabber. We had VOTE YES posters and SAVE MR. TERUPT posters stuck in store windows and staked up on lawns all over town. We even spent several afternoons standing on the corner by school, holding our special HONK FOR MR. TERUPT signs. It felt great every time we heard a beep, but whenever a car drove past without tooting its horn, it reminded us we were in for a fight. I wouldn't say that scared me, though—that would come later.

When Mr. Terupt didn't show up at church Sunday morning, I got another one of those funny feelings. Something was wrong. Later that evening, my funny feeling had blossomed into an itch that I had to scratch.

"Grandma, can we go over to the church?"

"What for?"

"I've got to see if Mr. Terupt is there with the candles again. I hope he's not, and then I can just light one for him and we can leave, but I won't be able to sleep until I know."

Grandma understood. I didn't have to say anything more. She grabbed her car keys, I grabbed my designer kit, and we headed out.

I spotted him the moment we walked in. Grandma put her hand on my shoulder and stopped me.

"Let him finish," she whispered.

We sat in the back and waited. I prayed for him. He was there for a while, which scared me even more, but then he got up and started toward us. He wasn't his usual self. He walked with his head down.

"Hi, Mr. Terupt," I said, startling him.

He looked up. I'd never seen bags under his eyes before. "Hi, Danielle," he said, sounding even more tired than he looked.

"I'm sorry about your job, and this whole predicament," I said. "The gang's doing everything we can to help."

"My job? Is that why . . . That explains . . . But it's not my job I'm worried about, Danielle. I can get another one of those if I have to. It's Mrs. Terupt. She's in the hospital again. She went back into preterm labor, and this time they had to keep her. Her blood pressure was high, and they were worried about the baby, so they've got her and are monitoring things."

I caught my breath. He didn't try to pretend all was fine, the way adults sometimes do with kids. I felt so bad for him, but I didn't know what to say. It's a good thing I had Grandma with me.

"The bond between a mother and her unborn baby is a miraculous thing," Grandma said. "There's nothing else like it. A baby can sense everything that's going on with its mother. I'm sure this situation with the budget has your wife upset, even if she claims it doesn't. Once it's over, things will settle down and everything will be fine—especially after these kids get done."

Mr. Terupt nodded. "I hope so," he said. And then he walked out, his shoulders carrying so much worry.

Dear God,

For selfish reasons, I want you to make sure the vote passes so we can keep Mr. Terupt here forever, but that's not what I'm praying for tonight. Please, God, please take care of Mrs. Terupt and the baby.

Amen.

Jeffrey

Lukester was overseeing our operation and helping us every step of the way. He never ran out of ideas or suggestions. But as the date for the vote drew closer, we couldn't help but feel like we still weren't doing enough, especially after learning Mrs. Terupt was back in the hospital.

"What else can we do?" Jessica asked all of us.

No one had an answer. We were silent. Maybe that was what caught Mrs. Cross's attention, because she lumbered over to our table to see what was going on.

"How's it going, kids?" she asked.

"Not good," Luke said. "We're not sure we've done enough, and we're running out of time."

"Well, I know of some other kids who'd like to give you a hand," Mrs. Cross said.

We instantly perked up. It was like we had just found our second wind late in the third period of a tough match. Of course Terupt's sixth graders wanted to help! Any kid who had Terupt as his teacher knew how special he was and wanted to keep him forever. We didn't want to get Terupt involved, but that didn't mean *his students* couldn't get involved.

"What did you have in mind?" Luke asked.

"Well, if you're all okay with it, I was thinking I could have my grandson Kevin put a letter in each kid's mailbox or backpack instructing him or her to make more flyers or posters for your cause. The students could then give their completed work to Kevin. He'd give it to me, and I'd give it to you."

"Mrs. Cross, that's an awesome idea!" Peter yelled.

"Shh!" she hissed. "Need I remind you that this is still silent study hall?"

Peter shrank down in his chair.

"I wasn't born last night, Mr. Jacobs. I was a room mom years ago, and that's how we went about collecting things for teacher gifts."

"It's still awesome," Peter whispered.

The woman actually cracked a smile.

This new plan worked without a hitch, so well that Anna and Danielle even had a joke going about making Mrs. Cross an honorary member of the Spy Sisters—whatever that meant. Before we knew it, we had another hundred posters. We got them attached to stakes and put up on all those lawns that were home to the friendly people Lexie and Peter had met. The younger grades at Snow Hill School had made cards for Terupt following the Everything Fair but hadn't given them to him yet, so the sixth graders decided to send those to us to pass out rather than more flyers. The cards all showed how special a teacher can be. Peter's favorite one had a drawing of a boy holding a dog above a big snake. Lexie didn't like it, but the rest of us got a kick out of it.

Eventually, Voting Day arrived. And after all our hard work, there was only one thing left for us to do, and that was wait for the results. Not surprisingly, Lexie had an idea about how we should do that.

Alexia

It was Voting Day.

"Like, we need to have a party," I told everyone during silent study hall. "Remember, every campaign ends with a party."

"I don't know," Danielle said. "I'd like to be with all of you while we wait for the results tonight, but I'm not sure about another party."

"Don't worry," I said. "It'll be different this time. And if it makes you feel better, we don't even have to call it a party. We can call it—"

"A party," Jessica said, cutting me off. "Sorry, but we have to call it a party. That sounds happier and more optimistic, and we need that vibe right now."

"Okay, then," Peter said. "I'll see all of you at my place tonight. We'll have a party while we wait for the results to roll in."

"And don't worry," I told everyone again. "It'll be different this time."

By "different," I didn't mean for it to turn out worse.

anna

Lexie was right, this party was different. Sure, we had all the food and drink like we did the last time, and Peter played his music and we challenged each other in foosball, but we also had the budget results looming over us. When you're full of worry because of something like that, it's hard to go on laughing and having a good time. But Lexie came prepared to help us get through the night. She'd better grow up to be a party planner.

"Like, I've got something we can do," she said. "Everyone sit in a circle."

"No, we're not doing that again," Luke said.

"Chill out. I'm not getting a bottle. I brought something else." Lexie pulled out a round black object from her pack. "A Magic Eight Ball," she announced, holding it high for all of us to see.

"What's that?" Danielle asked. I wasn't surprised that she'd never seen one. It wasn't the sort of thing you found in church.

"It's our fortune-teller," Lexie said. "Like a crystal ball. You ask it a yes-or-no question, give it a shake, and then look through this little glass window and wait for your answer."

"How does it give you an answer?"

"There's a twenty-sided die inside with a bunch of different responses written all over it," Peter said. "The die floats
to the top, and one of its faces presses against the window,
showing you your answer."

Danielle still looked confused.

"Gimme that stupid thing," Peter said, grabbing it from
Lexie. "I'll show you. Does Lexie snore?" he said, giving it a
shake.

"You're a jerk," Lexie said, reaching for the ball.

"Ah, ah, ah," Peter said, holding it away from her. "You
have to wait for an answer once a question's been asked."

Lexie huffed and sat back.

"Here comes the answer!" Peter cried. "It says, 'Like a
bear'!"

"No it doesn't!" Lexie yelled. "That's not even on the die."
She grabbed the fortune-teller from him. "Does Peter fart in
his sleep?" she asked it.

That was how it went. Round and round the circle we
passed the Magic 8 Ball, each of us asking it our silly questions, then shaking it and waiting for an answer. It was ridiculous, but that thing entertained us for the next two hours.
After asking questions about the gang, we started asking the
fortune-teller things about our teachers.

"Does Mrs. Cross wax her mustache?" Jeffrey asked.

Peter thought that one was great, so naturally he had to
try to come up with one better. "Does Principal Lee wet the
bed?" he asked.

"Ugh! You guys are terrible," Jessica said.

Then Luke went ahead and asked the thing we all really

wanted to know, but were too chicken to say. "Will the budget pass tonight?"

Our circle sucked in one deep breath and waited for the cloudy blue water to clear. Luke peered into the glass opening. "'Outlook not so good,'" he read.

It was just a stupid plastic toy, but its answer took all the fun out of everything. That was the last thing we asked the Magic 8 Ball. Lexie put it away, and we gathered around the TV. We still had about an hour before the news came on and posted the results, so we found a movie to watch. We wrapped ourselves in blankets and began the waiting.

I thought all the excitement for the night was over until the results came in, but then something you're never going to believe happened. Someone started snoring, and not little tiny snores, but deep honking ones. The kind you only picture fat old men with hairy bellies producing. I couldn't believe she'd fallen asleep. I mean, it was late and all, but she was supposed to be the party animal. Lexie's head was tipped to the side, and her mouth hung wide open. Her whole body shook with each bellow. Those snores were coming all the way from her toes.

"Told you the answer was 'like a bear,'" Peter said, covering his mouth to keep from waking her with his laughter.

The rest of us had to do the same thing. We were dying. For Peter, this moment was too good to be true. He couldn't let the opportunity pass him by. He hurried over to the snacks and grabbed the container of Reddi-wip in one hand and a toothpick in the other.

"Peter, bad idea," I warned him. "I wouldn't do it." But like they say, some things never change. He wasn't about to listen to me—a voice of reason, and a girl.

"Forget it," Jeffrey whispered. "It's no use. He's got his mind set."

Danielle and I exchanged glances. We knew things were about to get ugly, we just had no idea how ugly.

Peter crouched down and slowly filled Lexie's right hand with the whipped cream, and he didn't give her just a little bit, but a pile of it. Then he took his toothpick and ever so gently dragged it along the bridge of her nose. He did it once. Twice. And then all of a sudden, Lexie's hand flew through the air and landed on the tickle she was feeling. She took that whipped-cream hand of hers and rubbed it right up her nose and all over her face! That was it. Peter couldn't hold it together anymore.

"Oh my God!" he yelled, and burst out laughing.

Lexie sat bolt upright. "What? What'd I miss?" We couldn't tell her because we were cracking up, but Lexie wasn't born yesterday. She knew we were laughing at her. She reached up and touched her face, looked at her hand, and then screamed, "Peter, I'm gonna kill you!"

"Shush! Shush!" Luke yelled. "They're starting to post the results."

Our fun and games ended. This was it.

Jessica

Dear Journal,

We'd done what we could with our voices. Now it was time to wait for the numbers. It was time to find out if letters or numbers had won in our war. My fingers were crossed. . . .

Jeffrey

There must've been budget votes all over the place because I kept seeing the results for different towns flashing across the screen. Where was ours?

Alexia

Like, I rubbed my eyes to make sure I was seeing things right, that it wasn't the whipped cream blurring my vision. I wanted it to be the whipped cream.

anna

I couldn't hold back my tears. I wasn't strong enough for that.

Peter

"No way! That's wrong!"

LUKE

The results came in.

YES 2,349
NO 2,456

Danielle

*D*ear God,
  We've been crushed by the full weight of the storm. Please help us.
  Amen.

LUKE

It was time for more drastic measures. There was no way I was allowing this to happen. These people had made a mistake.

Jeffrey

After the numbers came up on the screen, I had a hard time breathing. It was like I was in the hospital—with Michael, with Coach Terupt—all over again. I had to get home. I needed to see Asher.

I called Dad. He'd been watching the news like the rest of us, so he knew the results.

"Jeffrey, I'm sorry, Son."

"I need you to come and get me now."

"I'll be there in a few minutes."

Dad didn't know what to say during our ride home. I wasn't interested in talking anyway. I was only thinking about Asher. When I got in the house, I hurried into his room. I placed my hand on his shoulder and gently shook him. I needed him to wake up. I needed him to open his eyes.

"Jeffrey, what're you doing?" Dad asked, startled by my strange behavior.

There was no time to explain everything. "I've got to see him."

"You can see him in the morning."

I shook the little guy harder.

"Jeffrey, that's enough," Dad said, pulling my arm away. But he was too late. My little brother started to stir. He rubbed his face and opened his eyes. I bent closer and looked. And I found what I'd been hoping for.

Staring back at me were the same eyes I first met when I rescued Asher from that field by the side of the road. The same eyes I'd seen when he had banged on our slider and yelled "My-my." The same eyes he had in the gym when he told Anna and me that Michael was there. Michael was with us again tonight. That was what I needed to know. With Michael, and with Asher, I knew we still had a chance.

Maybe we'd lost the battle, but we could still win the war.

MAY

LUKE

What do you do when things don't go your way? A toddler throws a temper tantrum, a teenage boy might opt for throwing punches, others choose pouting or implementing the silent treatment. Things had not gone our way, but none of these responses seemed appropriate or particularly helpful—except maybe the silent treatment.

There's power in silence. If you recall, I mentioned having felt that during my visit to Arlington National Cemetery. There's also power in numbers. When there's a group of people not happy about something, how do they respond? Sometimes they stage a protest, which might mean picket lines and marches. Such an undertaking would require more signs and materials, and that was simply too much for us to try to pull together this late in the game. But a protest could also be in the form of a boycott. This seemed more manageable and just as effective, and not only that, but *boycott* also happens to be a dollar word. Mr. Terupt sprang his dollar-word project on us back in fifth grade. In that challenge, each letter of the alphabet had a different cent value, and a dollar word meant that, when totaled, the letters in the word equaled one dollar exactly. Ever since, these words have had a way of speaking to me. A *boycott* (dollar word) was definitely the answer. The question was: What could we boycott?

As I thought and thought about it, knowing we needed to do something big, yet smart and safe, I realized it was civil disobedience that I was thinking about. History was alive with it. We didn't study and honor just our former presidents, but also great human beings like Martin Luther King Jr. and Rosa Parks, who were able to rally and unite people and inspire change with their nonviolent acts.

Luke Bennett was going to be next.

LUKE'S SEVENTH-GRADE SURVIVAL GUIDE
TIP #21: Let your heart be your compass.

Alexia

I thought I was the crazy one in our group who came up with the risky and dangerous ideas, like sending Jessica to New York City as me, but, like, Luke was even crazier. This idea of his was going to be one for the ages. And like, succeeding at this was going to give Mom the strength to win in her fight, too. I could feel it, like Danielle said she can sometimes.

Jessica

Dear Journal,

I wrote those letters to the paper with renewed energy. Was it because I wanted to save Mr. Terupt? Yes, of course! I wanted my time with him to be everlasting. Remember? But I also found writing the letters made me feel closer to Dad. He's still sending one a day. He hasn't missed once. Mom still hasn't opened any, and I have yet to reply, but they keep coming. Do you think it's possible for a string of simple words, or simple acts, to eventually add up to something significant?

Luke's persistence in our plight to save the teacher we loved reminded me of Dad. Despite failed attempts, Luke was going to keep trying, and his newest idea was genius. Mrs. Reeder had spent all year talking to us about important words, but it was our silence that was going to say the most.

Still fighting for Mr. Terupt,
Jessica

P.S. I want Mom to open Dad's letters, but how do I convince her to do that?

LUKE

To pull off something of this magnitude would take careful planning and management of resources. That wasn't anything that intimidated me. In the end, this was just another project. Last year, I was convinced that I'd never take on a bigger or more important task than overseeing the budget for Mr. Terupt's wedding. That was the only budget I'd ever cared about. But now, less than one year later, I found myself in this position because of a different budget, and the truth was it wasn't *just* another project. If you asked me, we were facing a life-or-death situation, because to imagine things without Mr. Terupt nearby felt like someone dying.

I had Jeffrey and Peter explain things to the eighth-grade wrestlers, who then spread the word among their classmates. Then they went and found Brandon. This was a really important connection because Brandon was a very popular kid, and he was also a huge Mr. Terupt fan. He had the power to rally most of the high school behind us—definitely the eleventh and twelfth grades. Lexie talked to Reena and Lisa, the high school girls she had befriended last year, and they agreed to help Brandon get everyone on board. I found all the other student council members and told them about my plan, and they got busy spreading the word as well. I had people working from all different angles. There was only one other key player we needed to reach so that he could help us pull it all together, and reaching that person was up to me. Abraham Lincoln once said, "Do I not destroy my enemies when I make them my friends?"

To arrange for our meeting, I did something I never do during class—I took the bathroom pass and excused myself. I knew I'd be missing something important, but sacrifices needed to be made. This was the best time to do something like this, because the halls were empty. I fast-walked toward my destination, not wanting to miss any more class time than was necessary. I popped into the bathroom, counted to sixty, and then started on my way back. No, I didn't even go. I didn't have to, but I was careful to make it appear as if I'd gone. Returning too soon could make my teacher suspicious. I dropped my note in Zack's locker as I hurried back to class. Phase one was complete.

The note wasn't a small scrap of paper as you might suspect. I chose a large piece of red construction paper. Zack wasn't the most observant kid—from what I'd observed—so I wanted to make sure he noticed it. The instructions I gave him said to meet me in the bathroom by the teachers' room at two o'clock, during ninth period. I chose that specific location because it was the least likely to have another student in there at that designated time, and also because there was a chance a teacher might hear me screaming for help if Zack decided to show up and beat the crap out of me.

I spent the rest of the day counting down the minutes. My hands wouldn't stop sweating, and my heart felt like it was beating in my throat. By the time ninth period rolled around, I had myself convinced that I'd made a terrible mistake.

"Luke, you're looking rather pale," Mr. Brobur said when I walked into Science. "You feeling all right?"

"Not the best," I said. "I might need to step out if I start feeling worse."

"Sure. Okay. Whatever you need."

Perfect, I thought. Now I have a reason to go to the bathroom without causing alarm. Being a good kid sure paid off. Mr. Brobur never doubted me. I'd have felt bad about that, but this was important. I just hoped he didn't decide to send someone to check on me—or maybe I did, in case Zack was using me to mop the floor.

At 1:53, I got up and left science class without Mr. Brobur saying a word. I practically ran to the bathroom. I intended to get there first so I could get in a comfortable and confident position, but when I arrived, I found Zack already standing there, blocking any chance I had for a fast getaway.

"Whatever it is, Bennett, it better be good," he said. "My coach may have helped me out with some of my . . . anger issues, but I still owe you one for that hallway stunt, so if I don't like what you've got to say, I think you'll go swimming in that toilet over there—the dirty one."

I gulped, unable to imagine a worse death. "I arranged for this meeting because I—we—need your help."

"You've got guts, I'll give you that," Zack said, taking a step forward, "but you must be stupid. I can't believe you showed up here to tell me that. You better hope one of those turds works as your life raft."

A second gulp and a step back. "We're trying to pull off

a school-wide sit-in to protest the teacher cuts," I croaked. "We're trying to save our old teacher, Mr. Terupt. If you knew him—"

"Wait a sec. Mr. Terupt? I do know him. He's an awesome dude. He's the coach who helped me at wrestling and stuff this year."

Whew! Maybe I wasn't going to get stuffed into that toilet after all. "We need your help if we're going to save him," I said.

"What do you need me to do?"

"Get the word out to the ninth graders. Make sure they know the sit-in will take place this Thursday. Everyone should come to school same as always, but instead of reporting to homeroom, they need to go to the high school gym. That's where we'll be gathering."

"Who's going to be there?"

"The entire school," I said. "We've got all the other grades covered."

"Whoa! This is going to drive Principal Lee crazy!"

"Yes, so it's got to be kept secret," I reminded him. "And we need *everyone*."

"Yeah, yeah, don't worry about that. You forget who you're talking to."

I stuck my hand out and we shook. "Thanks," I said.

"You're all right, Bennett. You don't have to worry about watching your back anymore. I've got it for you."

Zack left, and I stayed behind. Honest Abe had been right about making enemies your friends, but he forgot to mention that I'd need to check my underwear after doing so.

Peter

Principal Lee exploded through the gym doors. I hadn't seen him this mad—ever. Not even when I slopped coffee all over his boy parts. He stormed to the middle of the floor, his megaphone in hand. No one said a word. He didn't need to raise his arm or blast his air horn because we were already dead quiet, and it wasn't for him. He saw all our signs. He knew what this was about. Principal Lee was the man who was always in charge, always in control—but suddenly he wasn't. This was *his* school—but not right now. How dare we do this on his watch! He loosened his tie, which I thought was an excellent idea because he already had splotches of purple dotting his forehead, and he hadn't even started yelling yet. Slowly, he lifted the megaphone to his mouth.

"I want to know who's responsible for this extreme show of disrespect and insubordination," he said, using a firm but low voice. He waited, fighting to keep his composure, but it was no use. The gym remained silent, and then Principal Lee lost it. "*Now!*" he shouted through his megaphone.

More silence.

"Fine," he said, back to using the low but firm approach.

"We can do this the easy way or the hard way. Give yourself up, and the consequences won't be as severe as they'll be if I have to investigate and find out the truth. Turn the guilty person in, and you'll be rewarded. However, if no one chooses to come forward, then each and every one of you will pay the price, and this act of defiance"—here Principal Lee started shouting again—"*will go on your permanent records!*"

Our silence persisted. You could feel us growing stronger with each passing minute of our standoff, but Principal Lee wasn't throwing in the towel yet.

"I was hoping to avoid this, but you leave me no choice," he said. "Miss Ferguson, you can follow me. We'll start with you. As president of the senior class, I'm sure you had some say in this. It's unfortunate that this rebellion will need to be reported to the college you've chosen to attend next year, which will almost definitely jeopardize your acceptance, and after all the hard work and sacrifices you made. What a shame."

I didn't know "Miss" Ferguson from a hole in the ground, but to see an innocent person being marched off because of something you've done is not an easy thing to let slide. Luke was ready to crack. There was no doubt about it. He started to stand, but I grabbed his shirt and yanked him back down.

"We need you in this fight if Mr. T has any chance at all. Don't say a word," I hissed in warning to him. Then I jumped to my feet. "I'm the one behind it," I said.

"Peter, what're you doing!" Luke whispered.

"Shut up," I said.

Principal Lee spun around and glared across the gym. He

was wild with anger and couldn't wait to see who'd dared to challenge his authority.

"Mr. Jacobs. You expect me to believe that a puny seventh grader foolish enough to put hair dye all over his face could pull this off? Very noble of you to take the blame for someone else—noble and stupid. You can follow us. After I'm done with Miss Ferguson, I'll have fun expelling you."

What? Expelling me? He couldn't do that! Could he?

"Actually, I'm the one who planned it, not Peter," Jeffrey said, rising to his feet beside me. He had my back.

"No, I'm the one who planned it," Jessica said.

"I'm the one who planned it," Zack said.

"It was me," Brandon said, standing among the sea of high schoolers.

"It was me," Reena said.

One by one, my friends and kids I didn't even know stood and claimed to be the person responsible, until the entire student body was standing and in unison began chanting, "Save our teachers. Save our teachers."

Was this going to be enough to save Mr. T? I had no idea. It was enough to send Principal Lee storming out the doors, though—without "Miss" Ferguson. We didn't break into celebration—not yet. Instead, we sat back down and let our silence press on, knowing that we still had a long ways to go.

Jeffrey

Peter did one of the bravest things I've ever witnessed. I suppose I shouldn't have been all that surprised, because he'd done the same sort of thing last year when our class was divided between royalty and peasants during Mr. Terupt's *Whipping Boy* project. Peter made his stand for the peasants, and I had thought that was the bravest thing I'd ever seen, his sacrificing Field Day and all, but that was nothing compared to this. What we were dealing with now was no make-believe ordeal. It was a do-or-die situation. We were playing with fire, and Peter wasn't backing down.

Peter was on his feet and telling Principal Lee that this was all his doing. Lee didn't buy it for a second, but he was more than happy to make an example of Peter. He never liked Peter to begin with. Again, Luke tried to stand, but I yanked him back down.

It was my turn to be brave. Even though I couldn't see Michael, I felt him there helping me. I reached down and grasped Anna's hand. She gave mine a squeeze.

"You heard what he said," I warned Luke. "Not a word." I stood. And after me, Jessica did. And then Zack. And Brandon. And then all of a sudden the entire gym was on its feet, Luke included.

I had chills after beating Scott Winshall, when the referee raised my arm and everyone went wild cheering for me, but that didn't compare to what I felt in that gym, standing together. My skin tingled.

Knowing there was nothing he could do, Principal Lee turned and slammed through the doors. Gone for the moment, but we knew he'd return.

"Now what?" Anna asked.

"We stay," Luke said.

"For how long?"

"Until they give us Mr. Terupt back." He sat down, and the rest of the gym followed, ready to stay the course.

Were we on our way to winning the war?

LUKE

Principal Lee never suspected me. He was wild with fury, determined and desperate to find someone to blame for it all, to nail the culprit, but he never even looked at me. But Mr. Brobur did. Mr. Brobur maintained a straight face and acted as if he didn't know anything and was only there with the rest of his colleagues, supporting Principal Lee. But when he looked at me—in a moment that was invisible to everyone else—it was clear that he saw my phenotype. There was a twinkle in his eye. He knew. And here's what *I* knew—he wasn't going to tell on me. But why?

LUKE'S SEVENTH-GRADE SURVIVAL GUIDE
TIP #22: It's in your best interest to make your teachers allies. You'll want them on your side as you navigate seventh grade and beyond. I suggest you go about this with good old-fashioned hard and honest work, and not through brownnosing efforts.

Danielle

The one thing we hadn't discussed was what to do at the end of the day. If nothing had resulted from our pilgrimage, what were we going to do? Luke was prepared to stay there all night. He wasn't budging until they gave us Mr. Terupt back, and none of us were trying to talk him out of it. Principal Lee's temper tantrum had tricked us into believing we were winning, when really we weren't.

Superintendent Knowles and Mr. Murphy, president of the school board, showed up next, but, unlike Principal Lee, they didn't lose their cool and start yelling. They commended us for our efforts on behalf of our teachers, but they also assured us it wasn't going to change anything. Given the results of the vote, and the current state of the budget, the cuts had to be made. It was already decided.

"We understand that's difficult to hear, but we have no other choice," Dr. Knowles said. "I'm sorry. You can go to class now."

Even then, we didn't call it quits. Luke had predicted this would happen, and he had emphasized to everyone that we absolutely had to continue with the sit-in after they tried talking us out of it, otherwise nothing would change. We had to be brave and determined—and we were.

It turns out the only person who was able to get us to stop was the person who got us started in the first place. Mr. Terupt arrived later that afternoon. He walked into our gym alongside Principal Lee. It was obvious he hadn't seen our campaign signs for him or known how much effort we were putting in to save him, because he came to an abrupt halt when he entered the room. I hoped it was because he felt the magnitude of our love. We were there for him.

Mr. Terupt turned to Principal Lee and said a few things. What, I don't know, but I could tell Principal Lee wasn't in agreement by the way he started shaking his head and waving his hands. That was when Mr. Brobur joined them. He and Mr. Terupt talked to Principal Lee, and a minute or two later, Mr. Brobur, Principal Lee, and the other teachers exited the gym, leaving just Mr. Terupt. The gym remained silent, with all eyes trained on him as he walked over and sat down with us.

"Hey, gang," he said. He was talking in a low voice. "I didn't realize until I ran into Danielle the other night that you even knew what might happen with my job. I see now that you've been fighting for me all along. And you still haven't quit. You guys are the best. This means so much to me. . . . But . . . it's time to stop now. Your voices have been heard, but at this point, I fear your continued silence might start doing more harm than good. You have your parents, teachers, and other caring and compassionate adults in your lives very worried. Besides, I just got Mrs. Terupt back home, and when she hears about this she might get all excited and go into labor again," he joked.

We cracked tiny smiles, but this was no laughing matter. My prayers about Mrs. Terupt and the baby had been answered, but that didn't make losing Mr. Terupt any easier.

"The board is in a difficult position," Mr. Terupt continued, turning serious again. "It's not like they wanted this to happen, but it did. They can't change that now. If they could, they would. But trust me when I say to you that what you've done here in the last month might not have saved me, but it will make a difference for all those who come after us."

We didn't say anything. We huddled together, sharing that moment with our beloved teacher, wishing there was a way we could keep it forever. There's no telling how long we would've sat there, but I started feeling shaky. I didn't want to be the one to ruin things, but I didn't have a choice. My sugars were dropping, and I didn't have any snacks with me.

"Guys, I'm feeling shaky. I've got to go to Nurse Sharon's and get some juice."

It took so much work and planning on Luke's part to get everyone gathered in the gym, but after I said that, Mr. Terupt, with Luke beside him, explained to everyone that it was time to get back to class. We got up and started leaving, and it was all over in a matter of just a few minutes. When I got to Nurse Sharon's and tested my blood sugar, I discovered that I wasn't low. I was feeling shaky because I knew there wasn't anything more we could do. We had tried—and we had failed.

Dear God,

I thank you for the days I did get with Mr. Terupt, and I ask you to please be with him and his family when the time comes for them to move away. Help them find a place that loves them like we do, but also knows how to keep them.

I pray that you help my friends and me stay together when he is no longer in our community.

Amen.

ANNA

After our sit-in, after our failed attempt to save Mr. Terupt, there was a sadness that we carried with us every day. I had another wedding in my future—the one I'd been dreaming about—a dad and a sister, my friends, Jeffrey, so much to be happy about, but the realization that we were losing Mr. Terupt was always with me.

We transitioned from trying to save our hero to trying to savor our remaining time with him. We wanted our seconds to feel like minutes, our minutes like hours, and our hours like days. I took pictures whenever we got together, but those snapshots just brought us closer to the end. No matter how many photos I took, it wasn't freezing us in time.

We spent the last few weeks of May visiting Mr. Terupt whenever we could. It was like we'd resumed Thursdays with Terupt, but it happened on any day of the week. Mrs. Terupt was doing better. She was still on bed rest, but it was close enough to her original due date that her situation wasn't a scary or stressful one anymore, so Mr. Terupt was able to spend time with us after school. We chose not to arrive until his day of teaching was over. We liked his sixth graders very much, but we wanted them to enjoy their final days without us interfering, and we also wanted *our* time with him to be only ours. We weren't interested in sharing. Maybe that sounds selfish, but that was how we needed it to be.

We busied ourselves on those afternoons by doing our homework—though Peter refused to consider us a homework club—and by helping Mr. Terupt. We helped him gather boxes and, little by little, we packed up his belongings. We started early because we worked slowly. It was hard to put his things away, knowing we wouldn't see them again. It reminded me of when we moved him to the annex before our sixth-grade year, but this was different. Mr. Terupt wasn't moving to another classroom. He was moving out.

Jessica

Dear Journal,

For my essay on words in Mrs. Reeder's class, I chose to write a letter. Here's how it began:

Dear Dad,

My English teacher, Mrs. Reeder, has had us thinking about important words all year long. She challenged us on the first day of school to do something important with our words. Now the time has come for us to write a paper of reflection on this very topic, and while I know I've said and written heartfelt and meaningful things this year, I also know I haven't yet said or written everything that I need to.

You taught me at a young age that, if strung together with thought and care, words can tell incredible tales. I have one for you now. It's about my amazing teacher—Mr. Terupt. . . .

Writers say the work needs to come from inside, that we must put emotions into the marks we scratch on paper; I was a kaleidoscope of emotions as I began writing to my father. In my letter, I told him about our journey with Mr. Terupt, from day one in fifth grade to now, describing our struggles to save him and how our ride had come to an end. I told him how Thursdays with Terupt had ultimately led me to New York City, where I found him. I told Dad that, like us, Mr. Terupt was a fan of happy endings—and *our* ending was still left to be written, so I hoped he'd keep trying.

I handed my paper in yesterday, and Mrs. Reeder kept me after class today. "Jessica, I wanted to talk to you about your essay," she said.

"Was it okay?" I asked.

"I read it last night . . . four times," she said, "but I didn't mark it up or put any sort of grade on it. Jessica, what you've written is far more important than any essay for my class. You need to send it to your father. It's beautiful."

Earlier tonight, I sealed my letter in an envelope and addressed it. Then I went and asked Mom for a stamp. She was reading. "I'll put one on it and get it in the mail for you tomorrow," she said, never looking up from her book.

"Thanks," I said. I left the envelope sitting next to her and quietly slipped away.

I knew she'd see who my letter was going to when she put the stamp on it. I still wasn't sure how to talk to Mom about Dad, but maybe this was a start.

Drained,
Jessica

P.S. There's a level of excitement that I feel with the letters to and from my father, because I find I'm hoping they might be a beginning. But to think I'll have nothing more than letters with Mr. Terupt is a sad thought.

Alexia

There were boxes on top of boxes in Teach's room, and like, I got used to them being around. So I didn't even think about it when boxes started showing up in my house. I was more concerned with the upcoming test. No, not some stupid math test or science test or any other test in school. Mom was going in to have her scan to see if the cancer was gone— or not.

If I'd had to choose between losing Teach or Mom, then I'd have picked Teach. Don't hate me for saying that, but, like, it's the truth.

And those doctors had better not tell me I was losing both!

JUNE

Jessica

Dear Journal,

I had fooled myself into thinking all stories with Mr. Terupt delivered happy endings, but fairy tales aren't real. You don't always get a happily ever after.

Glancing around his classroom, I felt like I was in a graveyard, with each box representing a coffin and a different set of memories being buried forever. Our days together had been wiped from his walls and tucked away. His books that I loved to gaze at and hold and read were no longer out to provide me with comfort; they were huddled together in darkness, afraid of their untold future. I imagined they felt like me.

With all those special stories and words taken away, Mr. Terupt decided to fill that empty space with his own, taking a page from Mrs. Reeder's book. "You know what else I really like, other than happy endings?" he asked me on an afternoon when I was huddled over one of the final boxes.

I thought about it, and then I remembered. "Surprises," I said. "You love surprises. That's why you wouldn't let Mrs. Terupt find out if you're having a boy or a girl."

"That's right." He smiled, not at me, but at the mental

pictures he had playing out in his mind. "I guess we'll know pretty soon," he said.

I nodded.

"You know what else I like?" he asked again.

I shook my head. I didn't have an answer this time.

"I like it when I know about a planned surprise and get to keep the secret, and then spring it on someone else later. That's fun, too." He smiled again—this time at me.

That got my attention, and I was about to say something to him, but our moment was interrupted by the sudden ringing of his phone. Mr. Terupt always encouraged us to eavesdrop when he was conducting reading and writing conferences, so I thought of his phone conversation as one of those and did my best to listen in.

"Now?! It just happened? Are you sure? . . . Dumb question. Sorry. I'm on my way."

Mr. Terupt ended his call and then looked at all of us. There was nervous excitement in his eyes.

"That was my wife," he said. "I've got to go. Our baby is on the way!"

Smiling,
Jessica

P.S. I hope it's a little girl.

Danielle

It was time for another gathering in our gym. Not one organized and masterminded by Luke, but one that we knew would be coming. It was our last day of school, and I will admit, the junior high had managed to plan something that I'd been looking forward to. It was Yearbook Release Day. Anna and I were anxious to see the results of our hard work.

Before heading to the assembly, I went to check my blood sugar with Nurse Sharon. It didn't matter that it was the last day of school. When Anna and I arrived, we found Nurse Sharon and Mrs. Rollins carrying on the same as always, whispering like crazy in their hushed voices. There was just one difference today. For some odd reason, they zipped their lips as soon as we got there. They hadn't even reacted that way when it was the budget cuts and Mr. Terupt they were gabbing about, or any other thing for that matter. What in heavens they could've been discussing on the last day of school that was so important, I hadn't a clue.

"What do you think they could've been talking about?" Anna asked as soon as we stepped out of Nurse Sharon's office. She'd noticed their strange behavior, too. The Spy Sisters didn't miss much.

"I don't know," I said, "but that sure was weird. Something's up."

We made it to the gym just before things got started. The entire seventh and eighth grades sat in the bleachers, excited for the release of this year's junior high yearbook. There wasn't a kid who didn't look forward to getting it.

Naturally, Principal Lee had to start things off for us. It was his lectern, and before anyone else could use it, he needed his moment. I noticed he didn't seem to stand quite as tall at it anymore. Whether that was because it was the last day of school or we'd shrunk his ego with our sit-in, I don't know, but he didn't threaten us with his air horn or even raise his hand. We simply fell silent without giving him any sort of attitude. You could say it was because we'd had plenty of practice at being quiet, but I think it was more that our budget struggles had left both sides tired of fighting.

"This is always one of my favorite events of the year," Principal Lee began. "I'm very proud of the work Mrs. Reeder and our students have done to create this beautiful yearbook. This is something that I know will bring you fond memories for many days to come. It was, after all, a truly memorable year.

"I wish all of you a happy summer. And now, here to announce this year's yearbook dedication is Mrs. Reeder." Principal Lee stepped away from his lectern and Mrs. Reeder came forward. I was on the edge of my seat.

"Ladies and gentlemen, your student yearbook committee has done a wonderful job. You'll find your yearbook is full of beautiful moments, photos, and artwork. The cover was designed by our extremely talented Danielle Roberts." There was sudden applause, which made my face flush—something that usually only happened when my sugars were high. "The campaign posters Danielle created during our student government elections were so striking that we took her storm sketch and reworked it for the cover. How fitting that turned out to be, because you most definitely took this year by storm. You've done important work, work that hasn't gone unnoticed, work that has done more than you realize."

Mrs. Reeder paused, giving us a chance to absorb what she'd said. Then she took a deep breath and continued, "As voted upon by the students, this year's junior high yearbook is dedicated to . . . (drumroll) . . . our remarkable science teacher and wrestling coach, Mr. Brobur."

The gym erupted in cheers and clapping and whoops that continued until Mr. Brobur took his place at the podium. He would take a minute to thank us for the honor, and then it would be time to pass out the yearbooks. That was how things were supposed to proceed. But we were just getting started with the big announcements.

LUKE

I wanted to know how Mrs. Reeder could stand up there and tell us we'd done important work, and that it hadn't gone unnoticed and had done more than we realized, when we hadn't saved Mr. Terupt. There wasn't anything about my work that left me feeling good or proud—but that all changed when Mr. Brobur stepped forward.

"I want to thank all of you for this touching honor," he said. "It means a tremendous amount to me, and it's the perfect parting gift."

Mr. Brobur paused. He had to. There was an explosion of whispering throughout our student population after he said that, with everyone asking the same things: "What did he say?" "What does he mean?" "Is he retiring?"

"Yes, I said 'parting gift.' I have decided to retire," Mr. Brobur announced.

Again, he paused to allow for more whispering. I didn't say a word. I couldn't. I was stunned. First I was losing Mr. Terupt, and now my favorite teacher in the junior high was leaving.

"I've been a member of this community all my life, having gone to school here and spent the better part of thirty-plus years teaching here," Mr. Brobur continued. "This place is my home, and I care about it tremendously, as I do you and your futures, which is why I became a teacher in the first place. This is also why I know the time has come for me to step aside.

"I do not speak of English and literature and words in the way that Mrs. Reeder does, but make no mistake about it, you have inspired me with the important words you've spoken, the sentences you've written, and the silence you've kept. It's been a privilege watching you. And to show my sincere gratitude for all that you've done, I wanted to give you one last thing in return. Taking over the reins as your new junior high school science teacher and wrestling coach, I present to you . . . Mr. William Terupt."

At that precise moment, Mr. Terupt walked into our gym. He'd been saved.

LUKE'S SEVENTH-GRADE SURVIVAL GUIDE
TIP #23: If you have a goal that you do not achieve, this does not guarantee failure. If you've worked extremely hard, and if you've been honest in your pursuit to attain it, then you will have accomplished far more than you realize.

Mr. Brobur had spent his career talking about science and concepts such as survival of the fittest. He'd taught us that it's not necessarily the biggest or fastest individuals who survive, but the ones most responsive to change. Mr. Terupt was a survivor.

The changing environment in our community hadn't influenced only my phenotype, but Mr. Brobur's as well. He was much more than a teacher and coach. Much more.

anna

We rushed from the bleachers and swarmed Mr. Terupt, engulfing him in our hugs. It was the last day of fifth grade all over again. He was back, bringing us another surprise happy ending.

Jeffrey

"I've got another surprise for you," Terupt said, after the rest of the gym had emptied outside.

"*Another* one?" Jessica said, unable to hide the excitement in her voice. Did she know what he was going to say? I sure didn't.

"Yeah. C'mon."

We followed him. Once we stepped through the front doors and continued toward the parking lot, I knew where he was taking us, and understood why Jessica was excited. Sitting on a nearby bench, cradling their new bundle of joy, was Mrs. Terupt. Their newborn baby was perfect, a beautiful little angel. (I guess I have a soft spot for babies since Asher.)

"T, is it a boy or girl?" Peter asked.

"Are you *serious*?!" Lexie cried. "She's a girl, you dope. Don't you see her cute pink hat?"

"Oh," Peter said, sounding like the dope Lexie had called him.

"What's her name?" Jessica asked.

"Hope," Mrs. Terupt said. "That name feels right to us— mostly because of you guys."

"That's pretty," Anna said, bending closer. "Hi, Hope."

We smiled.

"Guess you'll need to try again to get your wrestler," Peter said.

"Why? Girls can wrestle," Terupt said.

"Oh, no!" Lexie cried. "She is *not* a wrestler!"

"We'll support her in whatever she wants to do," Mrs. Terupt said. "That just won't be wrestling."

We laughed.

The third period of a good wrestling match can be a flurry of action, and that was exactly how the final months of seventh grade had felt. There was one thing after another, but we ended with our arms raised in the air. We'd won the war. And with Terupt back in our corner, I knew we had many victories yet to come.

Peter

After T and his family left, we spent the rest of the day having fun in the sun. The afternoon was ours for a cookout, time to sign yearbooks and soak up the rays. It was when I went to grab another slice of watermelon that I bumped into Principal Lee—not literally this time.

"With Mr. Terupt around here next year, I'll have another pair of good eyes on you," Lee warned me. "And I'm going to be on you like white on rice, Jacobs. You better not *slip* up."

"Don't worry," I said. "I'm always at my *best* with Mr. T around."

Alexia

I remember how excited I was for my first day of junior high school, but like, that was nothing compared to our last day of seventh grade, a day marked by all sorts of special moments. First there was Mr. Brobur's announcement when we learned Teach was still going to be with us. I didn't think it could get better than that, but then Teach took us outside to meet his precious little daughter, Hope. I still say Lexie would've been a better name, but Hope's nice, too. I can't wait to make her a pair of cute little booties to match her hat—pink for a reason other than cancer.

That day, Vincent was there to pick me up after school. Mom and Margo sat in the passenger's seat. I was so excited to share all the good news that I ran right up to her window.

"Guess what? Teach gets to stay! Mr. Brobur is retiring, and Teach is taking over his position."

"That's awesome!" Vincent said. "Now it's our turn."

I stopped breathing and froze.

"The test showed I'm clean," Mom said. "Cancer-free."

I leaned through the window and squeezed her. Margo pushed and rooted with her nose to get in between us, whimpering and whining. Then she started licking at my face, tasting the salt on my cheeks.

"I love you," Mom whispered in my ear.

"I love *you*."

Margo started yipping and barking after that. "Oh, and I love you, too," I said, picking her up in my arms. I climbed into the back, and then Vincent pulled away from the curb.

"Where are we going?" I asked.

"Home," Vincent said.

Sitting next to me was another box, one like the others that had been showing up in my house. I smiled. Teach wasn't the only one moving closer. I hugged Margo.

Danielle

Dear God,

Mr. Brobur might be a man of science, a man who spent the better part of his life talking about evolution, but what he did for us was something that only a person living with you could pull off. He's a saint. Keep him healthy and happy during retirement. And do continue to keep an eye on Mr. and Mrs. Terupt and baby Hope.

I need to go now. Anna and I are going wedding-dress shopping with Jessica and Lexie. Our moms are coming too—and Grandma.

On second thought, before taking care of Mr. Brobur and the Terupts, you probably better keep an eye on us. If Lexie tries to get Grandma in that bra store, we might need another miracle down here.

Amen.

LUKE

Jessica's the one who has a knack for words. I couldn't come close to writing something in her book that would sum up our year and express my feelings. Plus, I didn't want everyone else who would sign her yearbook reading what I had to say, so instead, I asked her to go on a walk. My compass pointed the way.

LUKE'S SEVENTH-GRADE SURVIVAL GUIDE
TIP #24: If you follow Tips #1–23 and play your cards right, not only will you survive seventh grade and potentially achieve something great, but you just might get the girl, too!

Jessica

Dear Journal,

I found Mom reading Dad's letters later that night. She'd been through many, but I wasn't sure if she had a bigger stack of letters or tissues by her side.

I walked over and wrapped my arms around her.

"You write like your father," she whispered, "from the heart. You feel his words."

I squeezed her harder.

Love,
Jessica

P.S. I know I didn't tell you about my walk with Luke. You don't need to know everything.

P.P.S. To describe it would require especially beautiful writing.

Peter

All good things must come to an end, but with the end there also comes a beginning. And eighth grade was a beginning we couldn't wait for!

JUNIOR HIGH SURVIVAL GUIDE:

Helpful Tips from the Old Gang!

Jessica
Read good books. Make good choices.

Alexia
Parties are fun, but stay out of the closet—
and don't fall asleep!

Peter
You'd be better off getting a tattoo than trying to dye
the peach fuzz on your face.

Danielle
There are plenty of highs and lows, but with your family
and friends, you can make it through anything.

ANNA
Junior high is no different from looking through a camera.
It might take you a while to get the right angle and the right
lighting and to bring it all into focus, but once you figure
things out, you'll have a moment in your life you're going to
want to save forever. So take lots of pictures.

Jeffrey
Don't be afraid to let go. You have people rooting for you who
you can't even see. And if you come up short the first time,
you've only lost the battle. You can still win the war,
so go for it.

LUKE
It's easier to believe in yourself when others believe in you.
So believe in each other. That's what friends are for.

Jessica
Everyone deserves a second chance.

LUKE
Stand up for your friends,
but remember to stand up for yourself, too.

ANNA
Sometimes it can be hard to share how you feel with someone.
It's important to know who you can trust, but also important
to know when it's okay to open up.

Danielle
If you're having trouble of any kind,
don't be afraid to ask for help.

Alexia
Looking fabulous can help you feel fabulous. But keep things
in perspective when you have a bad hair day—
it's nothing a little hair spray won't fix!

Peter
Just kidding. Don't get a tattoo.

ACKNOWLEDGMENTS

Thank you to all the teachers, librarians, and booksellers who continue to bring Mr. Terupt and his students to life, and to my many readers who have written asking me for more—and sometimes asking to be in the book and its dedication.

To John Irving for always being there to share your wisdom and stories.

To Paul Fedorko for your faith in me and continued work on my behalf. And to Sammy Bina for your work behind the scenes.

To Beverly Horowitz for being there every step of the way.

To my wonderful editor, Rebecca Weston, thank you for loving these characters—from the beginning. Thank you for your insightful comments and feedback, for your honesty and careful attention, and for your magical touch. Mrs. Reeder gives you an A+.

To all my friends and family who continue to spread the word, better position my books in the book stores, and provide rock-solid support and positive encouragement, I can't thank you enough. And a special thanks to my mother, Joanne Buyea, and mother-in-law, Mary Dame, for making the trip to North Andover on numerous occasions so that you can watch the grandchildren while I travel to schools near and far.

To my gang, Emma, Lily, and Anya, thank you for being so understanding, patient, and helpful when it came time for me to do the revision. And for listening to me read aloud my drafts—sometimes over and over—though you still haven't heard it as many times as Jackson (our dog). I love you!

And lastly, to Beth, who, along with Karlene's help, filled Missy's hand with shaving cream and tickled her nose. We always love your stories—the naughty ones, especially. I couldn't do any of this without you. I love you more every day.

ABOUT THE AUTHOR

ROB BUYEA taught third and fourth graders in Bethany, Connecticut, for six years before moving to Massachusetts, where he taught high school biology and coached wrestling for seven years at Northfield Mount Hermon. He now lives in North Andover, Massachusetts, with his wife and three daughters and is working as a full-time writer. *Because of Mr. Terupt,* his first novel, was selected as an E. B. White Read-Aloud Honor Book and a CYBILS finalist and has won seven state awards and been named to numerous state award lists. *Mr. Terupt Falls Again* and *Saving Mr. Terupt* are companion novels to *Because of Mr. Terupt.* The books continue to reach classrooms near and far and have given Rob the opportunity to visit with students all over the country—something he loves to do. Rob spends his summers at Cape Cod enjoying family adventures, entertaining friends, and writing. You can visit him at robbuyea.com.